$5-

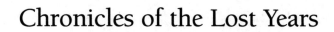

Chronicles of the Lost Years

Chronicles
of the Lost Years

A Sherlock Holmes Mystery

Tracy Cooper-Posey

Published by Ravenstone
an imprint of Turnstone Press
607–100 Arthur Street
Winnipeg, Manitoba
R3B 1H3 Canada
www.TurnstonePress.com

Turnstone Press gratefully acknowledges the assistance of the Manitoba Arts Council, the Canada Council for the Arts and the Government of Canada through the Book Publishing Industry Development Program.

Canadä

Cover design: Doowah Design

Interior Design: Marijke Friesen

Printed in Canada
by Friesens for Turnstone Press.

Canadian Catalogue in Publication Data

Cooper-Posey, Tracy, 1962–

Chronicles of the lost years

ISBN 0-88801-241-1

I. Title.

PS8555.O59238C48 1999   C813'.54   C99-920156-5
PR9199.3.C646C48 1999

To Mark.
Thank you for being born
the same day as me.

ACKNOWLEDEGMENTS

My deep thanks must go to the Western Australian Sherlock Holmes Society. I had immense fun while I was there, and learned lots—most of it having nothing to do with the best and wisest man I have ever known. I miss you all.

Posthumous thanks go to Robert Stephens and Jeremy Brett for their inspiring interpretations of an endlessly fascinating character.

Table of Contents

Chapter One

It will come as a considerable shock to readers who know Sherlock Holmes only through my writings in *The Strand* magazine that my assertion that he was unique and certainly the most fascinating of subjects was fraudulent. There was another I knew who was equally as fascinating an individual. Her name was Elizabeth Sigerson.

It would seem appropriate that these two highly individual people should meet, and indeed they did, in the spring of 1891, when Holmes was expending nearly all his energy in his final battle of wits with Moriarty.

Because I have omitted to give the public all the facts concerning my very singular friend Sherlock Holmes, I feel I should complete the record here, and if by some chance this memoir comes to light in a distant time, then so be it.

To begin at the beginning and include all the facts, I must go back to the winter of the year 1891. That winter was unruly and unpredictable. I cannot recall another season so out of character. Experts spoke of magnetic flux about the globe and the more common folk pondered the unusual extremes of temperature and weather. Record levels of snow fell for two days, then unseasonable days of sunshine turned the snowfalls to floods.

The weather appeared to affect every person's temperament, and the number of crimes rose to a remarkably high level. Sherlock Holmes was kept extremely busy investigating a number of mysteries, and would often of an evening arrive at my fireplace to bemoan the sheer quantity of his work, and its correspondingly poor quality. Always he remarked on the common underlying cause of each motivation.

"Always it is the weather that is blamed, Watson."

"Impossible! In every single circumstance?"

"No. I admit that the little puzzle I was asked to solve today was not a result of the weather, but the weather did cause me to become acquainted with it sooner than some person anticipated." He stretched his feet out to the fire.

"What puzzle was that?"

"A set of clothes found upon Dartmoor," he answered shortly.

I felt a small disappointment. "That seems a little ordinary," I ventured to remark. "Clothing is abandoned and lost every day."

"Not clothing like this." Holmes stood and removed a cloth bag from the hat rack, and emptied its contents onto the table. I moved closer and examined the clothing, trying to utilize my powers of observation as Holmes did.

I fingered the items, separating them. A shirt. A pair of trousers, waistcoat and jacket, collar and cuffs, and their pins. All were cut in small proportions and were exceedingly dirty. On the shirt, waistcoat, and jacket a small tear appeared in correspondingly identical positions. It was obvious that whatever instrument had caused the tear had passed through the material of all three garments in one pass. It must have been exceedingly sharp.

Holmes was watching me, and I shrugged. "Perhaps the suit belongs to a youth. It is a peculiar size. Beyond that, I cannot guess."

"These clothes were made for a woman," he told me. He held up the trousers, displaying the length of leg. "The size of the waist is disproportionate to the leg for a man, but for a tall female, these would suit. The woman who owned these clothes was in her late twenties to early thirties, and a liberal thinker. Unmarried, red-headed, and neat.

And if it were she who secreted them, she is a forward planner, and is in trouble of some sort. She is also in hiding from some person or agency, and these clothes would distinguish her too readily if found in her possession. My general impression is that she is highly intelligent, Watson, and uses her mind logically. A unique woman I would very much like to meet, but I am afraid that is out of the question."

I looked again at the clothes. "How on earth . . . ?"

Holmes smiled good-naturedly and threw himself into the chair. "I had a slight advantage, Watson, for I saw where this cloth bag had been secreted, and well hidden it was, too. It was sheer chance they were discovered. They were buried out on the moor, beneath a stone covered with snow. Whoever it was who buried them—and I strongly suspect that it was the owner of the clothes, for she would not be the sort to let them fall into a stranger's hands—she obviously intended that the clothes remain safely hidden under the snow. The weather has undone her plans."

"But to conclude she is red-headed and unmarried. . . ." I prompted him with disbelief tingeing my voice.

He moved his hand toward the clothing. "I gave you a clue, Watson. I drew attention to the proportion of waist size to leg. The neatness of the waist indicates that she is young, and has had no children yet. A married woman's husband typically would not allow the frivolous activities indicated by these clothes, so she is unmarried. She is a liberal thinker and that is indicated by the styling of the clothes. Whatever their purpose, it would take a woman of rare talent to exploit them. She is neat, because the clothing has been cared for and was neatly folded inside the bag. This also indicates they have not been entirely abandoned. She is a redhead, as several long strands of hair about the collar of the jacket indicate. That she is a planner is indicated by the removal of any identifying tags at the neck and waist of each garment, and their careful hiding place, which also indicates her desire to keep their owner's identity a mystery. She thought she might need to retrieve the garments one day, and did not throw them in the river or down the sewers. Hence my impression that she is intelligent and in trouble."

"And the logical thinking?" I asked, allowing my admiration to reveal itself upon my face.

"She has carefully obliterated any possible evidence near the hiding place, and has managed to successfully disappear into the city and remain hidden for the two days I have been searching for her. The trail is cold now, and I won't find her without considerable effort." Holmes leaned back in the chair, stretching out his legs. "No, she is a very clever woman, Watson, who is hiding very successfully. It is a pity we will never have a chance to unravel the mystery, but my time is too limited."

That should have been the end of the affair. I was concentrating on my medical practice; there were many cases of the elderly, frail, and infirm succumbing to the rigours of this peculiar winter, and I was busy.

For the greater part of January Holmes was in Europe, going about his affairs. Just as the winter deepened its hold in February, I received a new client. The lady's name meant nothing to me, so it was with something of a shock that I found myself facing a tall, red-headed woman. A quick glance at her left hand confirmed her status as an unmarried woman. She complained of a series of headaches. These are easily remedied with an application of salicylic powders, which I prescribed for her. Throughout the short interview I found myself wondering if she was Holmes' mystery lady.

But by the time I showed her to the door I had convinced myself that coincidence did not stretch that far. There would be a good many red-headed ladies in London, even tall, neat, and beautiful ones. The chances that Holmes' redhead had actually called on me professionally were too slim.

Again, I all but forgot the incident. Holmes returned from Europe in March for a very short sojourn before taking up his activities in France once more. I called to see him on one of the nights he was not out and about on business, and we shared a companionable meal before settling in front of the fire and exchanging the news of each other's lives since Christmas.

It is here that my story departs from that other I have previously related. For as I was searching my memory for any other scraps of news that Holmes would find interesting, I recalled my red-headed patient.

"Do you remember that mysterious redhead you were trying to trace, the one with the male costume?"

Holmes nodded, his eyes closed and his pipe jutting out aggressively.

"Last month I had a new patient who could have doubled as your mystery lady. It surprised me. I thought your redhead herself had appeared."

Holmes sat abruptly upright, dropping his pipe into his hand. "Describe her," he commanded.

"That's just it, Holmes. Her description tallies almost exactly with your conclusions. Redhead, tall, trim, neat. It's difficult to judge forward planning and intelligence with a ten-minute interview, but she certainly wasn't a fool."

Holmes stood and moved to the mantelshelf. "And her name?"

"Miss Elizabeth Sigerson." I felt a little bewildered by his reaction. "You don't think it was your redhead, surely?"

"Why not? It makes a certain kind of sense, Watson—quite apart from an inner certainty I have had that we would one day meet."

"But it is stretching coincidence a bit, isn't it?"

"I wish you had told me earlier. As it is, I shall have to hurry the arrangements. Would you be able to arrange for her to meet you at your consulting rooms on a professional basis?"

"Yes, certainly, if you require it. But why, Holmes?"

"For some reason she is afraid of me. She wants her clothes back, Watson, and she is making an indirect approach through you. She fears that if I see or speak to her I will deduce some truth she is keeping secret. We must woo her cautiously and time is limited. I'm due back in Paris tomorrow, so it will have to wait until I return. I will send you a cable when I know the date, and you can arrange for the appointment."

I felt a bit winded. I had related my trivial story only to amuse Holmes. "Yes, of course," I agreed slowly.

"Good. Now, tell me all about her, Watson. Every detail . . . every nuance."

On April the 20th, a Monday as I recall, I received a cable from Holmes informing me he would be arriving back in London on the Thursday. That was all the cable stated, but I had not forgotten his instructions, and set about arranging the interview with Miss Sigerson. I sent her a note stating I wished to review the effectiveness of the treatment I had prescribed for her and requesting her presence on Thursday afternoon.

I received back a prettily worded letter asking to change the time to seven o'clock in the evening, for she was employed as a typewriter and could not arrive earlier. On Holmes' arrival I informed him of the interview and invited him to share our supper before Miss Sigerson arrived.

Accordingly, he appeared on my doorstep in the late afternoon, looking tired and much used, yet with the same keen look in his eyes he had whenever he was on the scent of another mystery.

I questioned him concerning his health, and confessed my curiosity over his doings in Europe, but apart from hinting heavily about the gravity of his deeds, he would say nothing more.

"It is all settled now, Watson. And in four days it will be over. I wish to forget it for now and enjoy myself with this lighter, more unusual mystery."

At seven o'clock we descended the stairs to my consulting room, and I pushed the door open to enter, only to fall back in confusion. I held onto the doorknob, preventing Holmes from following me into the room.

"Miss Sigerson," I said, both in greeting to her and as a warning to Holmes.

"Doctor." She stood. "I suppose I must apologize for waiting in your room, but it is late, and I preferred not to wait in the street."

"Yes, of course. That is quite all right." I was unsure whether to enter and close the door, and risk exposing Holmes, or to back out on some pretense. I had been caught completely by surprise. All the investigative tasks Holmes had coached me to complete during the interview fled my mind.

Miss Sigerson studied me carefully with her candid, green eyes, and I saw her glance thoughtfully at the door. Then she put her head to one side.

"Doctor Watson, you have asked me here under a falsehood."

I stared at her blankly.

She shook her head. "Never mind. I will see to it myself." She moved to the door, stepped around me and into the corridor. I saw Holmes straighten from his resting place against the wall. "Mr. Holmes, why don't you come inside?" she asked him. "It is cold out here."

"Miss Sigerson." He walked into the room. "Never mind, Watson." He patted my shoulder.

Elizabeth looked at me kindly. "Your face gave you away, Doctor Watson. Do you ever play whist?"

Holmes sat against the edge of my desk. "Yes, and he loses—quite badly." He studied Elizabeth. "Red hair, trim, neat. . . ."

Elizabeth allowed him time to scrutinize her properly. She held out her hands. "My sleeves, Mr. Holmes. You find a woman's sleeves most revealing, I believe."

He leaned forward to examine them. "Thank you," he said gravely. "Why did you not want me to see you?"

"I believed you to be in Europe."

Holmes examined her face closely. "You are not denying you consulted Watson as a means of regaining your clothes?"

"I had genuine reason for seeking a doctor. I merely combined the two. Are you prepared to return my clothes to me? They are very difficult to replace. Understanding seamstresses are hard to find."

Holmes smiled. "Yes, I sympathize. You may have them back. They are in my rooms, at Baker Street."

"Thank you." She turned to pick up her gloves.

"Where is the knife that cut them?" Holmes asked, addressing her back.

Elizabeth slowly turned back to face him. Her face was quite still. "I beg your pardon?"

"The knife. It was a knife that caused that very neat tear. Through so many layers, too. Aimed right here—"and he touched his breast pocket. "Whoever was wielding it was in deadly earnest. I was wondering what became of the knife. It wasn't with the clothes."

"I'm sure I don't know what you're talking about. The clothes were not torn when I . . . left them."

"Of all the very small mistakes you have made, that is the most telling." Holmes straightened from his slouch. "I have trained myself to observe the most minute details of a person's attire and deportment. Anyone who moves through a normal day will have dozens of such clues about their person, yet you have none. Such absence of detail can only mean you have taken great care to remove them. You have secrets, Miss Sigerson. I consider any secret an irresistable call to action. Doctor Watson will assure you that I am more persistent than Job when confronted with a riddle."

Elizabeth bit her lip. "This is what I feared," she confessed. "That if we ever met face to face you would detect my . . . covert motivations."

"There is no need to fear me if your intentions are good," Holmes replied. "But you must explain these discrepancies."

Elizabeth wavered.

"Come, Miss Sigerson, explain. I have about me at this very moment some of the most dangerous, desperate criminals of the century. I cannot afford to play loosely with even the slightest of suspicions. Tell me."

Elizabeth shook her head. "I cannot. Please believe me when I say I wish I could. I have nothing to do with these criminals you fear, and would clear myself if I could. My intentions were benign. I have nothing but deep admiration and respect for your abilities, as reported by Doctor Watson."

"Yes, that is clear by the length you went to avoid my scrutiny."

Elizabeth sighed. "I want my clothes back. That is my chief aim. I believed you to be in Europe and thought it would be an ideal time to approach Doctor Watson, establish contact, and eventually ask his help in reclaiming them, thus staying out of your way and creating the minimum of disturbance."

"That was most considerate of you," Holmes replied dryly. "It must have dismayed you to learn the police had asked me to examine the clothes when they found them."

"Considerably, at first, but then I realized the authorities would have appealed to you sooner or later. It was inevitable. I knew they would find no answers."

"Yes, you made quite certain of that. However, you fear I might, and that is why you want them back."

"I blame myself entirely for this mess. At the time I was dazed and sick, and not thinking clearly. I should have destroyed them utterly." She finished quietly, almost to herself, "It is a mistake I won't make again."

Holmes frowned. "The person from whom you were hiding— they are no longer a threat?"

"I have solved that problem," she replied.

Holmes walked up and down the room once, thinking. "If you would care to accompany us, Miss Sigerson, you can collect your clothes now."

"And then?"

"And then you are free to go."

"I will believe that only when you replace the safety catch on the revolver you are holding in your pocket," Elizabeth replied.

Holmes glanced at her sharply. Then, with a short laugh, he pulled out the revolver and ostentatiously replaced the safety catch before dropping it back in his pocket. "Come, Watson, let us collect Miss Sigerson's cherished possessions."

Holmes called up a hansom and handed Elizabeth in before climbing aboard. I followed. He gave his address, settled back into the seat, and closed his eyes. Elizabeth kept her gaze on the passing scenery. The entire trip was silent. On our arrival, Holmes opened the door, hurried up the stairs, and threw open the door of his sitting room while I paid the cabby. I climbed upstairs, and found him removing the cloth bag from the top drawer of a bureau. Elizabeth stood just inside the door.

He tossed the bag on the sofa.

Elizabeth picked it up. "Thank you."

"I've not solved your mystery, Miss Sigerson," Holmes said suddenly. "I have other, more pressing matters on hand that prevent me from following up your puzzle. You should consider yourself fortunate, for it is clear you fear my discovering the truth."

"No, I do not fear you, Mr. Holmes," Elizabeth replied, her voice mellow. I detected a hint of amusement. Evidently Holmes did, too, for he fixed her with his keen gaze, but a sudden shout out on the street made him whirl towards the window. He withdrew his gun from his pocket, and carefully pulled the curtain aside by a small fraction to peer out.

"I suggest you leave, Miss Sigerson," he said shortly.

Elizabeth studied his tall, motionless figure and the gun in his hand. Wordlessly she turned and left.

I moved to the other window and peered out, too, but there was nothing remarkable to be seen. Holmes dropped the curtain and looked about the room. With a shrug he pocketed his revolver and looked at me.

"I shouldn't have returned here. This place is not safe for me at the moment."

"Then come home with me."

"No. I will remain here for the night, now. I need to think, and I prefer my own hearth for that."

"Then I will remain here, too."

He was pleased. "Thank you. That would be a great comfort to me."

"Holmes, won't you tell me what this is all about? You've dealt with Miss Sigerson now, and had your leisure. It is clear you consider yourself in danger. I would be of more assistance to you if I knew what was happening."

It was then Holmes told me of Moriarty and his gang, and of the plans Holmes had been painstakingly following for nearly twelve months in an effort to outwit the most dangerous criminal in England. He explained to me the details of his expected coup in four days' time, and the waiting game he was now playing.

I spent an uneasy night in front of the fire after that, and it was with some relief I watched the sun rise outside the windows. Holmes read my thoughts easily.

"It is not a sign to relax our vigilance," he warned me. "Moriarty is a clever man. He understands that night fears disappear in daylight and he will use it to his advantage. But there is no need to starve while we wait. I will scare up Mrs. Hudson and request a large breakfast."

We were almost through the excellent meal when there was a knock on the door, and Moriarty himself entered. I have written elsewhere about this extraordinary interview, and the repugnance the man created in one. In my public account of the event which appeared in *The Strand*, I omitted the fact that I was there. In this account I am free to describe the conversation as I saw and felt it.

Moriarty and Holmes exchanged words that held the form of politeness, but they were really taking the measure of each other as part of their preparations for the final combat due in three days' time. From my observations I deduced I was right to be as uneasy as Moriarty made me feel. Menace radiated from him even though he spoke civilly.

I also omitted Moriarty's parting words from my account. For he turned at the door, and looked back. "There is one other thing we share, Holmes."

"Oh?" Holmes replied coolly.

"Our taste in redheads. She is very beautiful." He laughed and slipped out the door.

Holmes' face held a momentary shock, then his eyes narrowed thoughtfully. I fell back into my chair. "I didn't believe we would come out of that alive," I confessed.

Holmes threw off his dressing gown and reached for his jacket, dropping the revolver into the pocket.

"Quick, Watson! We haven't a moment to lose." He grabbed his coat, rushed out the back door, and hailed a passing hansom. He rattled out the address as he climbed in. I recognized it immediately.

"Why, that's Miss Sigerson's address."

"Exactly," Holmes agreed. He remained silent for the remainder of the short trip and sprang to the pavement as the cab slowed. "Pay the driver to wait, Watson!" he called over his shoulder.

I hurriedly dispensed coins and instructions, and followed Holmes up the steps into the house. It contained an extraordinary amount of activity for the time of morning. Holmes was asking rapid questions of a matron in dressing gown and nightcap, and her answers were shrill.

"Screaming, hysterical screams, and thumps and yells, and deep voices," she was saying. "Then heavy bootsteps on the stairs, and muffled noises. I just froze to my bed."

Holmes turned to me. "Send for the police, Watson, if someone hasn't already." He turned toward the stairs and climbed rapidly.

I, in turn, looked at the matron.

"We have already sent for the police," she said primly.

I followed Holmes up the staircase. On the first floor a door stood ajar, and Holmes stood in the middle of the room it served, carefully observing the furniture.

"We're too late, Watson," he said softly.

"I don't understand, Holmes," I said. "Miss Sigerson said she was no longer in trouble."

"Moriarty," Holmes replied shortly. He straightened from his examination of the bed and picked up an envelope on the bureau. It was addressed to him. Rapidly opening and reading it, he gave a snort of disgust, crumpled it up, and threw it on the floor. I picked it up and smoothed it out.

> *I doubt this note is necessary, but I will trouble myself with explaining the obvious to ensure the situation is perfectly clear. If you insist on continuing with your plans, Miss Sigerson will be delivered to your door— one piece at a time.*
>
> *Moriarty*

Chapter Two

I READ THE NOTE ONCE MORE, APPALLED. "Holmes, we've got to get her from him."

"Possibly," Holmes said absently, examining the carpet.

I felt myself spluttering indignantly. "We must!"

Holmes straightened and placed his lens back in his pocket. "There is no point rushing in heroically until we have established that Miss Sigerson needs saving." I was still puzzled, and he added patiently, "It could be a bluff, Watson."

"You mean she is part of Moriarty's gang?"

"It would certainly explain some of the mystery surrounding her, wouldn't it?"

I considered the matter. "I find it hard to believe," I admitted.

"That is because you have been charmed by her looks," Holmes replied. He glanced around the room once more, then closed and locked the door. "I could be wrong about her. I will put the Baker Street Irregulars onto it. I certainly cannot move about the city freely, and they will soon discover where she is."

Our return to Baker Street was uneventful, and the wait long and tedious. As Holmes had pointed out, there was little else he could do. He had put in motion the only avenues of inquiry open to him, and any public movement by him would threaten both his life and Elizabeth's.

"And I cannot jeopardize the plans, Watson. Three more days is all I need."

Finally, about two o'clock that afternoon, one of the leaders of Holmes' squad of street urchins appeared in our doorway. He tipped his hat at Holmes. "Guv." He handed Holmes a scrap of paper, and Holmes dug into his pocket and extracted several coins. The boy accepted them and scampered from the room.

I pushed my notes aside as Holmes read the scrap.

"A warehouse, dockside. Appropriate enough," he said briefly. "The boys were attracted by a woman's screams for help."

I felt the beginnings of horror. "Holmes, surely that must tell you she is innocent."

"I refuse to speculate where Moriarty is concerned. I will accept only facts. Let us go and observe."

Forty minutes later we found ourselves scaling a large expanse of roof shingles. Our object was a skylight that Holmes had spied on the building next door to the warehouse to which we had been directed. He hoped it would provide an indirect approach to our target.

I lagged somewhat behind on account of my leg, and Holmes reached the skylight before me and peered through the glass. He pulled back instantly, as though the glass were hot, and waved me to silence and caution. I crawled over the final feet of shingle very carefully.

"The Irregulars seem to have made a mistake concerning which building Moriarty is in control of," he said quietly. "Unless he has both. Look very carefully, Watson."

I peered cautiously into the skylight. Immediately below me was what appeared to be an empty room, dusty and disused, the floorboards dark with age and possibly discoloured with oil. Outlines here and there seemed to suggest machinery. The machines had all gone and the only furniture in the room was a low divan. Elizabeth lay on the divan, resting on her side.

I pulled back carefully. "We appear to be in luck."

"It seems a little too easy," Holmes replied, looking about the roof.

I felt a tiny flame of irritation. "Oh come, Holmes. You're really carrying this a bit far. You are entitled to a piece of luck every now and again."

He smiled at my irritation. "I will keep that in mind."

I took another long look through the window. "She is either asleep or unconscious."

"Asleep," Holmes said shortly. "I imagine she is sleeping off the effects of the concussion she received from the blow to her head." He was busy uncoiling rope from around his waist. "Did you notice the bruise on her forehead? Or the handcuffs? Or the guard by the door?"

I hadn't, and looked through the pane yet again, confirming Holmes' observations.

"It appears she has been caught up in this adventure against her will," Holmes continued. "Moriarty may have read more into our relationship than was there, but her innocence ensures I am as tied as Moriarty intended. So we must save her as you wished, Watson." He loosened the final twist and piled the rope onto the roof. "Are you comfortable?"

"Comfortable enough."

"Good. We may be here until nightfall. If you would be so good as to check through the skylight regularly, Watson, and let me know when she wakes?" He settled himself full length against the pitch of the roof, and closed his eyes. I suspected it was the only uninterrupted sleep he'd had for the last few days. Only Holmes could manage to relax so completely right in the very heart of his enemy's lair.

Just on sunset, I saw Elizabeth begin to stir. I pushed at Holmes with my foot to wake him, and we both watched her rouse from sleep.

Holmes looked about him again. "There is nothing we can use for a lever or pivot," he said. "Unfortunate. Still, I don't believe Miss Sigerson will prove to be an impossible weight." He coiled the rope carefully. "We cannot open the skylight until the last moment, for the change of air pressure will alert the guard. On my word, Watson, I want you to lift the frame open as fast as you can and then wait until I have hauled the rope up. You will help Miss Sigerson out."

"Do you think she will understand what is required of her?"

15

"I have no doubt she will. Ready? Now!"

I hauled the skylight open, throwing back the pane. Holmes tossed the rope down into the gap, and settled himself into a stance that would give him maximum purchase on the shingles, the rope in his hands.

I peered into the room. The rope had landed right in front of Elizabeth, and she glanced up quickly. I waved her on encouragingly, and she lifted her cuffed hands and caught the rope between them. "Now," I told Holmes, but he was already hauling on the rope, hand over hand, his eyes glittering with concentration and his jaw clenched with effort.

I watched Elizabeth's ascent anxiously. The guard was racing toward her, and she was barely out of his reach. However, Elizabeth remained clear-headed enough to wait until he was within range, then she kicked out with her boot and caught him a well-calculated and powerful blow in the face. It was enough to keep him occupied with his own miseries for the few seconds she needed to be drawn high out of his grasp.

When her hands reached the lip of the skylight, Holmes stopped hauling, and by the expedient of reaching down and grasping her waist in one arm, I managed to lift her up onto the roof. She lay full length, her eyes closed, and I could well imagine the fear and relief mixing in her blood.

Holmes dropped the rope and crouched beside her. With one of his fine metal instruments he unlocked the cuffs about her wrists.

"How bad is your concussion, Miss Sigerson?" he asked.

Elizabeth sat up, rubbing her wrists. "For goodness' sake, call me Elizabeth. Miss Sigerson is such an awkward mouthful." She was smiling.

Holmes looked at me inquiringly.

"Very mild, I'd say," I judged quickly, studying her eyes. "She is coherent enough."

Holmes looked amused. "Very well—Elizabeth. We must hurry."

We reached my consulting rooms two hours later, after completing a tortuous route to throw off any pursuers. Our escape from the roof of the warehouse had been dogged by several guards, whom we fought off before escaping into the alleys and subways of the London dockside. Holmes' familiarity with the myriad little ways and paths was our saving, I believe. The trouble we had reaching safety did quell Holmes' concern that the rescue had been suspiciously easy.

I locked the door behind me and sat Elizabeth in a chair to examine her injuries. There was some bruising about a small cut on her forehead.

"Did it bleed much?" I asked.

"I don't know. It knocked me unconscious. When I came to, somebody had already dressed it."

"So you were unconscious for a while."

She nodded. "They attacked me outside my room last night. That's not when I received this." She touched her temple. "I tried to raise as much noise as I could, but they held a rag to my face. It smelt. Would that have been chloroform?"

Both Holmes and I nodded.

"When I woke I was quite ill, and I found myself in that room in which you found me. My hands were cuffed. There were two guards, who took turns watching me. I could hear traffic somewhere nearby and decided I would attempt to draw attention to myself again. I began shouting and calling for help." She looked up at Holmes. "I am aware of what you call your Baker Street Irregulars. Is that how you found me?"

"Yes."

"Then this bruise has been worth the pain."

"The guards hit you?" I asked, appalled.

"To keep me quiet, yes." She smiled at my expression. "They warned me several times to stay silent, but I persisted."

I reached for my medical bag. "I have something for the headache. How do you feel otherwise?"

"I don't feel either weak or ill now. The fresh air and the exercise have done me the world of good."

I turned to Holmes. "Let me look at your hand, Holmes."

"It is nothing," he said absently, briefly examining the broken skin about his knuckles before sliding his hand into his pocket. He was leaning against my tall bureau, frowning. "Perhaps you will explain to Elizabeth the events she has became involved in while I consider our next move?"

I nodded, and proceeded to give her the facts concerning Moriarty as Holmes had related them to me the previous evening by the fire. She listened quietly and without interruption, her eyes focussed on my face. Finally, she turned to Holmes.

"I appear to have been a nuisance to you, Mr. Holmes. I do hope I haven't spoiled your plans?"

"No, not now we have retrieved you. Did you see Moriarty at all?"

"I saw no one who resembled Watson's description of him. I believe I was being held by employees. It puzzled me, the attack, for I could fathom no reason for it, but now I understand."

"You are both going to have to travel with me," Holmes said, his mind apparently settled. "Moriarty has introduced a new twist to the match, and I haven't the time to shore up my defence. Everything I have planned will come to fruition in three days' time, so for three days I must keep myself and both of you out of harm's way. We must leave England."

"Just like that?" I queried.

"Do you wish to die?" Holmes asked me harshly. "For obvious reasons I cannot leave Elizabeth here. For those same reasons I will not leave you behind. Come, Watson, you're always looking for adventure. Here is one for you, filled with genuine danger and difficulty."

"Of course I will come," I replied. "If only to keep your neck firmly attached to your shoulders."

"Thank you," he said. He turned to Elizabeth. "I am afraid I must insist, Elizabeth. For your own safety."

"I concur," she agreed simply. I was delighted to see Holmes' disconcerted expression. He had not expected such a commonsensical response. "When are we to leave?"

Holmes outlined his plan.

Holmes warned Elizabeth not to return to her room, and she readily agreed. While Holmes and I were puzzling on how to protect her for the rest of the night, she said simply, "Provide me with ten pounds, and I will look after myself. It is clear we cannot remain together. I will meet you tomorrow on the train."

Holmes gave her the funds without demur, and she bid us good night before slipping from the room and disappearing through the tradesmen's entrance at the back of my house.

The next day at dawn we began to execute our individual roles in Holmes' carefully coordinated escape from London. My own part I have already related, and I have indicated Holmes' task. I arrived breathlessly at Victoria Station the next morning. I had just tussled with an Italian priest who had insisted on my services as translator, and was heading for the train when I collided with a Sister of Mercy. The thought occurred to me that I was beset by the church, when I focussed on the startling green eyes beneath the wimple.

"Elizabeth?" I breathed softly.

She nodded a little and picked up her carpet bag again.

"Let me help you, Sister," I said more loudly for the benefit of eavesdroppers. I assisted her onto the train. "I didn't know you," I said quietly as we made our way to our compartment.

"It was the only way I could think of to disguise my hair. Holmes hasn't arrived?"

"No." I made a small sound of annoyance as we reached the compartment, for the Italian priest was sitting quietly on the seat, his cane between his knees. "I have just had the most infuriating conversation with that silly priest. He wouldn't accept that I don't speak a word of Italian."

Elizabeth put her fingers to her lips, suppressing a smile. "Oh," she murmured simply, examining the priest through the glass.

I strode into the compartment and attempted to explain to the man that he was in the wrong seat. I found both my voice and my temper rising. After a moment, Elizabeth put a calming hand on my arm.

"Leave him. He seems harmless enough."

I threw myself into a seat. "Where's Holmes? That is what I want to know."

Elizabeth sat opposite me, next to the priest. "I have no doubt he will be on the train in time. Relax, Watson."

I continued to watch through the window, growing steadily more anxious with each passing moment.

"Well, Watson, aren't you going to greet me hello?"

I jerked my head back to look at the priest.

"My god!" I breathed, as the face filled out into the familiar lines and planes of my friend's.

Elizabeth laughed softly. "I told you, didn't I?"

Holmes turned to her, his face sinking back into the aged creases of the priest. "What gave me away?"

"You knew?" I asked of her.

She pointed to the hands resting on the walking stick. "You made a casual movement with your hands when we walked in, and moved them into a position that looks quite awkward. It could only have been to disguise your knuckles, which you shredded last night."

"I am impressed," I said.

"Moriarty does not know of my knuckles, so if that is all that gave me away I am safe. For the moment. Now, I suggest we behave like strangers, at least until the train departs."

Obedient, we studiously ignored each other until the train had pulled away from the station. Then Holmes rose and shed his priestly garments, and became once more the familiar figure I knew. He relaxed back into the seat. "I am glad to see you both made it through. Did Mycroft say anything to you, Watson?"

"Mycroft?" I repeated blankly.

"He was the large coachman who drove you here."

I shook my head, bewildered.

"Elizabeth, did you notice anything strange or unusual on your way here?"

"No. I don't believe I was followed. I spent the night at the convent where I was raised, and I travelled here with a group of nuns. Moriarty couldn't possibly have traced me."

Holmes considered her. "No, I don't think he would have out-guessed your movements." I heard just the smallest note of amusement in his voice and studied Elizabeth anew. She appeared to have unsuspected talents.

Holmes lit a cigarette and fell into an introspective silence. Elizabeth, remaining in character, drew out a small pocket copy of the Gospel and read quietly. I, having lacked the foresight to bring any reading matter with me, sat back and gazed out the window at the passing scenes.

We were nearly to Canterbury when Holmes spoke. "I don't for a moment suppose Moriarty has missed all three of us. I know he traced one of us as far as Victoria, for I saw him scanning the platform as I came on board, and he will guess my plans to leave the country. So we are going to have to abandon our luggage and our comfortable berth, and alight at Canterbury." He gave us his plans to cross the country to Newhaven and then cross the channel to Dieppe, on the French coast.

"So we are limited to taking only what we can carry ourselves. Elizabeth, can you limit yourself to essentials and a few days' rough living?"

She nodded and pushed at the carpet bag at her feet. "I only have this bag." She stood up and tugged at the fastenings of her habit. "Holmes, could you help me? These things are not designed to be cast off quickly."

I stared up at her in amazement. "Elizabeth!"

Holmes smiled at my discomfort, and reached up to untie the fastenings at the back of her wimple.

"Holmes!" I exclaimed, fast becoming horrified and confused.

Elizabeth quickly shed the long, black, flowing habit and threw it aside. She stood revealed in men's trousers, shirt, and waistcoat, her hair tightly fastened at the back of her head. I fell back against my seat, lost for words and not a little relieved.

She opened the carpet bag, and pulled out and donned a soft-brimmed hat and jacket. I watched in fascination as she adjusted the hat to cover her hair and shade its burnished sheen.

"Do I pass?" she asked Holmes, who had watched the transformation with detached, clinical interest.

"Straighten your tie and pull your cuffs down," he said, after a minute inspection. Elizabeth complied. "If you remain silent and keep your face from close inspection, you will pass. It would be wise to keep your hands in your pockets to disguise them, and to act as a callow, sullen youth. It was an excellent piece of planning."

"Then you didn't suggest it, Holmes?" I asked.

"No."

"But you expected it. You knew," I pointed out.

"You forget, Watson, what first brought Elizabeth to our attention."

"Ah, yes," I said, recalling the other set of men's clothing.

Elizabeth smiled. "I foresaw we might have to flee on foot. I thought it best to be prepared for the possibility at the very least. And running is difficult in skirts."

Holmes peered out the window. "Canterbury. In about three minutes." He stood and picked up his hat.

I have related in my public account how we found ourselves hiking across to Newhaven and our race across western Europe. Holmes and I were old hands at fast, cross-country travelling. I suppose I expected our progress to be much slower with a woman in the party, but it was not so. Indeed it was I who had trouble keeping up.

On the third day we paused at a stream to refresh ourselves, and I offered the flask to Elizabeth from which to drink. She sipped and handed it back.

"You look exhausted, John," she said, tucking her long legs up against her chest.

Holmes turned to study me. "Elizabeth is right. Is your leg troubling you?"

"A little," I answered reluctantly, rubbing the knee. "It is nothing."

"I want to reach the Swiss border tonight. Think you can manage it?"

"I will manage," I said shortly.

Holmes examined me again, then turned away. He and Elizabeth exchanged looks before he abruptly walked away.

Elizabeth turned to me, troubled. "Are you sure you can manage?"

I watched Holmes' retreating back. "In truth, I don't know. So far the knee hasn't started to swell, which is good. Swelling is usually a sign I am going to be laid up for a while."

"Why didn't you tell him that?" she asked.

"He has the bit between his teeth. I have seen him like this before. If we weren't with him he'd probably walk all day and all night. I know of one occasion when he worked five days without cease. He collapsed afterwards, of course, but only when he'd solved the case." Her candid eyes were troubled and I looked away, a little embarrassed. "He is worried," I told her truthfully. "He cannot keep in touch with the London police out here and he is afraid they will blunder the job of rounding up Moriarty's gang. He feels the weight of responsibility for us, too."

"And you don't want him to worry any more?" she asked softly. "No."

"You're very loyal, John," she told me. "What if I ask him if we can rest in an inn for a couple of days? Would that help your leg?"

"It might, but I wouldn't suggest it. He is very single-minded, and any delays would make him impossible to be near."

"Perhaps after he has heard from London he will relax a little," Elizabeth suggested. "I could try then."

For the next forty-eight hours, Elizabeth was never far from my side, and whenever I felt myself back-sliding or faltering she was there with a helping hand or quiet word of encouragement. Holmes was not aware of her subtle delaying tactics. On one occasion she pretended to have a cramp in her side, giving me five minutes' grace in which to rest my leg, while Holmes fumed and scanned the horizon anxiously. She buffered his impatience and kept me going, and by the time we reached Strasburg and the hotel to which Holmes had arranged to have his most urgent cable addressed, I was quite in awe of her abilities.

Elizabeth was kicking the ground like a sulking youth, and I was resting on a flat rock in the low rays of the sun, when Holmes emerged from the hotel foyer with the cable in his hand.

"Well?" I asked simply as he reached us.

"Moriarty escaped." Holmes crumpled the cable and threw it to the ground. "He escaped." His voice was deeply bitter. He looked out across the mountains, screwing his eyes up in the sunlight. Abruptly he turned and walked away.

I sighed. "Unfortunate. He has spent nearly a year building the trap and in the end it fails to catch the mouse."

Elizabeth picked up the cable, smoothed it out, and read it. "All the others were rounded up. All except Moriarty."

I rubbed my leg wearily. "I wonder what Holmes will decide to do next?"

Elizabeth considered carefully. "We will have to leave Strasburg. Moriarty may trace us here through the cable. Can you go on tonight, John?"

"I will have to."

"I will try to help."

"You have been," I assured her. I felt a sudden, bitter frustration. "I am getting too old for this sort of thing."

"Nonsense," Elizabeth scoffed. "You're no older than Holmes."

"Holmes thrives on this. It is his meat and bread. Now he knows the outcome, you watch him. He seems to quiver with the excitement of it all." I sat up. "I prefer to live my excitement vicariously."

Holmes returned then, striding rapidly. "It is clear Moriarty will flee London. He has nowhere to go. I have had my revenge on him, yet he is still at liberty, his organization in ruins. He will come after me, and when we meet, death will be on the agenda." He studied us both. "You must return to London. It is safe enough there for you now. Certainly it is much safer than my company."

I protested. "I refuse to even consider it, Holmes. I could be of help." It was the beginning of an argument that lasted for nearly thirty minutes. I insisted on remaining with Holmes, and he was his usual intractable self, demanding I return. Elizabeth stayed well out of the argument, merely observing our heated exchanges. I did not like her hearing some of the truths we threw at each other, yet I judged the situation important enough to ignore such considerations.

Finally Holmes drew her into the argument. "Very well, then. If you will not return for my sake, do it for Elizabeth. You can hardly countenance her continuing on this dangerous adventure. You must take her back to London."

I laughed shortly. "I have you there, Holmes. With all due respect to Elizabeth, I will not leave you even to return her to London. You cannot argue that she will slow you down because for the last three days she has more than kept up with you, and managed to help me along as she was doing it."

"I know," Holmes replied, surprising both of us. He waved his hand impatiently. "I will find you a *pensione* to stay in," he told her.

"I am coming with you," Elizabeth said flatly. "You're not discarding me like a cast-off shoe. You insisted I come this far. I insist I continue."

Holmes threw up his hands. "Can I not make you understand? Moriarty is going to search for and find me. When he does, he is going to do his very best to kill me. He is not going to concern himself with preserving innocent bystanders. If you come with me, you will be in equal danger."

"We understand that," I said, speaking for us both.

"Very well, Watson, it is your decision. However, in all conscience I cannot allow you to come, Elizabeth."

Elizabeth put her hands on her hips. "Tell me, Holmes, have you always been so damned obstinate?"

I sucked in my breath, shocked. I turned to where Holmes stood, motionless, his thin features frozen. Then he smiled, the expression blossoming with humour. "I know my assumptions are right. Why should I salve your pride by doing what I know is dangerously incorrect?"

"Pride has nothing to do with it. I owe you my life, Holmes. You hauled me out of Moriarty's grasp in London. You could have left me there. I was of no importance to you and you had more urgent business to think about. So I stay. Besides, I could be of some use to you. Give me your revolver."

Holmes gave her his gun.

"John, throw that glass up into the air, please."

I picked up the tumbler the inn had supplied with our lunch, and threw it high into the air. Elizabeth aimed and fired, then dropped her chin as glass fragments pattered about the ground around our feet. She held out the revolver and calmly brushed glass pieces from her hat brim.

I laughed, delighted.

Holmes silently replaced the spent bullet and put the gun back in his pocket.

Elizabeth pushed her hands back into her pockets. "Besides, I will not sit back in safety and let a fellow human being go off and get himself killed—not while I can do something about it."

Holmes turned his back on us and paced about the gravel, thinking. I merely watched. Finally he half-turned and said over his shoulder, "I want to be well on the way to Geneva tonight. We leave in ten minutes."

Elizabeth caught my arm in her hand in a spontaneous expression of comradeship. Holmes walked away, his hands deep in his pockets.

"I believe, deep down, he is touched and pleased," I told her.

"So now we must deliver our promise and watch out for him. And ourselves," she replied.

Chapter Three

WE CONTINUED OUR JOURNEY through springtime Europe. On any other occasion it would have been a wonderful walking tour, but that week held hellish overtones.

Holmes' awareness of fate lurking around the corner I did not exaggerate, nor the counterpoint charm of the countryside. Elizabeth was a cheerful, energetic, and thoughtful companion, and I believe Holmes all but forgot her womanhood, so well did she fall in with our habits. However, he did not forget the last, small, lingering cloud of doubt hovering over her—not until she cast it aside for all time.

It was an evening around a campfire. Elizabeth had proved her capabilities to us by this time and we thought nothing of sitting down where we were to spend the night. We had passed over the Gemmi that day and a falling rock had nearly taken Holmes. Holmes had instantly assumed foul play, despite the protestations of the local guide we had employed to show us the way over the pass. He had become increasingly tense after that, dampening the holiday spirit that had begun to develop. Eventually, even our guide became uneasy. We paid off the guide at the next village, and Holmes insisted on continuing while daylight lasted. Consequently, darkness found us in a low, deserted valley, and we stopped for the night.

"You are wondering if you have brought your fate along with you," Elizabeth said quietly, some time later. I looked up, surprised at her voice and words. They were facing each other across the fire, Holmes watching her steadily. I sensed some sort of dénouement was about to take place. I put my notebook down quietly.

Holmes looked away from her and threw a small twig on the fire. "It would not be the first time I have been betrayed by a woman."

"You cannot brand womanhood with the same tainted brush because of the doings of one woman."

"I did not say just one. Every woman I have dealt with professionally has had ulterior motives."

"I see. So now you are wondering what my own motives are?"

"You have a surprisingly long list of skills and talents, all tied up in the prettiest of packages. The combination is disconcerting and could have been designed to have just that effect."

Elizabeth studied him. I sensed she was judging him. "Very well," she said softly, yet I could hear the steel quality of decisiveness in her tone. "I will put myself in your hands. I will give you the leash that will tie me to you, and you may do with it what you wish." She paused, choosing words. "You were seeking the location of a knife. Do you still wish to know its whereabouts?"

"Where would I look?" Holmes asked sharply, his eyes narrowed speculatively.

"In the same grave as the man who was wielding it."

"You killed him?"

"And buried him, yes."

Holmes sat back, regarding her, his eyes glittering with satisfaction and eagerness. "I suggest you give me the complete story."

They had forgotten me completely. I was still staring, astonished, as Elizabeth continued.

"Dressing in male costume has been a habit of mine since I was fourteen. I enjoy the freedom of movement and social independence it allows me. However, I am not blind to the possible complications that could arise, so I also carry a gun whenever I go on my excursions over the moors. I learnt how to use it, too, as I could not see the purpose of threatening if one couldn't deliver on the threat."

I must have made some small sound in reaction to this, for Elizabeth glanced at me. She must have read disapproval into my expression, for she shrugged. "I have been alone in the world since I was three years old. A foundling soon learns the hard facts of life. And because I am a woman, I was doubly disadvantaged. I have had to work to support myself, and the only positions I could obtain were as governess, teacher, or nurse. None of them appealed to me. I held a job as a typewriter before this adventure, and even that was beginning to pall. My only pleasure was my long solitary walks upon the moors. Last winter the trouble against which I was always prepared to guard myself occurred."

Holmes lit a cigarette. "A man . . . a shepherd?" he guessed.

"Yes. I came too close and he saw me for what I was. He was too fast for me, and trapped me against an outcrop of rock and the bog. He had a knife, as you have already surmised, and his intentions were perfectly obvious."

I felt an ache in my hand and glanced down to find my hands both tightly fisted. I willed my fingers to unfurl and lifted my gaze back to Elizabeth's face.

She drew in a deep, shaking breath and forced herself to continue.

"He thrust me to the ground, and I believe that had I been wearing skirts my fate would have been quickly sealed. As it was, he had trouble with . . . the fastenings." Elizabeth stopped and swallowed. "Must I continue?" she asked Holmes.

He leaned forward. "You shot him with the gun you always carried," he said, sparing her.

She nodded. "I could see no other way out of my predicament. I shot him. I managed to lift his body off me, and I dragged him toward the bog, intending to throw him in. But the shock of what I had done struck me then and I lay for a while, too sick and dazed to do anything. After a time—I do not know how long—my mind began to work again. I knew that what I had done was murder, yet I had killed only to defend myself. The man was a . . . an animal." She whispered the word with abhorrence. "He had boasted to me of other conquests while he was preparing himself, but I knew no one would believe me if I attempted to recite his claims."

She stopped and looked into the flames, her eyes distant, her mind focussed on the memory. "So I buried him. I knew the bog would eventually reveal its booty if I dumped him there. It was clear nothing but burial would do. I found a suitable place and pushed the snow aside, and with a rock, his knife, and my bare hands I carved out a shallow grave. I rolled him, the knife, and the gun into it, and covered him over. I knew the snow would obliterate any trace of the grave by the time the ground thawed. I very carefully removed any sign of human activity in the area, then changed back into my skirts which I carried with me in a pack. My walking clothes were wet and filthy, so I washed them in a stream and carried them five miles away, where I buried them under a rock. I knew I could not walk off the moors carrying wet, stained, and ripped men's clothing, for if the body was ever found, I would be remembered. Neither did I dare put them in my pack as I normally would. I was afraid I would be stopped and questioned, and my pack examined." She grimaced. "By then, I was not thinking very clearly. Burying them seemed like the only sensible thing to do. I intended to come back for them in the spring. Then I destroyed any clue in the area that might point to my identity."

She looked up at Holmes. "I kept your reputation in my mind as I did so, and tried to match my wits against yours. I believe that to a certain degree I succeeded."

I let out my breath. "It must have taken you hours!" I exclaimed.

Elizabeth nodded. "Two days," she said softly. "I was very ill by the time I felt I could safely leave, and not be noticed and remembered."

Holmes threw his cigarette into the fire. "Your mistake was contacting Watson."

"Yes. I knew that even as I contacted him. But I had been ill for weeks, and dazed, and when I finally recovered, I didn't know if the police had discovered the body, or the clothes, or if the game was up. I was desperate to know what my fate was to be. I combed through back issues at the newspaper office and found a very small article stating my clothes had been found, and Sherlock Holmes had been brought in to investigate. You can well imagine my terror. I didn't believe for a moment I had managed to outwit you. I was quite sure I had overlooked that one vital clue that you would discover, and that it was only a matter of days before you would arrive on my doorstep to arrest me. When that didn't happen, I became more deeply disturbed."

She stared into the fire. "I haven't had much practice as a criminal. I believed you were playing with me. So I learned John's address and consulted him on a medical matter. My intention was to coax him into talking about the clothes, to see if I could gain an indication of what was happening in your investigation. As soon as I walked into the room, John started and stared at me as if I had the word 'murderer' tattooed on my forehead. It was all I could do to carry through with the interview and leave. There was no need for me to trick him into talking about the case; I'd already had my answer." She sighed. "So when you wrote to me, John, asking me to return, I believed it was the end. I fully expected that when I arrived the police would step in and arrest me."

I gasped. "Yet you still came!"

"I couldn't see the point in prolonging the inevitable. And I truly did believe it was the inevitable, with the famous Sherlock Holmes on my trail." She gave a very small laugh. "You can imagine my amazement when I realized a few minutes into the interview that, contrary to my belief, you hadn't solved the entire puzzle. I was quite lightheaded with relief. And up until Moriarty's men abducted me, I thought I could finally reclaim the reins of my life."

We sat in silence for a long moment. I was filled with horror at what Elizabeth had put herself through. Quite apart from her narrow escape on the moors, she had lived a life of silent dread for months.

Holmes said softly, "Have you proof of any of this, Elizabeth?" His words were the gentlest I had ever heard him address towards her before.

She frowned. "I am not sure it is evidence, but it will corroborate part of my story." With an embarrassed hesitation she unbuttoned her waistcoat, pulled her shirt and undergarments up, and twisted her body around so that we could both see a vicious, recently healed scar on the skin high up over her ribs.

I sucked in a breath in reaction. "Who doctored those stitches?" I said, appalled. "He should have his licence withdrawn."

"That would be difficult," Holmes replied, "as the doctor was never qualified in the first place."

Elizabeth lowered her shirt and looked at me. "I did it," she said softly.

The enormity of her undertaking shocked me anew, and I shook my head, unable to express myself.

Elizabeth looked at Holmes as she tucked her shirt back in. "So there you have it, Holmes. I am in your hands now. As you can see, I have nothing to do with Moriarty, my mystery has been cleared up, and you have the means to keep me immobilized. As you are renowned across Europe, you have merely to inform the police at the next large town we call on, and they will ensure you are rid of me."

Holmes studied her closely for a while. "I am not a court of law," he said softly.

"Your reputation is built on a zeal for justice."

"As Watson will tell you, my definition of justice and the law's sometimes conflict." He sat back and lit another cigarette. "Besides, neither of us can judge you guilty of murder when we ourselves have both killed in self-defence."

"I don't understand," Elizabeth replied, her voice low and strained. That was, I believe, the only time I have ever heard her utter those words.

"You have paid enough for your mistake," Holmes replied. "Your secret is safe with us."

Elizabeth's face seemed to crumple and for a brief moment I thought she was about to cry. She dipped her head and when she lifted her chin again, her face was smooth and under control. "Thank you," she said, her voice hoarse with unshed tears.

Holmes got to his feet. "I suggest Watson give you his professional opinion on your needlework," he said, indicating her side, and walked away.

Elizabeth's secret was full of horror, courage, and resilience. My admiration for her lifted even higher after her confession. I do not believe my conscience was ever troubled over what was technically a murder. To me, the world was short one shepherd, and well rid of him, at that. As Holmes pointed out, we had both killed in self-defence, too. However, I am not sure I would ever be able to compete with Elizabeth's self-control in attending her own wound.

It also explained her cheerfulness under our rough camping conditions. In comparison to what she had already lived through, our walking tour must have felt very much like a stroll in the park.

The events that culminated in that week are well chronicled. Not only did all the major English and European newspapers report the facts and speculate endlessly on their interpretation, but I also attempted to clear the confusion with my own account, which appeared in *The Strand* magazine some time later as "The Adventure of the Final Solution."

The facts are grim enough. Moriarty did find us, eventually. He contrived to draw me back to our hotel with a false message calling for my medical skills, leaving Holmes alone to deal with him.

On May 4th, 1891, Holmes and Moriarty met, grappled, and fell into the fatal depths of the Reichenbach Falls. Elizabeth's fate as an innocent bystander appeared to be as deadly as Holmes had predicted, for her body was not found, either. Although I could speak publicly only of my grief over Holmes' death, privately I was mourning for both of them. And even then my sorrow for the loss of Elizabeth was no less than that I felt for Holmes.

Holmes' dramatic return three years later was the dawning of a new era after a long dark night. For three years I had thought him dead while he evaded Moran, Moriarity's most able lieutenant, who hounded him all across Europe and into Asia. He had only returned to London when Moran had grown lax and embroiled himself in a situation that Holmes could use to put away the beggar for good. The murder of the Honourable Ronald Adair was the event that gave Holmes his opportunity to deal with Moran, and to return to London.

I believe that from the moment Holmes revealed his identity to me in my consulting rooms and I was acquainted with the gigantic deception he had played on the world, up until the time of Moran's arrest, I was mildly bemused and possibly even a little hysterical. I took no notes of the events at all, and later had to prompt Holmes into reminiscing when I came to write up the case. I spent most of that evening watching Holmes, and marvelling that the man was actually alive and here in London. Later that night, when we were settled in front of the fireplace at Baker Street, the solid reality of it began to filter through.

Holmes stretched himself out in the chair. "Ah, Watson. It is good to be home."

I sat back, sipping my brandy. "Holmes, you have been very good to give me the broad spectrum of your journeys, but one particular has been overlooked."

Holmes smiled. "Nothing has been overlooked."

"Well, then, what has happened to Elizabeth? You assured me she was well and safe. But where is she?"

"Standing behind you, John," Elizabeth said quietly, right beside my shoulder.

I jumped to my feet and turned, startled beyond measure. "Elizabeth. It is good to see you," I said truthfully.

She held out her hand in greeting and I drew her closer towards the fire so that I might look at her. She was quite as tall as I remembered, and her hair the same glorious, burnished copper.

"It is so very good to see you, John," she said, smiling. "You do not know how hard I found it to watch you from that ledge above the Falls. It was only Holmes' own, more dangerous situation that kept me silent."

"I am glad you survived. When I thought Holmes dead, I believed you were, too." I paused, hesitating to voice the next natural question.

Elizabeth smiled, and answered my unspoken thoughts. "Yes, I travelled with Holmes on his journeys."

I glanced at Holmes, and some of my shock showed, I know, because a glimmer of amusement pulled at his mouth. I am afraid my gentlemanly instincts proved too ingrained, and I sought a change of subject.

However, my curiosity was provoked. Although no plain answers surfaced that night, no matter how I probed with my eyes, certain insights were afforded me as time went by, small signs that would have gone unnoticed had I not cued myself to look for them. Chief among them was Holmes' barely perceptible air of contentedness. He had never been a demonstrative man, and he treated Elizabeth with no more affection than was normal, at least in my presence. Yet often I would catch him following her with his eyes, or observing her closely when she spoke. His pride in her expanding abilities was boundless, and could have served as applause for his own apprentice.

While Holmes had been away, I had lost my dear wife. Because of my recent widowhood, I often found myself in the well-remembered rooms at Baker Street, toasting myself by the fire. During those hours, Elizabeth was always there, a new partner in the old friendship. Outside, when Holmes was working, it was much as I remembered. Since his return, however, I spent much more of my time following his career. And I confess my motive for doing so was almost purely so that I could attempt to understand his now-reserved personal life.

The first step towards the more comfortable affection we used to share came from Elizabeth. I should have expected that, but I was surprised when I called at Baker Street one morning to find Holmes already gone about his business without waiting for me, and Elizabeth standing at the top of the stairs, looking out for me.

She drew me in towards the fire, for it was a cold, wet March morning, and settled me comfortably, pouring me tea from the silver pot sitting on the tray.

"I confess I am surprised Holmes is about so early," I said.

Elizabeth stood before the fire, a hand keeping her skirts from the grate and the other against the shelf, as she studied the dancing flames. She lifted her head at my statement and smiled.

"That was my idea," she admitted.

"I have no idea why you would suggest such a thing," I replied carefully.

"I felt it was time I broached a subject you find distasteful so that Holmes may have his old friend Watson back. Some truths need to be aired."

I arranged my answer carefully. "Distasteful is inaccurate. Awkward would perhaps be closer."

Elizabeth nodded her consent at my amendment. "So I am afraid I am about to make you feel awkward. You are jealous of me, John."

That was the very last thing I had expected her to say, yet immediately she spoke the words I recognized the barrier that had arisen in my dealings with Holmes. I felt words of protest bubble to my lips but honesty made me force them back. Elizabeth was watching my mental struggle as it appeared on my face, and I answered with the unadorned truth, for I knew she would accept no less.

"Perhaps you are right. I was Holmes' friend first and I never expected someone would take my place as his closest confidant."

Elizabeth nodded sympathetically. "And I miss the John Watson I learned to like and respect while trooping around Europe. Then we were companions and comrades in the fight for the well-being of Sherlock Holmes. He misses the old familiarity, John, although he will never speak of it. And I am afraid that is my fault."

"Perhaps fault is too strong a word," I suggested.

"Perhaps. You are the wordsmith." She moved away from the fire and refilled my teacup. Unexpectedly she changed subjects. "I read your account of Moriarty's death in *The Strand*. It reached us in Khartoum."

"I was forced to give an account. His brother, James Moriarty, was raising a dreadful fuss in the papers."

Elizabeth sat in Holmes' old armchair. "You carefully edited any mention of me. Why is that?"

I forced myself not to prevaricate despite my discomfort. "I didn't know how to include you. Your conduct was. . . . "

"Unbecoming?" Elizabeth asked, with a smile.

"I was about to say courageous and admirable. But the truth would have caused a furore in Fleet Street, to say nothing of among the public, if *The Strand* had dared publish it at all." I shifted uneasily. "Elizabeth, I admired you immensely for your perseverance and courage, and if there had been some way of making that clear I would have done so. All three of us understood the necessities that drove us, but the public is less sympathetic."

"Don't apologize," she said. "Your wisdom will prove far sighted. But that is another matter. For the moment we are dealing with, well, with the future. Tell me: you were hurt when Holmes did not immediately ask you to move back here to Baker Street, weren't you?"

"Yes."

"You do know that he will never ask?"

"I have suspected so for a while." I felt myself beginning to relax. Although we were nearing the core of the matter, Elizabeth's straightforward attitude made it seem easy to deal with the blunt truth. It occurred to me that this was in part what attracted Holmes to her. He had always preferred dealing with logical facts than with slippery emotions.

Elizabeth eyed me. "There is no point in resenting the fact, John. Or resenting me. New facets have been added to Holmes, but if you look past these new facets, you will find you still have the efficient thinking machine you admired so much in your writings."

"I cannot see where I fit into these new facets," I confessed. "I have spent six months attempting to understand."

"I know. That is why I am trying to help you now. You were once Holmes' self-appointed chronicler. Have you retired from the position?"

"How can I chronicle what I do not understand?"

Elizabeth sat back. "Given time, there is much you will understand. That is clear in your work; that you grasp subtleties. But to begin, why not write up a story from when you both shared these rooms? I am sure going through your notes and revising your old friendship will show you just how much things haven't changed."

I considered her words. "A sound suggestion." I could feel the old enthusiasm beginning to warm my bones. There were notes on several cases of Holmes' laying in the bottom of a trunk in my rooms that were worthy of being written up. I immediately recalled the details of the case on the moors and the beset Baskerville family. "Yes. I will do that. And then, perhaps I should deal with your return from the dead."

"Holmes' return from the dead," Elizabeth amended. She sat forward. "And now it is we reach the matter I spoke of earlier. I cannot exist on the printed page, John."

I stared at her.

She continued quietly. "Remember Moriarty? Remember how I became involved in the adventure? Because Moriarty is dead is no guarantee the same cannot happen again. As long as Holmes is out there making enemies in the criminal world, we must minimize any risks that he may be distracted." Then she laughed. "Besides, as you have pointed out, it is awkward attempting to explain me away."

I found myself smiling. Elizabeth offered me another cup of tea and we settled down comfortably.

"May I ask you something?" I ventured.

"Of course."

"Did you really walk all the way to Constantinople?"

"Every step. With Moran on our trail we didn't dare risk using the rail system."

"Tell me about it."

Holmes strode into the room sometime later to find us deep into a discussion of their journey. Those uninterrupted hours were invaluable to me, and will forever be enshrined in my memory as the start of a new and wholly fulfilling stage of my life. They also served as the key that unlocked the old friendship. Both Holmes and I were enriched professionally by having Elizabeth as part of our lives.

On that wintry day I caught a glimmer of the complexities and depths of Elizabeth's character. Like Holmes, she was bohemian and hedonistic in her attitudes, as their shared experiences in some of the more remote regions of Asia and Africa served to underline. Yet, she had learnt through hard lessons in life as a foundling and woman to contain these attitudes within a demure, proper, and altogether beautiful exterior, and her practised charm and grace also served to baffle the unwary.

In contrast, Holmes had never attempted to hide his bohemianism. In his chosen career it had not mattered, and he cared little for reputation—save professionally.

As I was to discover more fully later, Elizabeth was Holmes' intellectual equal. She had not had the advantages of a broad education, nor the training Holmes had put himself through. But she had been taught to read and write by the Sisters at the orphanage she was raised in, and she read voraciously. She soon devoured Holmes' extensive reference library, and she even worked her way through my more obscure medical works. She had Holmes' quick, observant eye, and she practised assiduously all the many techniques he employed in his career. Holmes aided and abetted her in this education, and they would compete endlessly with each other in intricate mind games.

Holmes' supervision of her education did not neglect the physical skills. Elizabeth was already a marksman with the revolver, as we had both discovered in Strasburg. I do not believe Holmes went so far as to teach her boxing, but I do know he taught her all his martial arts skills, which proved useful to her, by and by.

One day I discovered them duelling with Holmes' foils. I paused in the doorway until the round had finished, and coughed.

"Good morning."

They both turned to face me, Elizabeth with the smile I like to believe she reserved only for me, and I kissed her temple in the little ceremony that completed our pleasant greeting ritual. She was wearing trousers and shirt, a costume I had become used to, and even secretly enjoyed seeing her wear.

"You appeared to be giving Holmes worthy opposition," I observed.

Elizabeth laughed. "Never. I don't have his reach, to start."

Holmes took the foil from her and, after pushing the sofa back into place, threw both foils beneath. "She could have been a champion if she had started young enough and been a man."

"Well, there you are," Elizabeth said simply.

I tossed a copy of *The Strand* I had brought over to Holmes, who caught it deftly.

"The celebration of your return to Baker Street," I told him. "Along with the requested distortions of the truth."

Holmes sank into a chair with his sleeves still rolled up and began to read the story.

Elizabeth exchanged a glance with me. "Excuse me," she murmured, and left quietly. She returned, the men's attire swapped for more elegant skirts, and turned her back to me. "Would you mind? I can never reach the middle buttons."

Holmes closed the magazine and rolled it. "Catch!" he said abruptly and threw it to Elizabeth. She shot out her left hand and caught it neatly, and Holmes nodded approvingly. He sprang out of the chair. "You have not lost your habit of wringing drama from every fact," he told me.

"I have discovered I have a formerly unsuspected creative talent, too," I told him somewhat sourly. "I am beginning to consider a work of fiction."

Holmes glanced at Elizabeth, who was already absorbed in the falsified article that had unfairly expunged Elizabeth's place in the history books.

"It is best this way," he said softly. "No one would ever try to subdue you, Watson, for your reputation is well known and respected."

Later Elizabeth gave me her opinion on my story. "To me, I can feel you are holding something back. There is a reservation, a distancing, that was not there in your earlier works. But that's the price I believe you must pay for not telling the whole truth."

Knowing I was keeping Elizabeth safe was more than adequate compensation for the shield of lies I continued to publish after the release of "The Adventure of the Empty House." This fact comforted me whenever my conscience prickled.

Ah, hindsight! Had I known my successful efforts to keep Elizabeth from the public gaze would have such tragic consequences, I doubt I would ever have written another word.

Chapter Four

As Elizabeth predicted, our old familiar partnership returned. I believe Holmes was secretly relieved I knew of their intimate relationship, for neither of us had to guard our tongues. Even so, I found I never referred to their relationship directly, taking Holmes' reticence as my example.

Naturally I wondered how Elizabeth had managed to slide under his armour and claim such a unique place in his heart.

I don't suppose I would ever have heard the story and thus gained my answer, if I hadn't developed a fever one autumn. It took me a long while to be rid of it, and my recovery was slow. I cannot remember now whose suggestion it was that I recuperate at Baker Street, but it struck all of us as a sensible solution, and I was duly installed in my old room. Elizabeth became my temporary nurse.

With such an arrangement, Holmes' domestic affairs were wide open to my scrutiny, and as I lay in bed day after day, I found my observations both educational and entertaining. I had supposed myself a man of the world, well versed in the habits and ways of women in their homes, but I was soon to discover that I knew very little indeed.

Elizabeth was an excellent nurse. Always helpful and kind, and deft in her ways, she never became overbearingly cheerful or solicitous. Doctors can make the very worst convalescents, I know, but I did try my best to remain patient. Elizabeth would spend long hours curled up in the armchair by my bed, telling me stories of their journey about the remote corners of the world, or otherwise entertaining me in the comfortable way she had. Indeed, I often found myself relating events I considered unfit for a lady's ears; not only would Elizabeth appreciate the tale, she could usually better it.

One afternoon, when Elizabeth was reading to me, I reached out to close the book and requested from her the story of how she and Holmes had become, to all effects, man and wife.

She put the book on the floor. "Holmes would never tell you," she said.

"I wouldn't dare to ask," I admitted. "But I feel I have been handed a *fait accompli*. Holmes meets you, you both disappear for three years and when you reappear, it is all over and done with."

Elizabeth smiled. "I do believe there's a romantic hiding under that exterior of yours. Yet you spend so much time writing about Holmes' feats of logic and deduction."

"Emotions and logic are like oil and water," I said. "The two do not mix."

"Oh, but they do. Very well," and Elizabeth laughed at my discomfort. "Dear John, you have requested a story that will embarrass you, I know it. I cannot relate it without using unpolished truth and details." She looked at me fondly for a moment. "You're curious because Holmes presents such a cold exterior to the world, aren't you?"

I admitted I was.

"I believe you think that I threw myself at Holmes," she said, with her mischievous smile. I knew she was testing my resolve to accept the blunt facts. I smiled back.

"It is difficult to imagine it happening any other way."

"You would have the end of the story before you have the beginning. No, if you insist on the tale, I must start at the beginning and you must wait for the end, or the storyteller's art is lost." She lifted her feet and tucked them under her, making herself comfortable for the telling.

"Holmes didn't wish to leave you believing he was dead. I argued that it was safer that way. I suppose he omitted to tell you that?" she asked.

Much surprised, I nodded.

"Yes, he is overprotective of me," she said half to herself. "Perhaps I should start there."

I will use Elizabeth's tale as my own, for the story is lengthy and complicated. . . .

Holmes' and Elizabeth's story began, appropriately, when in response to the fraudulent plea for my medical help back at the inn at Meiringen, I left them paused on the path that led to the steep drop down into the heart of the Reichenbach Falls. Holmes smoked a cigarette in quiet contemplation whilst Elizabeth watched my departure. She actually waved goodbye to me when I turned for my one last look before scrambling over the hill and out of sight.

I didn't know it then, but that image of Holmes and Elizabeth quietly waiting on the footpath was to be my last sight of them for three years. Compared to what was to happen in the next few minutes, it was a composed, tranquil scene.

Holmes continued to smoke his cigarette in silence for a few moments, then glanced at Elizabeth. "Perhaps it would be as well for you to follow Watson. They may need some nursing assistance from an English woman."

Elizabeth considered the idea for a short second, then felt her blood run cold as she fathomed Holmes' true intentions.

Constantly throughout that week we had heard Holmes maintain he would consider his life's work complete if he could only rid the world of Moriarty. I had quoted verbatim to Elizabeth Holmes' breakfast-time conversation with that evil man—including Holmes' acceptance of death, if death was necessary to achieve his aims. These facts coupled in her mind, and she stared at Holmes, horrified.

"The note. It was a forgery!"

Holmes shook his head irritably. "You saw the note. It was signed by Steiler. Why would I send Watson on such a long goose chase with his poor leg if I even suspected it was false?"

But Elizabeth's quick mind had already leapt past the question and reached the answer. She looked around the jagged horizon, feeling very much trapped in a corner. "You wanted him out of the way. Now you're trying to do the same to me."

"Really, Elizabeth, paranoia suits you ill. However, I do think you must return to the hotel." He spoke quite firmly.

Elizabeth ceased her search of the horizon, and studied Holmes instead. "The message was a fabrication. You knew it was the minute you read it. And you knew Moriarty wrote it. He is setting up a trap."

Holmes merely returned her look.

"*Death is on the agenda,*' you said. And now you are calmly waiting for it to arrive."

"I also said that bystanders would be hurt. You must return, Elizabeth."

An artificial calm descended upon her at Holmes' indirect confirmation of her guesses. The panic left her as she comprehended that the final confrontation was mere minutes away. She had a promise to live up to.

"I am not leaving you alone," she replied.

"You must. For your own sake."

Elizabeth held out her hand. "Give me the gun."

"The gun will serve no useful purpose."

Elizabeth stared at him, dismayed and vexed. It was not part of her nature to accept the inescapable with Holmes' fatalism, and she knew no way of jarring him out of the mood, short of direct action.

With a swift, dexterous movement, she lunged and delved into Holmes' coat pocket—the one she knew carried the loaded revolver. She moved very fast—quickly enough to catch Holmes off his guard, and she succeeded in getting a grasp on the gun and half-withdrawing it from the pocket, before Holmes' iron grip snared her wrist. She looked up at him.

"If you won't help yourself, I must," she said.

"And you will be killed alongside me," he said firmly. He lifted her wrist, and held her hand steady, the gun between her tingling fingers. She could feel her grip loosening. "Go back," he told her, and reached for the gun.

It dropped from her numbed fingers and fell through Holmes' as he stretched to catch it. With a solid thump it hit the spray-drenched rocks at their feet and gave a little bounce up, over the edge, and down, irretrievably, into the mists hiding the foaming water beneath them.

They both looked over the edge, Elizabeth with a wordless cry of dismay. She wrenched her hand from his loosened grasp and grabbed his lapels, and shook him.

"Damn it, Holmes, do something! Don't just stand there. Think of a plan, work out a strategy. He can be beaten!"

Holmes looked down at this extraordinary woman. He had not had a finger laid on him since boyhood, and he certainly hadn't been shaken. Her vexation was beginning to communicate itself to him. Firmly he pulled her hands away.

"I have been building strategies and laying plans for a whole year—and it all leads to this." He in his turn shook her a little, for emphasis. "Go back to the hotel, Elizabeth. Now. I insist."

The sound of falling rocks alerted them, and they looked up the cliff path. The hunched, crooked figure outlined in the last of the evening sun was unmistakable. Moriarty had arrived.

Elizabeth didn't need confirmation of Moriarty's identity. Holmes' quick, exhaled breath was all the verification she required. She rubbed her wrists as Holmes let them go.

"Too late," he breathed.

Elizabeth looked back at the figure slowly making its way down the path that ended where they stood. There was no way out.

Holmes pushed her gently to one side. "Now I must win," he said. "Or you will die, too." He stepped in front of her, and faced Moriarty as he approached.

Moriarty halted a few paces from them, and glanced at Elizabeth before returning his steady gaze upon Holmes.

"Foolish. You should have got her out of the way, Holmes." The words were innocent enough, but Elizabeth realized with a jolt that her death sentence had been pronounced. The grim surety behind the casual verdict made her shudder.

Holmes remained silent, seemingly relaxed, yet Elizabeth could sense his whole body was tense and waiting.

Elizabeth expected Moriarty to continue, to give some twisted justification for what he was intending to do, but the man fell silent and simply watched Holmes. There was no need to declare himself, she perceived, for everything that could be said had already been spoken. The entire year's convoluted strategies and complicated actions led to this moment.

Suddenly Moriarty sprang, and threw himself at Holmes. They grappled, and Moriarty's weight carried them back toward the edge of the path. Elizabeth flattened herself against the cliff face, stifling a gasp as Moriarty leapt past her.

On the very brink of the path, Holmes and Moriarty struggled against each other as Elizabeth watched, frightened. It did not occur to her that the path was clear now, and she could make her escape. She stayed, waiting for the fatal outcome.

The test of wills and power came to a sudden end, for Moriarty found a superior grip on his opponent and, with a rasping cry of glee, prepared to throw Holmes over the ledge. But on the very verge of losing his balance, Holmes twisted and broke free, throwing himself aside.

Moriarty's cry changed to a scream of rage as he fell, without his prey. Holmes rested on the lip of the cliff, watching Moriarty's descent.

Elizabeth moved to his side and looked down. She saw Moriarty's body strike some rocks and bounce aside, still falling. Then the swirling, floating spray closed over the body, and Moriarty was gone.

Elizabeth shut her eyes, her body shaking with giddy relief.

Holmes stood, moving slowly, and then lowered himself gingerly to sit upon a broad rock close by. He delved into his pockets and pulled out a pencil stub and his notebook, which he opened.

Elizabeth stared at him. "What in the world are you doing?" she asked.

Holmes wrote rapidly and without hesitation. "I am about to die," he said.

Elizabeth felt her jaw drop. "You are?"

"Moriarty was the leader of a very clever gang of criminals. At least three of his lieutenants are almost as ingenious as he, and all of them have as much reason as Moriarty to wish me dead."

Elizabeth nodded. "You want them to think you dead so they will not come after you," she surmised.

"Yes, and not only they. I have other enemies, not connected with Moriarty. It would suit my purposes if they fell to the same erroneous conclusion. If they are truly convinced I am dead, they will grow lax and careless. They will make mistakes, and I can then destroy them."

Elizabeth considered the plan. "Am I to die, too?" she asked.

Holmes glanced up from his page. "I am afraid so. You heard Moriarty: he was going to deal with you as he tried to deal with me. If you walked out of this canyon and claimed that Moriarty had killed me, and let you live to tell the tale, his men would know without a doubt that it was a bluff." He looked back down at his page. "Besides, I do not trust your ability to carry the bluff convincingly. You would be cross-examined by some of the shrewdest minds in England, and nothing but the truth would be allowed by them."

"I see," Elizabeth said. "How are we to die?"

"This note to Watson should take care of the details," Holmes said, tearing out the pages and folding them. He took out his cigarette case and rested the notes beneath it on the rock he had leant his cane against. He pointed to Elizabeth's feet. "Do not move any farther up the path. I want our footsteps down to the end of the path to be perfectly clear and easy to read."

Elizabeth stayed where she was. "And how are we to get back up the path to the top?"

"We don't," Holmes replied.

"There is no other way out—unless you intend to fly?"

Holmes pointed up the almost sheer cliff face beside him. "There is a shadow up there that suggests a small ledge about twenty feet up."

Elizabeth gazed upwards and bit her lip. There was no need to ask Holmes if he seriously intended to scale the cliff; the situation was entirely inappropriate for jest. Instead she told herself firmly that this was something that had to be done, and that was that.

The climb taxed their nerves and sinews, for the cliff was wet and slippery, and they strongly felt the urgency to reach cover before I reappeared. Several times one or the other nearly slipped as grass pulled out by its roots, or their footing gave way beneath them. But they persevered, and at last made the safety of the minuscule ledge.

And there, laying full length, they watched as I returned. While Holmes had struggled with Moriarty, I had returned to the inn at

Meiringen to find that Steiler had not sent for me at all. I immediately fell on the truth: Moriarty had removed me from the scene with a simple ruse. I hastily organized a party of men and had hurried back to the Falls, only to find the path empty, footprints leading to the edge of the cliff, and Holmes' note.

The note made it all too clear to me what had happened. Moriarty had allowed Holmes a few moments to compose his last thoughts before their final, deadly confrontation. As well as bidding me a last goodbye, Holmes expressed his satisfaction that his death would accomplish what he had set out to achieve: the end of Moriarty.

Defeated, saddened, and weary, I ordered the rescue party back to the inn, where I would begin the formalities of Holmes' death, while above me, Holmes and Elizabeth kept silent vigil.

As the rescue party moved out of sight of the Falls, the pair relaxed, only to be shocked by a huge rock falling past them.

Holmes looked up and ducked as another large rock bounded by barely a foot from his head. Elizabeth flinched against the cliff face, in relative safety. He looked again, and his face remained expressionless as he identified the figure. "Moran."

The name meant nothing to Elizabeth, but there was no doubt in her mind that Moran was dangerous, for Holmes immediately set about descending the cliff face again. The hail of deadly missiles continued, and Elizabeth threw herself forward and began to climb down. They slipped, slithered, and scrambled down the cliff face, tearing skin, shredding knuckles, elbows, and knees, and ripping fingernails, as speed took the better part of their caution in their race for the sanctuary of the footpath. Halfway down, Holmes fell, and landed heavily on the footpath below. He picked himself up, and reached up to assist Elizabeth down onto the path.

They took to their heels, the beginning of a long race across the countryside, attempting to lose Moran.

It was almost fully dark by this time, and their footing was unsure and their speed retarded. Constantly they stumbled and sometimes fell, yet Holmes kept up a punishing pace, pushing forward into the darkness.

They were also climbing steadily, and despite their exertions,

Elizabeth felt a chill settle into her bones, and she was breathless beyond what her hurried gait demanded.

It seemed many hours of exacting and ceaseless effort had passed when Holmes slowed and began to look about him. On their right a bulky shadow defined itself from out of the night, and Holmes led her toward it. Its square angles bespoke manmade shelter, and the lack of light its emptiness. As they drew closer, details became apparent, and Elizabeth recognized it as an alpine hut—one of those dotted about the lower and middle slopes of the mountains, designed to serve as shelters for anyone caught out in the harsh winter weather. There would be wood, water, and a stove for warmth.

Holmes explored the hut's perimeter, then opened the door and inspected the inside before drawing her in.

"Rest," he told her. "We've succeeded in losing him, I think."

Elizabeth lowered herself wearily onto the hard, wooden bench next to the door.

Holmes opened a chest next to the rotund stove in the corner and pulled out a small, wooden barrel. "Water." He put it on the table, and inspected the stove. "We can risk a fire, I believe," and he discarded his jacket and set about making a fire of the wood stacked on the other side of the stove.

Soon the fire was burning cheerfully, and they had supped inadequately on the contents of the barrel. At least refreshed, they sat back to consider their situation.

Elizabeth was the first to speak.

"Moran is, I assume, one of Moriarty's lieutenants of whom you spoke?"

"Yes, and the most dangerous one." Holmes frowned. "I confess I was surprised by his appearance, but I should have foreseen that Moriarty would take steps to ensure he had some assistance. I suspect Moriarty contrived to have Moran released from prison shortly after Moran was taken."

"Just Moran, or would he attempt to release all his lieutenants?" Elizabeth asked. "Do we have to deal with more than one?"

Holmes weighed the facts. "I know Moriarty lacked time as the key to my plans to defeat him was speed. If Moriarty and his men were to be successfully rounded up, then it was essential they be arrested all at once, so they could not send warning to their associates. That is how Moriarty escaped, I suspect—he was given just enough warning to evade the police and begin his hunt for me. If he was to find me, he could not afford to dally for long in London. That is why I hadn't planned on Moran's presence. Consider this: Moriarty was following us, avoiding the police, attempting to warn his gang of criminals of the trouble I had brewing, and yet he still managed to have his head henchman released from gaol." Holmes frowned. "If he could manage that, he could manage it twice. But not, I think, more than twice." He thought silently for a moment, then nodded. "Yes, that is what I would do in the same circumstances. Free two of my men to assist me."

Elizabeth, following this fragmented answer, said, "Moran is one. Who is the other?"

"In all probability, Mr. Straker. He is as capable as Moran of working on his own. Also, he works well with Moran."

"What does he look like? How will I know him if I see him?"

"Straker is very easy to identify." Holmes held up his left hand. "His hand is missing. He was once a failed thief on the east coast of the Mediterranean."

"Failed?"

"In that part of the world, a thief who is caught loses his hand. The first time."

"And the second time he is caught?"

"The other hand," Holmes replied. "I do not know what the punishment is for a third offence—I doubt a third offence often occurs."

Elizabeth shuddered. "And Moran?"

"Colonel Sebastian Moran, formerly of the First Bengalore Pioneers. It is unfortunate we have him stalking us. Moran is one of the best hunters in Europe. He has written books on the subject. He is a good practical soldier, and a superb gamesman and strategist."

"He sounds formidable."

"He is. But he has flaws, one of which is a vile temper he cannot quite control, and which distorts his judgement at times when speed of thought and reaction is necessary. It is that which has put him in trouble throughout most of his career." Holmes reached for his cigarette case, then remembered where he had left it. Instead he delved into a pocket and brought out a single, crumpled cigarette. He lit it before continuing with his lecture. "Despite that, Moran will be the leader, no matter who the other man is. It is Moran whom we should consider our opponent, now." He exhaled a cloud of smoke. "We should deem ourselves lucky on one point, however. He didn't have time or opportunity to retrieve his airgun."

Holmes went on to explain to Elizabeth the power and stealth of this remarkable weapon, and the danger it represented when wielded in Moran's hands.

"The man is a crack shot, and if he had had his airgun this evening, he could have easily picked us off one by one whilst we lay on that ledge, and saved himself considerable effort and frustration. I am glad we do not have to contend with it now, for Moran will not abandon the chase to go back for it. If we run into him in the future, however, we must be cautious."

"And the immediate future?" Elizabeth asked.

Holmes waved toward the bunk. "Sleep for you, rest for me. In the morning we must continue across country. Beyond that, I will have to decide. For now, we must play hare and outwit the most dangerous hound in Europe."

Chapter Five

ELIZABETH HAD WOKEN ON THAT FIRST MORNING in the hut and found herself stiff, sore, and still weary. Her sleep had not been an easy one.

Holmes had reached several decisions during his night vigil and he shared them with her as they prepared to continue their march.

"I intended that you would return to England once the deception had been established, but Moran knows we are both alive, so I cannot send you back. You are now inextricably involved, and as long as Moran roams the earth you are in danger.

"We must continue. I have decided we should head for Italy. Last night we covered nearly ten miles, and that was in a southerly direction, so we are moving toward the Italian border already. I am almost sure Moran will expect us to go west, toward England, and the familiarity of France." He stood, and looked at her. "Are you ready to leave?"

They spent the next week hurrying across the rugged alpine country of southern Switzerland. Elizabeth remembered it as an encapsulated period of time with a distinct beginning and end—but time within it grew flexible. Sometimes it seemed to pass quickly and at other times it was drawn out immeasurably. The constants were the countryside, the veiled pursuit, and Sherlock Holmes.

Holmes was her often-silent companion and guide. His stride was tireless and his strength of purpose unwavering. His concentration never waned, and her respect for Moran's hunting skills grew as she witnessed Holmes' unceasing caution. He never ceased planning or devising new strategies. Whether they were sheltering on the lee side of a tree through a shower of rain, or standing on the edge of a cliff or riverbank, Holmes was always scanning their surroundings, trying to outguess and outmanoeuvre the man he now called the most dangerous man in Europe.

They moved fairly rapidly across the countryside, for neither was burdened with any sort of luggage. Holmes avoided any population centres larger than the smallest of villages, working his way around sizable towns with painstaking caution.

It was necessary to enter some of the small villages to plumb the local knowledge of the terrain, for Holmes was attempting to navigate across the shoulders of the Alps without a guide, and it was essential they know which were the safest mountain passes to use.

On the occasions when they were in need of food, Holmes would leave Elizabeth safely hidden, and approach isolated farmhouses and chalets, and purchase their requirements with the last of the funds he carried with him.

Shelter was whatever derelict building, empty barn, or ruin they found toward sunset. Once it was the lee side of a ravine, high up on a lonely mountain pass, with the calling of wolves for fellowship.

Their companionship wrought changes on them both. Holmes began as taciturn and reserved. Elizabeth's womanhood was a barrier. However, he was helped by her male attire and her determination not to allow her assumed weaknesses headway. At night they would talk of inconsequential things. They explored each other's tastes in music, philosophy, fiction, and other trivial matters. Once or twice she actually managed to make Holmes laugh, and she was pleased.

On the third day it occurred to her that despite the pursuit and the hardships they were suffering, Holmes was enjoying himself. They had paused at the crest of a long climb, and stared out across the breathtaking vista spread beneath them, while Holmes considered their direction anew. Elizabeth recovered her breath, for they had been maintaining a fast pace for several hours.

She watched Holmes casting about, looking across the valleys toward the horizon and studying the countryside. His manner was alert and relaxed, and his eyes were keen. The chase was stirring his blood.

On the fifth day, as they traversed another high mountain pass, Holmes put his hands on his hips and took a deep breath. "I believe we will make it to safety, now."

"You speak as if we've achieved some sort of goal," Elizabeth remarked.

"We have. We've just crossed the Italian border. Moran will be hard pressed to track us here. We've seen no sign of him for four days, and we're well out of his grasp now." He glanced at Elizabeth's rumpled attire. "I think we can safely allow you to revert back to a lady, and I need to contact Mycroft. He can wire me some money." He paused. "I won't make too many plans. If we can reach the outskirts of Varzo tonight, I will be content."

Two days later they reached Florence.

Mr. and Mrs. Sigerson, Holmes wrote with a flourish. Elizabeth read it over his shoulder, and surreptitiously slid her left hand back into the glove Holmes had purchased for her.

The porter picked up their single piece of luggage and led them up the sweeping stairs to the best suite in the house. Holmes tipped the porter and inspected the room.

"I am going to cable Mycroft and Watson," he said when they were alone.

Elizabeth looked up from her inspection of the contents of the bureau. "Why cable Watson?" Her voice was a little sharp.

A faint puzzlement crossed Holmes' features. "To tell him we're alive, of course."

Elizabeth closed the drawer and moved across to face him. "You can't, Holmes."

"*Can't?* Why not?" He looked a little astonished at this dissension.

Elizabeth explained. "You have just spent a week tirelessly establishing to the world at large that you are undoubtedly dead. You brought me along to help the illusion, as you insisted I could not maintain the fabrication had I been left behind. Correct?"

"Yes."

"Holmes, if you do not trust my ability to carry the hoax, how much more can you rely on Watson not to give the game away? He plays cards badly, and lying is not part of his nature." She shook her head a little. "It is entirely possible that his joy in learning you are alive may cause some sort of indiscretion which will be your undoing. And they will be watching him, Holmes. Moran knows you are alive somewhere on the continent. Having lost you this time around, he will hurry back to London and watch your rooms, and keep a very careful eye on Watson so he may learn your location as soon as Watson does. What of those others who wish you dead? Is it not possible that they, too, will watch Watson to see if the story of your death really is true?"

Holmes looked away, and Elizabeth knew she had made her point. She was content with that, and let the matter drop. It was never mentioned again, and neither of them acknowledged that Holmes had nearly made a bad tactical blunder. His concern for me was implicit and understood, and no further discussion was needed or welcome.

The hour before dinner that evening they spent in the lounge, reading week-old newspapers that the ferret-faced desk clerk had rummaged out from underneath the desk after some monetary persuasion from Holmes.

The story of Holmes' death had been reported in the major European papers barely two days after it had supposedly occurred, and in England the day after that. Holmes and Elizabeth read all the accounts available to them with some curiosity and concern.

"So much for murdering me," Elizabeth said. "It appears I never existed in the first place."

Holmes looked amused. "There does appear to have been a remarkable oversight. I sense Watson's hand in this."

"John? How?"

"Only one, perhaps two, journalists would have been *in situ*, and their stories would have been syndicated or simply plagiarized in the other papers. Watson would have seen to it that Steiler and his staff kept their silence, and the journalists had no other source through which to learn that there was a third party at the Falls."

"But why?"

Holmes shrugged, suddenly bored with the subject. "If your presence was disclosed, your background would have been investigated, and we both know how undesirable that would be."

They were interrupted by the arrival of the telegram boy, who held out his tray towards Holmes. He took the cable and read it, then thrust it toward her.

"My brother. I requested of him both funds and news. He suggests we avoid returning to London just yet. I suspected as much."

Elizabeth read the cable. It was in free cryptic, but she had enough points of reference now that she could decipher its message. "So what do we do now?"

"Do you speak Swedish or Norwegian, Elizabeth?"

"Not at all. Why?"

"Sigerson is Scandinavian," Holmes pointed out.

"My ancestors were Norwegian. I was born in Hertfordshire."

"Your Italian is not good enough for you to pass as native, either."

"Why? What are you planning?"

"I believe it might be better if we parted company. I was thinking of settling you in some sort of *pensione*, and I would travel. Moran, given a choice of two targets, will come after me."

They went into dinner, and over the meal discussed the necessary arrangements for settling Elizabeth in a safe situation.

The next day, Holmes departed to survey the city, searching for a suitable *pensione*. After a substantial lunch Elizabeth collected her meagre possessions and took herself off on a walking tour of Florence's beautiful architecture.

It was quite late and fully dark when she returned to the hotel. As she approached the front door, she observed the ferret-faced desk clerk talking to a stranger who passed a handful of lira over the desk. Her heart leapt with alarm—the stranger's left hand was missing.

She stepped back into the shadows at the side of the doorway. She knew it was vital she warn Holmes, and so she must somehow get past the desk.

She slipped back farther into the shadows and moved along the street, looking for an alley or mews or some access to the back of the building. Her intention was to indulge in some creative hotel-breaking, and reach their rooms without alerting the desk clerk of her return.

A dismal alleyway presented itself and she glided down its length, moving silently. It eventually opened into a courtyard that held an untidy assortment of crates and other miscellaneous rubbish. A set of rusty iron steps led up to a narrow door. The hotel's service entrance.

With an outward confidence, Elizabeth climbed the steps and boldly turned the handle. She was more than a little surprised when it gave way and the door swung open. She pushed it further ajar and slid inside, looking around for witnesses. Finding herself alone in the service hallway, she made her way along to the corridor she guessed would lead her to the service stairs.

Three minutes later she reached the floor their rooms were on, and stealthily began to work her way down the carpeted corridor towards their door. She could see a light from under the door and assumed Holmes had arrived ahead of her, but a week of being pursued had sharpened her cautionary instincts, and she moved slowly and quietly, alert to any sign of danger.

As a result, when she traversed an open doorway and a hand reached out, she was startled but not panicked. Holmes stepped out of the doorway and motioned her to silence, then drew her back into the darkness of the room.

"Straker is here," Elizabeth whispered urgently. "In the foyer. I nearly collided with him, and retreated around to the back and came up through the servants' hall to warn you."

"Straker, too? Moran is at this minute ransacking our rooms." Holmes shook his head in mock disbelief. "It appears our little ferret-faced friend is working for two masters." He took a quick look down the corridor. "It is as well we have so little luggage, for we must abandon it once more. Show me the way to the service door, Elizabeth. We have an appointment with the desk clerk."

At the witching hour, the desk clerk left the hotel and began the ten-minute walk that took him to his lodgings near the river. When two figures stepped out of the dark and confronted him, he looked up at Holmes and fear revealed itself on his pointed features.

"Yes, you have a right to fear me, little man," Holmes told him.

The man began to babble in Italian, his features writhing in panic. Elizabeth watched silently, almost immediately losing the sense of his outpourings, but Holmes followed it well enough.

He snapped out questions which the clerk answered, gradually turning from panic to snivelling supplication. Holmes' disgust was plain to see, although he continued to converse with the man. Finally the clerk fell to his knees and looked up beseechingly at Holmes.

Holmes waved him away, repelled.

The little man left, whimpering.

To Elizabeth's surprise, Holmes turned and held out his arm companionably to her, and led her back up the narrow street, heading for the city centre.

"You were discussing me," she guessed. "I caught references to my red hair."

"It is rather striking. Everyone notices it. The clerk felt that if we were seriously concerned with being discreet you should somehow disguise the colour."

"Moran was asking after me?"

"Yes. 'A beautiful redhead with green eyes.' No names were exchanged. I thought there might be a possibility that Moran would try a blanket search of this type," he continued. "If he paid for information from key personnel in each of a handful of hotels in the major cities surrounding our last known location, sooner or later information would reach him. I paid the clerk to remain silent should there be any inquiries about us. I knew he was the hungry sort by the way he inveigled a tip for the papers, but I did believe he'd stay bought once an arrangement had been made."

"I saw Straker paying him off in the foyer," Elizabeth replied.

"We're lucky in one respect—neither Moran nor Straker have seen either of us here in Florence. That is why Moran ransacked our room. He is looking for identification, which he will not find because I am carrying everything that could identify me. They must have raced to Florence at the clerk's first communication, only to find us both absent. If they had arrived a few minutes later, I would have been trapped in the room. As it was, I nearly walked in on them when I returned this evening."

They turned into a slightly busier thoroughfare, though even that street was quiet, for the hour was late.

"Are you up to another lengthy walk, Elizabeth?" Holmes asked.

"Yes, if needs be."

"Oh yes, it is a needy cause. I want to find a quiet little hostel somewhere on the outskirts of the city, and I wish to avoid leaving a trail that can be traced through cab drivers. That means walking."

"I can manage that."

"Good. Once we have arranged shelter for what remains of the night, we will talk."

They found a hostel high on the hill overlooking the city and the cathedral, and Holmes organized rooms. They settled into the two chairs in front of the window, which was showing a paling skyline. Elizabeth tucked her feet beneath her, and Holmes stretched out, a cigarette in his hand. The silence lasted for a few minutes, and Elizabeth finally prompted Holmes.

"Whatever you need to say or ask, speak without concern that I may be embarrassed. I won't be."

"I apologize for hesitating, and shall speak plainly." He extinguished the cigarette and placed his hands behind his head.

"I was hoping to be able to place you somewhere in safety and lead Moran along my trail, but it appears he is looking for me through you. A wise plan of action, in a way, as your features are so much more memorable than mine. But for you it is unfortunate, since I cannot leave you now. That much is clear."

"Surely he will not harm me if he is after only information?"

Holmes shook his head. "You've not experienced all the base qualities of humanity. If I left you and Moran found you, how do you think he would go about getting the information he wanted?"

"I suppose at first he would threaten."

"You would not betray me because of a simple threat," Holmes said, with complete certainty. "And Moran has less control and finesse than Moriarty. That is why he was not the leader. No, Moran would need to exert extreme effort to get his information and I do not want that to happen."

"I could feed him false information—lead him in the opposite direction."

"He would distrust information given so easily. Or if he did believe you, he would kill you once you had served your purpose. No, Elizabeth, Moran does not have the sort of control or logical purpose Moriarty had. You are forever tainted by my brush, and while Moran is alive I must protect you." He lit another cigarette. "You must travel with me."

"Holmes, why are you going to this effort? Why are you assuming responsibility for me?"

"I am responsible." He stood abruptly. "I involved you in this business through my damned inability to leave a mystery alone. I insisted Watson set up that interview because I wanted to learn your secret and as a result I have dragged you across Moran's path like a sacrificial goat." He leaned his elbow on the mantelpiece and his chin on his fist. "I can only thank god for your resilience, which allows me to suggest you travel with me. I know you accept the prosaic realities of the situation."

"So where do we go to first? Obviously Florence is not safe."

"I believe anywhere in western Europe would be equally unsafe. Civilization is our enemy. Moran knows how to use it to his advantage."

"Farther east, then?"

Holmes frowned. "I believe we should completely avoid the more populous paths of commerce. They're a natural bottleneck, and Moran will pick us up too easily. Constantinople perhaps." He dropped his fist softly to the mantelshelf. "We could go through Serbia, and across country. We'll have to cross Bulgaria somewhere, but if we travel in the north, and avoid the coast—"

"Do you really believe it will be that long before you can return?"

"Perhaps longer," Holmes admitted. "It may be that you and I will never be able to return. While Moran is alive we must keep one step ahead of him. We therefore cannot settle in one place. We must travel."

"Holmes, what about Watson?" Elizabeth said softly. "Will he be safe?"

Holmes rubbed his head wearily. "I believe so. It is me Moran wants. And he knows I am not there, in London. Once we lose him, he will return there to watch my rooms. As long as I am not seen there, Watson will be safe."

Elizabeth held out her left hand.

"I will need a ring if I am to pose as your wife. I cannot forever encase my hands in gloves."

Holmes tugged at a slender gold ring on his little finger. He tossed it into Elizabeth's lap. "Try that," he suggested.

Elizabeth slipped the ring onto the appropriate finger. "It fits." She looked at him. "Should I disguise my hair, do you think?"

"No. If it does put Moran on your trail, I will be there to deal with him. At least we will know where he is. Besides, if I must have a wife," he muttered with acute irritation, "I can at least take pride in her outstanding beauty."

Elizabeth smiled to herself as she related this to me. "I believe, even then, he was drawn to me. But he didn't realize it. I didn't realize it. We were just two companions on a race for our lives, and we didn't really stop running until we reached Constantinople. But once we had stopped running and paused long enough to catch our breath and look around us. . . ."

Constantinople, capital of the Ottoman Empire, was the gateway into another world, and they both sensed it. They stayed in an inn on the European side of the Bosphorus, but spent a part of each day on the Asian side, soaking up the contrasts and strangeness. Holmes found himself truly relaxing for the first time in more than a few months. With the knowledge that they could disappear almost instantly in the unknown and unguessed-at human subways that moved about this most ancient of cities, he could afford the time to sit back and think of his next step.

Elizabeth felt the same horizon-broadening possibilities.

They stayed in Constantinople for three weeks, while they savoured the many possibilities open to them, and tried to choose which option appealed the most. The advantages of being technically dead to the rest of the world were many.

During one of their excursions to the Hagia Sophia, Elizabeth ran into trouble. She had already discovered her colouring was a beacon in Florence, and now she found that it attracted attention she would rather do without. For a while her European dress and Holmes' company kept her safe, but it was merely a matter of time before a fellow with more than the usual boldness attempted something.

They were walking down the long colonnaded avenue that ran the length of the mosque when Elizabeth felt a brazen hand on her waist. When the hand slid quickly upwards, she clutched it, an involuntary shriek escaping her lips. Holmes pivoted around to intervene. He stepped towards the man and around Elizabeth, and she turned quickly to see what action Holmes intended. But she was not quick enough, for the man was already sprawled on the paving, hands clutched to his stomach, and his eyes rolling up into their sockets.

Holmes caught her arm and pulled her along into the crowd, putting distance between them and the scene.

The mild fracas caused almost no sensation in a busy street that witnessed at least one murder a week, but they both took the warning to heart, and Holmes began teaching her his self-defence tricks.

He was knowledgeable in Baritsu, the Japanese system, and his grounding in the fundamentals of defence was supplemented by his boxing, fencing, and singlestick interests. From his years of confrontations with the criminals and desperados who were the raw material of his profession, he had acquired a broad catalogue of techniques drawn from almost every known type of self-defence methodology, in addition to a not-inconsiderable supply of tricks that barely gave lip service to fair play.

The latter Holmes did not hesitate to teach Elizabeth in conjunction with more orthodox skills. His intention was to develop her ability to defend herself by whatever means necessary. There was a degree of self-interest in this: Holmes did not want to be wholly responsible for Elizabeth's safety and well-being, for their circumstances in the near future might put them in the position where he could not help her, and her survival would depend entirely on her own abilities. He reasoned that if she were to overcome her natural weight and power disadvantages, foul play must be included in her repertoire of defence.

Elizabeth was more than willing to agree with this philosophy. She had only to remember back to the moment upon the moors, when she had nearly been at the mercy of a shepherd, to see the logic in learning to fend for herself.

Lessons in violence therefore became a regular program.

Holmes also bought her a wicked-looking knife. Elizabeth showed me the knife, after first carefully ensuring Mrs. Hudson was out of the way. It was curved and sharp, and had a gold hilt embedded with green gems. It appeared ornately overworked, but the clever placement of the gems gave a perfectly comfortable grip. The gold was supposedly from the high ranges to the north of Tibet.

After the incident at the mosque, Elizabeth almost entirely discarded European dress, and she sensed her change in costume not only prevented curiosity about her, but helped Holmes relax his guard even more. She took to wearing the Arab headcloth to disguise the colour of her hair, and a burnoose for comfort and disguise.

It was the first time either of them had dressed "native," and once she had encouraged Holmes with her descriptions of ease and freedom, he, too, donned the burnoose and veiling headgear.

I gave a start at this, and Elizabeth smiled a little at my reaction. "We were not there to keep up the side, you know," she pointed out.

They found the local costume opened up doors for them that would have remained firmly locked otherwise, and they entered into a previously unsuspected world. This was the world of the Saracen, one that lay between the traditional regions of East and West, although sympathies in this strange world lay firmly to the East. They were already familiar with the challenges Islam made to their social and political traditions, but now they discovered sub-layers of complex cultures and exotic social structures, revealed—pearl-like—one layer at a time, drawing them ever deeper into the heart.

They explored this new world with the enthusiasm of children, crossing the strait each morning to wander at will on the Asian side of the city, sampling language and culture, soaking up the richness before returning each night to their European-style hotel.

"We were straddling a turning point," Elizabeth said to me quietly, fingering the blade of her knife. "At night you could hear the wailing and singing of the mosques mixed up with the tolling of the church bells. And everywhere you looked the same contrast appeared."

As they learnt more, the choice before them simplified. They could follow the traditional route of journeying British, and risk Moran following their trail, or they could throw all their concepts and prejudices aside, and sink into the other world that began in Constantinople.

The result of this busy intersection of chances was perhaps inevitable.

During the fourth week of their stay, they were forced to visit the Al-Sahib Square in the Arab quarter on the Asian side of the city. Communications in that part of the world are uncertain, and Holmes knew that the farther east they travelled, the less reliable they would become. He decided that his gold snuff box from the King of Bohemia must be sacrificed, for they needed ready cash. Nothing else would suffice.

Al-Sahib Square was a notorious trading place. Money merchants there would buy and sell anything without question, and their prices were often higher than those Holmes could have raised through legitimate dealers, who were subject to taxes, bribes, and legal overheads.

But Holmes took some precautions. It was vital Elizabeth accompany him—a lone Arab was an easy target. Women were unwelcome there, so she must go disguised as a man. The Arab burnoose she had been using, with its shrouding folds about the face, was the solution. Holmes was quietly confident that Elizabeth could handle any trouble that might arise, and he could foresee none, for he was confident of his own grasp of Arabic and he had been born a good bargainer.

They entered the square in the hour before the second prayers, about nine o'clock. It was a hot, dusty morning, with a stiff breeze, and they had a good excuse for muffling their features. Their only distinguishing feature was Holmes' height—which made him unusually tall for an Arab.

As they had agreed, they circled the square once, whilst Holmes established which agent would be the best to approach. Elizabeth's vivid description of the square will stay with me forever:

"It was crowded, as all the city is crowded, but there was not a Turk or European in sight. Everywhere you looked you saw only veiled Arabs. The square is quite small, and they crowded in until there was barely enough room to breathe.

"It smelt—unwashed bodies, untended animals, hot savoury food, and the heat of late summer. The noise was an assault on the ears. Everyone spoke loudly, and then there was the call of several minarets quite close by, and that strange undulating music that the Arabs love to hear, played as loudly as possible. Merchants were to be found around the edge of the square and in a large circle in the middle, squatting on their mats, and advertising their services at the top of their voices. All the animals were crying, bleating, and calling, and to be heard, one had to shout. With everyone shouting, you had to shout louder, and the noise level spiralled upwards.

"A lot of the people seemed to just be there simply for the atmosphere. They didn't appear to have pressing business, but they watched everyone with dark, suspicious eyes. Those who were there on business were prepared to bargain hard, and knew that the merchants would cheat them at the first opportunity.

"The menace was unmistakable. From the moment we entered I found myself holding the hilt of my knife inside my sleeve."

It was indeed a chancy place. Money turns the heads of most of the human race and all those in the square with business to transact were already risking much, or they would have gone to lawful dealers elsewhere. Elizabeth was alert to even the smallest hint of trouble, and she found herself falling back to keep Holmes' tall figure in sight in front of her.

Abruptly, a loud fight broke out on their right. The crowd surged in that direction and they were dragged along with the tide. Elizabeth tried to keep her eyes on Holmes, searching out the tall figure. She sighted him again just as three dirty Arabs closed in on him. Somehow he had been marked—possibly his height, or his way of walking. She felt fear chill her bones as a long, wicked knife rose and began to fall.

Chapter Six

FEAR TRIGGERED ELIZABETH INTO ACTION. She threw herself on the back of the nearest of the three assailants. With one hand she sought the Arab's chin, and gripped it to steady the head, and with a full, powerful swipe of her knife arm she slit his throat.

His gurgled cry, abruptly silenced, brought his two comrades' attention upon her. A powerful hand groped for her throat, and as she grabbed the wrist she heard Holmes' calm, instructional voice in her mind, directing her actions. She plunged her knife into the folds of the burnoose where her grasp on his wrist told her his stomach would be. He bent tiredly over her arm, and she pushed him back with her foot. She turned to locate the third attacker, but someone had already silenced him. He lay in a huddled heap, his own long knife protruding from his chest.

She wheeled about to look for Holmes, but a hand grasped her knife arm, spinning her around. She brought her other hand up to blind the attacker with a jab of her fingers, but a strong hand clamped onto her wrist. She found herself staring into Holmes' eyes. He pulled his headcloth aside a little so she could identify him.

"Fly!" he said, his voice rising over the deafening cacophony of reaction the fight had begun. "Run for your life!"

They turned and plunged into the crowd, which gave way in front of them like butter under a hot knife. Behind, a man called out in a mixture of Turkish and the bastardized Arabic of the city. Elizabeth understood only one word. "Kill." Her feet picked up speed.

Once outside the square they could run. People scattered from their path as they approached. Behind them they could hear the ground reverberate with the sound of many pursuing feet. Neither risked a glance backwards. Holmes changed direction many times, diving into alleyways and back streets. They cannoned into washing lines, and scattered chickens and pigs. Suddenly the sea was in front of them. The Golden Horn— and safety—lay directly opposite.

Holmes turned to his right and worked his way along the narrow shore to where a jetty pushed out into the strait. He pulled Elizabeth under it and they crawled to the other side, and crouched there, hidden from pursuit.

A couple of brown-skinned children perched on the end of the jetty watched them with large, solemn eyes, then abruptly skittered past them like frightened rabbits, and disappeared into hovels lining the shore.

Holmes pulled off his Arab headgear, lifted the burnoose over his head, and straightened up the western clothing he wore beneath.

"Drop your knife," he told her.

Elizabeth stared at him blankly, her breath loud in her ears.

He reached out to lift her arm so she could see her hand. It was still clutching the knife, and her hand and wrist and the sleeve of the burnoose were red and sticky with blood.

"Oh, my god," she whispered, the full horror of her deeds finally registering in her mind. She recalled the look of terror on the faces of the people who had scattered from their path, and the feel of the knife sliding into warm flesh.

Abruptly she dropped the knife, and turned and vomited into the sand. Holmes steadied her until she had finished, then sat her down with her back resting against a jetty pylon. With scraps of material from his burnoose he cleaned the blood from her hands and washed her face. She allowed him to administer to her while she shivered in reaction. Then he cleaned the knife in the river, dried it on another clean scrap of material, and held it out to her.

"Strap this back in its sheath. We may need it again."

She attempted to take the knife but her hand trembled too much. Wordlessly he pushed up her sleeve and slid the blade home for her. He studied her clinically.

"Take what time you need," he told her. "Bloodshed always affects a person to a diminishing degree. It doesn't please me that I can confirm it becomes easier."

Elizabeth finally found her voice. "I thought it was you they were attacking," she said hoarsely.

Holmes took her face in his hands, looking at her with an open fondness that took her breath away and made her heart trip-hammer. "I know," he told her quietly. Then he dropped a light kiss on her forehead before returning to the task of cleaning up the sleeve of her burnoose.

"We're not clear of it yet," he said in a matter-of-fact way. "Arabs love a hunt and they will keep on it until sunset if necessary. Besides, I heard someone call out in Arabic that he wanted us and would pay." He frowned. "I have an impression that it was the tall Arab whose life you so spectacularly saved." He shrugged. "I will probably never learn the answer to that. Regardless, we must get you out of sight, and the quickest way is to cross the strait and return to the hotel." He went back to the water to rinse out his rag, and when he returned he was laughing softly.

"Oh, what a merry joke! It would be inconceivable to them that the ferocious warrior they seek is a woman."

"Please. I can't laugh about it . . . not yet."

He shook his head, sobering. "It was well done, Elizabeth. You acted when you needed to act. Hesitation would have been fatal, and you did not hesitate. When arguments turn to bloody battles, you cannot afford to dilly-dally about. Do not assume you overreacted, for you did not." He sat back and threw the rag into the river, and pulled his sleeves down. "Do you think your legs will support you now? We must move from here. We've tarried overlong."

Elizabeth nodded, and Holmes helped her up. They climbed the rickety jetty, and crossed the pebbled shore towards the ramshackle hovels behind them. They traversed a narrow alley and emerged into a street lined with the more permanent oriental-style buildings characteristic of the city. Holmes checked his bearings.

Elizabeth waited. She noticed the children were back again, lined along one blank wall, watching them. Their eyes were expressionless, and their faces expectant.

Abruptly, a warning tingled in her mind and she reached for Holmes' sleeve, trying to voice it. But it was too late. A net, smelling rankly of overripe fish, descended over their heads. Elizabeth lifted her arm to ward it off. Her breath was cut off as another heavy layer dropped on them, and she was enveloped in a constricting, dark prison.

They were lifted and carried on a journey of considerable distance and time. The one significant detail Elizabeth could establish from within her muffled enclosure was that they were carried over the strait in a boat that rocked gently in the wavelets. She felt herself beginning to relax a little. It was highly unlikely that the Arabs hunting them for vengeance on their fallen comrades would carry them into the European sector—an area of the city with which they would not be familiar. They would have exacted a swift and merciless retribution. So whoever had ensnared them was a new player and would probably make himself known at the end of this journey.

Finally she felt herself being placed down on firmer ground, and she cautiously pushed at the tangle of canvas and fishing net. When her probing elicited no response, she rapidly untangled herself and breathed in fresh air.

Holmes sat in the midst of another pile of net and canvas next to her, casually rearranging his ruffled clothes.

They were in a room of palatial proportions. The ceiling arched overhead in graceful vaulted sections, and soared down to a row of massive pillars that marched along either side of the room. Between the pillars on her left was a wall hung with tapestries and carpets, and pierced in several places by ornately carved, double wooden doors which led further into the building. On the right the pillars opened onto a lattice-carved stone screen that revealed a view overlooking the city and the Golden Horn promontory. The view gave Elizabeth a small clue as to their location, for this section of the Bosphorus was lined with palaces, mosques, and gardens built by the sultans.

Apart from the end where they found themselves, the room was empty of furnishings. Beneath them lay a luxurious Persian carpet of grand dimensions, and before them was what Elizabeth immediately dubbed a throne. It was a wide chair of exquisitely carved marble and she speculated briefly as to how anyone managed to shift it. Sitting on the throne was a large, dark-eyed man. He was naked from the waist up, and another man in western clothes was attending to a cut on his back. Elizabeth inferred that the wounded man must be the Arab she had mistaken for Holmes.

She glanced at Holmes. He shook his head very slightly, and she guessed his message. *Stay silent.*

They climbed to their feet.

The Arab addressed Holmes in Arabic. "European? French?"

"English," Holmes replied.

"Ah, that is good. My French is atrocious," the Arab replied in unaccented English. "You must forgive the informality of my attire. I was bleeding like a stuck pig and had to have it seen to."

"May I know why you have detained us?" Holmes asked.

The Arab smiled. "I am Sullah Muhammad Zia-ad-din Ahmad. It is my miserable skin your friend there saved. I merely wished to thank you and return the debt if I could."

"Your methods are somewhat violent," Holmes pointed out.

"Ah, yes. I told my men I wanted you alive and unhurt. You must understand they had witnessed your skills in the square and were worried how they could approach you without being misinterpreted. Since they do not speak the Arabic of Constantinople, they were forced to be a little more direct."

"Then you are not Arab?" Holmes asked.

"Allah be praised!" he said with a mighty shout of laughter. "I am Persian."

Holmes relaxed, pushing his hands into his pockets. There was the beginning of a smile on his face.

"You're a long way from home," he said.

"As you are, my friend," Sullah replied. He pointed to Elizabeth. "Does your companion speak English?"

"Yes," Holmes replied.

Sullah addressed himself to Elizabeth. "I am grateful for your intervention this morning, friend. Never have I seen such ferocity. It would please me to look upon your face so I might recognize a friend in future, as I have allowed you to look upon mine."

Elizabeth glanced at Holmes for guidance. He nodded reassuringly. "Reveal yourself," he told her. "It is an insult if you do not."

Elizabeth pulled the folds aside, and her hair tumbled down about her face. She brushed the locks back and found Sullah staring at her, dumbfounded. Then the tanned, wrinkled face creased into folds of mirth. He began to laugh, a low, silent chuckle that quickly became a loud peal of hearty guffaws that left him shaking and helpless.

The doctor stepped back until Sullah had himself under control, and Elizabeth glanced at Holmes uncertainly. He was smiling, thoroughly enjoying Sullah's surprise and merriment. She felt a small smile pulling at her own mouth. Sullah's bellows were infectious.

Sullah explained that he was a merchant who traded in anything of value. Horses were his joy, and he found a constant demand in Persia for any Arabian horses he could lay his hands on. He followed the trade routes on the east coast of the Mediterranean for most of the year, and almost every spring he would arrive in Constantinople with carpets to sell to the rich European merchants, raising funds for the rest of the year's living expenses and for his hunt for the best of the Arabian breeds.

He had been educated in England, for his father foresaw the advantages to a man who could speak as an equal to the men with whom he wished to trade. His head wife was English, courted and married whilst studying, and as a consequence his households were a strange mix of East and West.

He had a small house in Baghdad, and a very large country establishment just outside Mashhad, on the foothills of the Elburz Mountains where he pastured his horses.

Once the initial mirth over Elizabeth's identity had passed, Holmes introduced them both. He cautiously used Sigerson as he had throughout their journeys, allowing Sullah to assume they were man and wife.

Sullah insisted they remain as his guests until either of them left the city. He was planning on staying for only another two weeks before setting out on the long, slow journey back to Persia. He did not wish to find himself still travelling when the harsh Persian winter arrived.

Their interview finished in the throne room (as it transpired to be). Sullah organized for their luggage to be collected at the hotel and graciously invited them to dine with him that night, after they had rested and recovered in the rooms he had put aside for their use.

A young girl in a simple white tunic came forward. "My daughter, Tayisha," Sullah explained while the girl bowed deeply towards them. "She speaks English well. She will show you to your rooms, and can assist you with any questions you have."

Tayisha smiled at Elizabeth. "This way, please."

Their rooms, all seven of them, were richly furnished in silks and carpets, and the vast, terraced windows looked out over the straits, the deep terrace, and intricately carved latticing designed to catch any stray cooling breezes, yet still maintain privacy. Tayisha explained the working of the amenities and clapped her hands. A woman in harem trousers and halter stepped forward and made obeisance to Tayisha. The girl explained that this was her mother's servant, and Elizabeth was to consider the servant her own while under Sullah's roof.

Then both withdrew, allowing Holmes and Elizabeth privacy.

Holmes threw himself on a wide, low divan, and lit a cigarette. He lay on his back, smoking.

Elizabeth checked the view from the windows, then carefully explored the extent of the room before turning back to Holmes.

"How much of what Sullah told us do you believe?" she asked.

Holmes smiled. "All of it—once you have interpreted it properly."

"He very carefully didn't say what he was doing in the square," Elizabeth pointed out.

"Neither did we," Holmes replied. He turned his head to look at her. "Which is why we are guests in his household. We are at this moment engaged in a game of bluff. He knows we know that he is not telling the precise truth, and he knows that we know that he knows we are not telling the precise truth. Who's truth eventuates as the least harmless will be the injured party."

"Do you mean that literally?"

"Not quite. He will not harm a hair on your head. He owes you the life debt. My head, however, can be more easily disposed of." He shrugged. "Once he realizes you made a mistake of identity, and I dealt with the third merely to finish the affair, he will be satisfied . . . I hope."

Elizabeth shivered. "Eastern people are never what they appear," she said softly.

"No one is." Holmes smoked for a few moments in silence. "But I like him," he said to himself, sounding surprised.

Dinner was a formal affair suited to the best dining rooms in England. The serving girl, whom Elizabeth discovered was whimsically called Sheba, arrived nearly two hours before the appointed dinner hour and took Elizabeth off to prepare her for the occasion. Elizabeth was bathed, dried, and pampered with an exotic hot-oil massage before dressing in one of three evening gowns presented for her inspection. Her hair was dressed skilfully by Sheba, who explained she had learnt from her mistress, who was "English like madam." Elizabeth assumed she meant Sullah's head wife.

Feeling gloriously feminine after weeks of rough living, Elizabeth entered the small room she was shown to, to find a small group of guests. She was somewhat taken aback, for she had not been expecting a party. She sought for Holmes amongst the strangers, and was relieved when he appeared by her side.

"I know," he said in answer to her expression. "It appears Sullah is entertaining his western business associates tonight. We'll just have to make the best of it."

"Holmes, I *can't*," Elizabeth breathed quietly. "I have never been to a dinner party before." The confession made her blush a little.

Holmes looked at her panicky face. "Never?"

She tried to explain swiftly. "I've no family or friends who would invite me to such an occasion." She touched his arm, and he could feel her trembling. "You *know* what my life has consisted of."

Holmes looked at her blankly, astonished. He abhorred social functions and expended a great deal of effort to avoid them, if he could. His was not an unfounded dislike, for he had, in his opinion, attended far too many social affairs of one sort or another.

Elizabeth had attended none. *Not one.* She was probably more terrified now than she had been during any of the dangerous adventures in which he had embroiled her.

Holmes was amazed to hear himself saying gently, "Just be yourself, Elizabeth, and you'll charm everyone here." He smiled reassuringly. "I will stay by you."

Sullah moved toward them, a European woman on his arm. Dressed in an evening suit, he could have passed as a well-tanned Englishman. He welcomed Elizabeth and introduced his wife.

Mary drew Elizabeth to one side, while Holmes was led away by Sullah, to be introduced to the other guests in the room. Mary kept Elizabeth by her side with idle and frivolous chat, the other women joining in. Elizabeth withstood it for only a few minutes before panic overtook her completely. She excused herself abruptly, picked up her train, and crossed the floor to where the men stood by the fireplace. Holmes made room for her in the circle in which he stood.

"My soul for a brandy," she said in an undertone.

"Try sherry," Holmes suggested, handing her his glass.

She sipped, and saw the women watching her and whispering amongst themselves.

Holmes picked up another full glass of sherry from the tray on the sideboard. "You seem to have stopped the conversation on this side of the room."

"Sigerson, is this beauty your wife?" The question was directed from Elizabeth's right, the tones hale and hearty country English.

"Elizabeth, may I introduce you to Lord Barrington Edgewater. My wife Elizabeth, Lord Edgewater."

Elizabeth held out her hand politely towards the dewlapped, portly lord, and Edgewater, after the minutest of pauses, took it in his own podgy hand and shook firmly. "May I call you Elizabeth?" he asked, extracting his hand, and mopping his gleaming face and shining, hairless head with his handkerchief.

"I would prefer it," she replied pleasantly.

"So, you have actually travelled on foot all the way from France?"

"Yes."

"A remarkable feat," Edgewater replied, studying her from top to toe.

"For a woman?" Elizabeth finished coolly, sensing his unspoken qualification.

Edgewater's brows rose. "You're not one of these damned suffragettes, are you?"

"Why? Does it make a difference?" Elizabeth asked with genuine puzzlement. She perceived she was falling foul of various unvocalized etiquette rules.

"I should imagine it would," another man said to her left. His accent was vaguely Italian. "At least to Edgewater here. He has been fighting them off for the ten years he has been in the House." He smiled at Elizabeth. "Carlo Ricco, at your service."

"Elizabeth Sigerson." She felt her hand being shaken.

"I wouldn't be offended by Edgewater," he continued. "He is a bit sensitive in that area. Your husband has been telling me about your journey here. It sounded like a good adventure. Did you have much trouble over the Alps? Some of the passes there are difficult, even in summer."

"We came via the coast," Elizabeth lied cautiously, maintaining the fictitious origins of their journey as Holmes and she had concocted weeks previously. "Through Monte Carlo."

"Ah! Monaco. That is a fascinating place. I am from Turin myself, but I have spent a lot of time up that way. Did you visit Grasse while you were there?"

Elizabeth cast about for an answer, lost.

Holmes turned to him. "You're on a commission for the Royal Family, aren't you?"

"Yes. Carpets, for the palace in Monaco ... which is why I am here."

"It is why we're all here," Edgewater replied. "Except you, Sigerson, I believe. At least, I've never heard your name around the traps. I thought I knew all the importers in England."

Elizabeth found herself relaxing a little. Holmes had deflected the conversation neatly from her and onto himself.

As promised, he stayed nearby, parrying all conversational openings directed towards her, giving her time to restore her confidence. She listened as he told the most outrageous lies with a perfectly sincere face.

He was deep into a discussion on the more intricate aspects of elephant herding in Africa—a subject Elizabeth knew for a fact he had no practical experience with—when she saw him cast a quick glance in her direction. There was a message in that glance, but it took her some time to interpret it, for Holmes had been spinning tale after scandalous tale since she had arrived, and elephant herding seemed no more or less extraordinary than any other conversation he had held.

But then she focussed on Lord Edgewater, and suppressed a smile as Holmes' message became clear. He was twisting their tails. He was dismantling their bombastic manners before her very eyes, and taking the essence of their insipid attitudes and throwing it back at them in hugely exaggerated proportions. He was telling her: *here, this is their substance. It is nothing.*

The humour was in their blindness. They accepted all Holmes said without a quiver.

Elizabeth finished her glass of sherry, accepted another from Holmes, then engaged in conversation with a young, nervous-looking youth to practise her own abilities at tail-twisting before looking for more fertile ground.

Some time later she found herself discussing hunting with Edgewater. By now, she had discovered that if she adopted a knowledgeable air she could say just about anything without being challenged.

"So, do you join in at the kill?" Edgewater asked.

"No, for I do not agree with letting the dogs have their way. It would be much simpler to slit the poor animal's throat," she replied unthinkingly.

"Oh, really," Edgewater replied, pouncing on her. "I suppose you would want the master of the hunt to dispatch the quarry. That's the way with you women who scream for equality. You want the best of both worlds, but will happily leave all the dirty work to the men."

Elizabeth looked quickly about her, for his voice had carried and the salon became quiet. She caught Holmes' eye. He was standing alone by the fireplace, watching her, his eyes narrowed slits of concentration. But there was a half-smile on his face and she felt he had been watching her for a while, appreciating her performance.

Over his shoulder she could see the woman grouped in a small, awed audience.

She smiled at Edgewater. "You really shouldn't assume so much, Lord Edgewater. I wouldn't be so silly as to become involved in politics. There are far more interesting things to do. And I do happen to believe that woman are quite as capable as men of dirty work. Why, for all you know, I could have been out slitting throats before lunch today."

There was a shocked, collective drawing of breath from the women, and a nervous twitter of laughter from the men. Then Edgewater let out a hearty bellow of laughter and thumped her on the shoulder.

"Oh, I like you," he said loudly. "I say, that's a grand notion, that. Here, have another port."

Elizabeth accepted the glass with a smile and a secretly drawn, shaky breath of relief, and looked about for Holmes. He was still standing at the ornately carved fireplace, his elbow resting on the mantel. He was quite alone, and had been waiting for her eyes to fall on him, for he lifted his glass in a mock salute, and communicated his approval with a barely noticeable nod of his head.

Elizabeth's smile broadened.

Holmes found her sitting on the divan, watching the moon over the sea, and the distant twinkle of stars. It was almost completely dark in the room, and the moonlight picked up the twinkle of sequins on her dress as her breath rose and fell. She was listening to the oddly modulated and weirdly attractive wailing songs floating up to the window from the many mosques about the city.

"Sullah said you had retired. Are you feeling unwell?"

She smiled reassuringly as he sat on the opposite side of the broad divan, facing her. "I couldn't stand the women's chatter—not after the fun of the salon. And they treated me like a pariah . . . not that I minded that so much."

"So you did have fun, after all," Holmes said quietly. "I thought you enjoyed deflating Lord Edgewater."

"Thanks to you. You showed me how. I was quite in awe of them all, until you pointed out their superficiality to me."

"That sort of people always find themselves pricked when they come up against ruthless realists."

"Am I ruthless?" Elizabeth asked.

"Reality is by definition ruthless. It cannot be anything else. Tonight both you and I discovered how far along that trail we have travelled. Whatever doubts I have about the future now, they are all doubts that nothing but time can answer."

"They seem quite blinded by their triviality," Elizabeth said sadly.

"Except Sullah. He was very impressed by you. I believe he would like to marry you if you were not already married . . . a fact I was greatly relieved to point out to him."

Elizabeth looked up at his face quickly, but could distinguish nothing but his usual watchfulness.

"And you call me ruthless," she replied lightly.

"You are. You have carved your way into my heart with the efficiency of a master swordsman, and without a single drop of blood spilt." His voice was casual, but the words caused Elizabeth to become quite motionless, her bosom rising and falling rapidly as her heart pounded.

Holmes reached up to pull at the pins holding her hair, and his hands trembled just a little. "You really are quite beautiful tonight. But I prefer your hair loose, like this." He removed the last pin, and let the locks cascade down about her shoulders. "Then I can do this." His long fingers slid into the copper locks, and Elizabeth shivered again.

"Holmes," she whispered.

"We've talked enough," he said, drawing her to him.

Chapter Seven

ELIZABETH FELL SILENT, STUDYING MY FACE. Then she smiled. "As you see, I threw myself at him," she added, reminding me of my guess. But after such a tale of the extremities of human kind, from murder to love, I could no longer feel embarrassment.

She was standing at the fireplace when she reached this point in her narrative. It had taken two days to relate the tale, and I had graduated to the sofa, pulled up close to the hearth.

I had maps and atlases spread about me, for I had begun tracing their route through the East, supplementing my own dim memories of the area from my minimal contribution to the Afghan Campaign. But the maps had fallen from my lap and my fingers played with the long, golden knife that had spent nearly three years strapped to Elizabeth's forearm, whilst she spun her tale of life under a foreign sky. She was a very good storyteller, for I could quite clearly see the cosmopolitan city that, for them, became their watershed. Constantinople with its conflicts and exotic contrasts suited them perfectly.

I held up the knife. "There are two gems missing," I pointed out.

Elizabeth laughed. "You have been fingering that knife for two days, Watson, and you have only just noticed?"

"I believe I grew interested in it only when I realized just what this knife represented," I told her.

"You have a gruesome turn of mind. The gems are not missing, John."

"Then where are they?"

"If you think logically, you will know where they are." And despite any more questions she refused to tell me any more. Instead she asked Mrs. Hudson for a pot of tea and set about making me more comfortable. The knife was hidden away again, and she picked up all the maps and neatened them.

"You're not going to leave me there, are you?" I asked.

Elizabeth studied me, her head to one side. "Haven't you had your fill of death and blood yet?"

"There is more?"

"Oh, yes, there is more. You do not travel around the remoter parts of Asia without some sort of trouble dogging your heels." She stood, the maps in her hand, and surveyed my face. "You're not trying to turn me into Scheherazade, are you, John?" she asked.

I am afraid I had to ask her what her reference was, and she told me the ancient Arabian story of the princess who kept herself alive by enthralling the king with stories, which every night she would leave unfinished until the morrow. Then Elizabeth added, "I thought I had given you your answer."

I was quick to assure her that she had, and that I had well satisfied my curiosity regarding the beginning of their unusual relationship. "It's just that . . . he is not at all the man I thought he was." And then I added, "And looking at you standing there, it is difficult to imagine you in a burnoose—"

Mrs. Hudson chose that moment to appear with the teapot and I fell silent. When she had left, Elizabeth poured, and handed me the cup.

She sat on the hassock in front of me. "I suspected that was it. Well, John, you are right. He has changed. Fundamentally he is barely the same man you once knew. Just as I am not the woman whom you remember from Switzerland. If we keep the same appearances and characteristics, it is merely habit and the comfort of not showing weaknesses." Her eyes lost their focus for a minute. "You cannot kill a man . . . or two men . . . and not remain unchanged." Then she smiled at me. "Had you been in Mashhad when we arrived, you would not have recognized him. For the further east we travelled, the more he changed. He was spreading his wings, John, just as he always wanted to. And he was tasting a life that just might possibly hold the answers he was looking for."

Holmes and Elizabeth remained in Constantinople for ten more days, and those were days of revelations for them both.

Sullah had quickly discarded all English affectations after the dinner party. "I have entertained my clients, and received much money from them. Goods were exchanged. They like it if they think they have bought carpets from the son of Ali Baba," Sullah told them frankly. "And the more silk and swags and slave girls I show them, the more money they give me. It is a pleasurable business in some ways. But I am much like you . . . their adherence to the forms to the exclusion of original thinking irritates me." He laughed. "You both have courage. You have it in here—"and he thumped his chest. "I thought to begin, well yes, it is very nice, the English ma'am can kill. But what is really in her mind when she kills?"

Elizabeth writhed under this frank discussion, but Holmes answered off-handedly, "That's the last thing you have to worry about, Sullah. You merely need be thankful that she can and did when you required it."

Sullah smiled. "Yes, but I believe I know now. I, too, listened when you were talking to Lord Edgewater, Elizabeth. I have always thought him a fool, but you thought so, and told him so. And he was too stupid to understand it." He laughed, one of his great shouts of laughter. "So much for the lord who is in trade. When you are next in a bad temper, I shall tiptoe around you. I hope you never mistake me for an enemy."

The reference was a reminder of Al-Sahib Square, for Sullah had been informed of Elizabeth's mistaken identification. And although he had not openly admitted it, Sullah had vaguely indicated he had been on possibly illicit business of his own, and the Arabs had somehow marked him as easy prey and acted accordingly.

Holmes had formed his own theory on Sullah's allusions. "There is a fairly heavy tariff for goods taken over the imperial borders," he told Elizabeth. "And Sullah carts caravans of goods every year or so. It would profit him to find a way of selling his wares without paying the duties."

"Smuggling," Elizabeth concluded, with a smile.

Holmes shrugged. "I shall be careful not to enquire too closely," he replied.

On the third day after the party, Sullah invited them to coffee, a Muslim way of opening a business discussion.

Holmes and Elizabeth had learnt a few lessons about Muslim customs by that time, so they dressed according to the standards acceptable to Sullah. Holmes wore the burnoose and a closely shrouded headcloth, which was a sign of respect. Elizabeth wore a head veil and kept well back behind Holmes, as was expected of women.

But even as she began to make her obeisance, Sullah caught her joined hands in his and lifted her back to her feet. "No, I will not have it," he said. "You have proved your right to stand at the same height as I." Deftly, he unhooked her face veil. "Sit, sit. I have business to discuss with both of you." He pointed to Holmes' headwear. "I would much rather see your face than your respect," he told him.

They joined Sullah at the low table, and waited politely until he had poured the first cup of strong Turkish coffee for each of them.

"I am leaving in a week," he told them gravely. "I will be heading back for my home beneath the Elburz Mountains." He passed a cup to Holmes, then Elizabeth. "I do not like to leave this city without all my debts and credits balanced nicely, for it is a year, and sometimes two, before I return. These modern times have speeded up, for often when I return, the faces are not the same."

They politely agreed with him.

"However, with you, Elizabeth, I owe the life debt, and that is a heavy debt to pay."

Elizabeth paused. It had been her first intention to pass over it lightly, but she realized that to do so would be to cheapen the quality of Sullah's life. Instead she nodded politely. "Indeed it was a happy day for me when I did save your life, for now I have a friend."

Sullah looked pleased at her response. "Exactly. Exactly. So I have been thinking carefully about what I can do to repay this debt, but nothing appropriate comes to mind. It is a little difficult, because I have never had to concern myself with what a woman considers important before now."

"Is it that you wish to ask me what I desire?" Elizabeth asked, maintaining a neutral face despite Sullah's candid admission.

"No. Because I believe I have a solution that will distract you until I do arrive at the answer." Sullah sipped at his coffee and they realized that the dramatic pause meant he was arriving at the purpose behind his invitation to coffee.

"It has come to my attention that you wish to travel east. Yes?" Holmes nodded.

Neither of them wondered how their needs had come to his attention. They had been surrounded by slaves, family, guards, and others in Sullah's retinue for two days, and had spoken extensively with Sullah and his business associates, as well as every other member of his household who spoke either English or Arabic. Somewhere during those conversations and through observation, report, and deduction, Sullah had learnt this information.

"I wondered why you have not followed the typical English custom of travelling by boat, steamship, or train to Bombay and thence to China, to do all the things that typical English do. But then you are not typical English. You do not think like typical English. You went to Al-Sahib Square dressed as natives so you could blend in and learn the truth. And I invite you to coffee, and you do me the honour of following my customs. You are very extraordinary people."

Even in three days, they had learnt that this expression was Sullah's highest form of praise. But he had not finished.

"So, I feel to pay off the debt I owe, I should put much thought into it. How long have we known each other? Three days? It is not long enough to learn all there is to know about a new friend. But then I discover that you want to travel further east. Perfect! I am leaving for Persia in a week. I could use two people as handy with their knives as these. I will ask them to travel with me and my horses, and protect us from harm. And that will give me much more time to discover what it is a woman could want in return for my life."

Elizabeth caught Holmes' eyes over the coffee cup. It was a perfect solution. They could travel at ease with a large group of people who knew the route intimately. And it gave them a direction, for which they had been searching. Persia. Mashhad.

Elizabeth nodded her head very slightly at Holmes' questioning look. He replaced his coffee cup, pushed it aside, and settled down to discuss terms.

"He employed you?" I asked of Elizabeth.

"Yes. We had our first assignment as mercenaries." She laughed at the appalled look on my face. "We were out of contact with England. Mycroft wouldn't have dared send us money even if he knew where we would be from one day to the next. We were on our own."

Sullah's offer was the standard terms offered to anyone who wished to work their way along the trade routes. They would travel with his caravan and give him any assistance he needed or requested, and in return he would give them food and shelter, and the protection afforded by travelling with a large group.

His caravan consisted of one hundred horses, thirty-six men, women, and children, eight long, heavy carts to be hauled by the workhorses, and a retinue of soldiers to guard them all. The caravan moved slowly; to travel fifteen miles in a day was considered good progress, especially through the mountainous country they would be journeying over towards the north end of the Euphrates Valley. Sullah generally allowed himself three months for the entire journey, and was anxious to get underway.

The caravan assembled outside the city and began the first leg of its journey to Ankara barely seven days after Sullah's proposal to Holmes and Elizabeth. By the time they had reached Ankara, they were well settled into the slow, easy routine of the caravan. They travelled only during daylight hours, so they would not miss any of the subtle navigation signposts. Camp was set up for the night in the last hour of daylight, and the precious horses corralled. The men set up shelter for the least hardy travellers, and the women cooked the only hot meal of the day on open fires while the children ran and played, and watched the activities of the men.

Holmes and Elizabeth, as guards, had no onerous duties at all.

They were privileged members of the caravan, and were treated with respect. At first, they believed their assigned duties were little more than a name and a status symbol for Sullah. But they were barely south of Ankara when they were disabused of the notion.

They had bent further towards the south to pick up the very beginnings of the Euphrates, which they would follow into Mesopotamia before branching off to Baghdad, where Sullah would trade some of his horses. On the second day out from Ankara, the caravan was set upon by mottled ragbag bandits whose main interest was in the riches Sullah carried on the heavily burdened carts. The bandits were most likely desperate beggars from the decrepit fringes that made up nearly two-thirds of Ankara's city profile. They were unskilled and, after first blood, unenthusiastic, and Sullah's soldiers chased them off very quickly. Neither Holmes nor Elizabeth fired a shot and their knives remained sheathed throughout, but it served to prove to them that their positions were anything but honourary.

All the guards rode on horseback to give them the extra speed necessary to protect the long tail of the caravan, and Sullah lent Holmes and Elizabeth a horse each. Both horses were among the pick of his purchases that summer and were beautiful.

Elizabeth liked to race ahead of the slow-moving caravan, her stallion's smooth, ground-swallowing gallop soothing and exhilarating at once. Sometimes Holmes accompanied her. More often she forged ahead alone. This freedom was far greater than any she enjoyed on her strolls about the moors; and she would achieve only a vague semblance of it once she had left the Persian mountains behind her. Holmes, with the growing intuitive understanding he would forever after share with her, allowed her to roam as she pleased. The deadly skills he was training in her were his gift towards her freedom. Some people would be appalled by Elizabeth's combat abilities, but these skills clothed her like an invisible shield potential enemies could sense, and trouble rarely came her way.

She roamed the mountains and valleys as she pleased, wearing the tight coat and gaily coloured cummerbund of the Kurds. Her hair was left loose, her sole concession to womanhood. Sullah outfitted them both with warm, fleece-lined riding boots, and she also adopted the trousers, finding them the most comfortable attire when she was astride a horse nearly all day.

She would move along the length of the caravan, talking to whomever she pleased, improving both her Arabic and Farsi, the Persian tongue, her bright red locks shining in the strong summer sun. She would walk Merlin, her horse, alongside a cart, talking to the driver, then perhaps race at full speed to the top of the caravan and exchange a few words with the guide.

Holmes frequently travelled alongside Sullah, talking quietly to him in Persian; he had mastered the fundamentals and a basic vocabulary at an astonishing rate. He also often sought out the elders of the family and spoke to them, as well. Sometimes he rode at the head of the caravan with the guide, discussing their route and the mountain passes, and what lay farther east, beyond Sullah's land.

Sullah found him there one afternoon and pulled his own wide-chested stallion alongside.

Holmes was watching the distant but unmistakable figure of Elizabeth, far down at the end of the valley they were traversing. She was astride Merlin and was galloping back to the caravan, her burnished locks flying behind her.

Sullah examined his English friend. "She is like a colt, is Elizabeth," he said. "Discovering the world and freedom before she is introduced to the bridle and bit."

Holmes nodded. "She knows it will come, though. But not for a while."

"Must you return, my friend?" Sullah asked softly. "It would be an unkindness to Elizabeth—and I would lose two remarkable friends."

Holmes looked down at his intricately carved saddle. "London is another world away. I could not imagine anything more unlikely than returning to its grimness. Yet we both belong there and one day it will be time to go back. Even Elizabeth will want to return."

Sullah watched Elizabeth's breakneck speed down the valley. "It seems unlikely. It is a very great gift you give her." And he laughed shortly. "She is the most admired woman in the camp. Every man lusts after her, yet none will dare approach her—so fierce is her reputation and the reputation of the man who watches her so carefully."

He glanced at Holmes covertly. "Is it not uncharacteristic of Sherlock Holmes to be so intimate with a woman?"

Holmes' head jerked around at Sullah's use of his name, then he relaxed a little, for only a scant handful in the camp spoke English, and none was within hearing range. He eyed Sullah warily. "You read too much into Watson's chronicles, Sullah. I am surprised *The Strand* reaches this far."

"Ah, yes, you relax despite my revelation. Then you know you can trust me."

Holmes nodded. "Implicitly."

"I am very pleased to meet the great Sherlock Holmes—and very puzzled."

"One day you will understand. For now it is enough that I tell you that the world believes Sherlock Holmes is dead and my life depends upon that misrepresentation remaining uncovered. Elizabeth's life, too. She is deeply involved in the machinations that bring us here."

Sullah held up his hand. "Peace. My lips are silent."

Elizabeth reined in her horse beside them, her eyes shining and her cheeks glowing. "You two are looking grim. Stop discussing politics, and enjoy this beautiful air and sunshine."

Sullah laughed.

They reached Sullah's home on the slopes of the Elburz Mountains north of Mashhad just as winter set in. Their caravan had diminished by that time, for parties had left the group as they reached their own destinations. It had been a long, indirect trip, for across Persia there are only two trade and travel routes, which follow the mountain chains, and only a fool would attempt to travel other than along their well-established paths.

The most populous route, and the one Sullah's caravan used, began in Baghdad and ran further south to skirt the western barrier range before turning northeast and heading directly for Teheran. Another route ran from Teheran across to Mashhad, following the long line of mountains that ended near Mashhad.

Their arrival caused excitement among the people who had remained in Sullah's home, for there would be many gifts and goods to inspect before the day was through. The travellers dispersed among their relatives and friends, and Sullah arranged rooms for Elizabeth and Holmes.

They stayed in Sullah's home for the remainder of that winter, a bitterly cold period of exceptional snowfalls. Travel would have been impossible, even if they had wanted to move on. But they were content to rest and regain some strength.

It was a time of waiting for Elizabeth, for she sensed that Holmes was still searching for their goal.

She spent her time making repairs to the few clothes and possessions they had acquired, and learning some of the herb lore of Persian cooking and medicine. The Persian skills in living off the land and conserving food and water were honed from centuries of constant travel.

Later, Holmes and Elizabeth would find themselves healthy and well fed in apparently barren country because of the nomadic skills they had absorbed during their journey with Sullah, and at Mashhad.

As they fell into the domestic routines of Sullah's home, Elizabeth noticed Holmes was spending more and more time with a strange little man who had travelled with them from Constantinople. On their journey she hadn't bothered to learn more about him, for he was a solitary creature who spoke Persian badly and Arabic not at all. He had tended the caravan's goats—a walking larder—with a deft hand and a keen instinct. At night he wrapped himself in skins and slept on the ground by his animals. The routine never changed.

Now that Holmes was showing such a deep interest in him, Elizabeth's curiosity was piqued. She asked Sullah about the man.

"He is from Tibet." Sullah looked over to where the man was tending the hooves of some of the young kids. "He came out of the mountains one day many years ago, badly cut by bandits, and with nothing to his name. We took him in and cared for him, for the frostbite had got him. We saved all but his toes; they were beyond help. In return he tends the goats."

"Doesn't he have any greater ambition than that? Has he ever expressed a desire to return to Tibet? To his home?"

Sullah shrugged. "If you ask him, he will say his home is here. I do not believe he has any relatives, and now he considers us his family. It is hard to get details from him, for he has never really bothered to improve his Persian. He is a wonderful man to talk to if you are looking for peace of mind. He understands the secret of life, I am sure. There is a placidness, a forgiveness in him that hints of higher wisdom. I am not surprised Holmes seeks him out."

Elizabeth returned to her affairs, pondering this new puzzle. Sometime later, as the sun was flattening on the horizon, she found Holmes still sitting upon his favourite flat rock, watching a spectacular display of colours playing over the face of the eastern mountains. His absent frown had disappeared, and his entire attention was involved in the enjoyment of the display.

She sat on the rock, appreciating its warmth now that the heat of the day had evaporated, and studied him overtly. Holmes eventually acknowledged her presence. He pulled the long skirts of his coat aside and lifted one knee to rest his chin upon.

"You want to travel to Tibet, don't you?" Elizabeth asked.

Holmes lit a cigarette before answering. "The old man—Ch'ang T'i—he has a placid wisdom that calls to me. And he tells me I can find it there. In Tibet."

"How?"

"Their leader, the Llama, is reputedly wise and humble, and will try to help all who approach him in need, no matter what their religion. The old man says this is the man I should approach."

"Could you find him?"

"Ch'ang T'i says he will lead us over the mountains, if we wish. But it is a dangerous journey, especially in the colder months. It is impassable in winter."

The implication was obvious. If they were not to spend next winter in some far-flung valley, or perish in an impassable mountain crossing, they would have to go soon. Holmes did not bother to spell this out to Elizabeth. He fully appreciated her mental prowess. Instead he sat smoking and waiting for her answer, tacitly giving her some say in the matter of their destiny.

"I started packing this afternoon," she said eventually. "We can be ready to leave in two days."

Holmes' gratitude for Elizabeth's uncanny empathy was revealed in the warm pressure of his hand on hers and his quiet, earnest thank you.

Elizabeth gazed at the distant, white peaks. "Sullah will be furious."

After a short silence, Holmes nodded. "Yes, he will be."

Sullah's disappointment was bitter enough to inspire two days' worth of invective, pleading, argument, and clever campaigning. All were useless against Holmes' resolve.

Eventually Elizabeth convinced Sullah his efforts were wasted, and he calmed long enough to consider Holmes' plans with a judicious and experienced eye. He immediately pointed out the difficulty of traversing the Hindu Kush from the west, and advised Holmes to follow the ancient and well-travelled Silk Road, which passed within a few miles of Sullah's land. This route skirted the Tibetan plateau, hugging the northern border mountain chains. They could travel as far east as Ch'ang T'i considered necessary, and then cross through one of the passes into the northernmost reaches of Tibet. It was a longer but easier journey.

Ch'ang T'i did not know the route, and Sullah offered one of his household guards as a companion and guide—the guard was Chinese and had once been employed by a trader who used the Silk Road. And with tears of emotion in his eyes, Sullah included the two priceless horses Holmes and Elizabeth had ridden from Constantinople.

The gift was inestimable for another strategic reason. Holmes was determined to begin immediately, even though winter was still lingering. Although they would manage to avoid the high mountain passes by using the Silk Road, it was much farther in distance. On horseback they would be able to reach the pass in time to cross into Tibet during good weather. On foot, they stood the chance of being caught by another winter.

So Holmes accepted the offer of the horses with much relief. It was arranged that their guide would go as far as the Tibetan pass before returning back to Sullah with the horses, for the animals would not be able to manage the mountain passes. Ch'ang T'i knew the way into Tibet from that point and could guide from there.

Within the two days promised they were ready to leave, and in the freezing air of pre-dawn they slid into their saddles, the bits clanking coldly as the horses pranced. Ch'ang T'i refused to ride his own beast, but consented to riding pillion with the guide, Ts'e.

Sullah stood watching, well wrapped against the cold in a bright handwoven cloak of goat's wool. Only a few other members of his household were present; the cold discouraged all but the most ardent well-wishers.

"On your return you must stop here awhile." Sullah shielded his eyes against the rays of the low dawn sunlight. "That is, if you are mad enough to try another winter passage, my friends. Then you can travel with me back to Constantinople."

Holmes looked down at the trader from his high perch. "We'll try," he said simply.

Sullah moved to Elizabeth's side and held Merlin's bridle as the animal fretted.

"Goodbye, Elizabeth, my dear."

"Goodbye, Sullah." She leaned down to drop a kiss on his cheek.

He turned to offer his hand to Holmes, who took it gravely. Sullah sighed deeply. "Be careful, won't you? And take care of her."

With no more ceremony the three horses were turned towards the sun and urged forward.

Chapter Eight

TIBET REMAINS ONE OF THE LAST EASTERN countries to be fully pene-
trated by Europeans. It rests at the highest altitude in the world,
surrounded by three chains of imposing mountains, and the breadth
of China to its east. Its geography guarantees a degree of isolation
that the Tibetans have sought to increase for generations.
Consequently, the rhythms of life on its semi-desert plateaus follow
customs that date from antiquity and have changed very little since.

The harshness of the life also encourages the ancient practices,
which have been honed by ruthless elimination. Survival is a primitive equation.

Most of the population are nomadic shepherds who follow the
centuries-old caravan routes that lead to Lhasa. Some are farmers who
subsist on crops of wheat, millet, and beans. All are simple people
who live with nature's patterns and follow a religion that nourishes
inner peace. It was this equilibrium in Ch'ang T'i that caused Holmes
to search out the country and seek answers of his own.

Perhaps Fate, in her wisdom, looked ahead and saw the answers
Holmes sought, and contrived to place him where he would discover
them. For as soon as they reached Tibet, his plan to find and speak
to the Dalai Llama was delayed.

At one of the waterholes that dot the trade routes they came across a lone woman. It was the time when shepherds were herding their animals to the high grounds at the base of the mountains on the Tarim Pendi—the northern plateau—where the sweet grasses grew. There, their herds of goats and yaks could breed and fatten, storing up nourishment for the lean winter months.

Yet the woman was too far south to make the feeding grounds in time for the breeding season. Her tent sat on stony ground next to a tiny lake. Dozens of wiry goats and tall, shaggy yaks milled around the water's edge, while the woman stood at the entrance of the round tent, watching the travellers' slow descent down the well-worn path to the watering hole.

Ch'ang T'i warned his companions to approach the camp cautiously. He feared a trap. Women did not travel alone.

The mystery was solved almost immediately, for as soon as the woman realized Elizabeth was a woman, she drew her away from the men and revealed a swollen abdomen beneath the layers of fur.

Elizabeth went back to Holmes. "She is pregnant. And her time is close."

Ch'ang T'i stepped forward and began a long, complicated, triangular, trilingual conversation with the woman and Holmes, which Holmes translated into English for Elizabeth. As the woman blushed and stammered, the story slowly emerged.

Her name was Ts'iang, and her husband had died nearly a month previously. By Ts'iang's re-enactment of the symptoms, Holmes guessed the man had died of appendicitis. Their camp had been much further north. Once Ts'iang had taken care of her husband's body, she had turned the flock southeast, hoping to reach her village before her baby was born. But her pains had started that morning, and she had set up camp, knowing she would need the shelter.

Elizabeth studied the woman. "She is not in labour," she judged.

After careful questioning and translation, Holmes shook his head. "No, she isn't. She said it stopped some time ago."

Elizabeth looked perplexed. "I don't know anything about childbirth. But that doesn't sound promising." She looked at Holmes. "What do we do?"

Ultimately, they did nothing. It was Ch'ang T'i, the goatherd, who delivered the baby some eighteen hours later, with Elizabeth's help. The day had long since drawn into night, and sunrise was close when Ch'ang T'i emerged from the round tent, grunted a few words at Holmes, and rolled himself up in his skins to sleep amongst the herd of goats.

"A boy," Elizabeth added tiredly, when she emerged from the tent.

Holmes threw more of the precious wood supply onto the fire. "How long until she is fit to move?"

Elizabeth frowned. "I don't know. We'll have to ask Ch'ang T'i." She glanced over at the motionless pile of skins. "Tomorrow."

The consensus was they would have to provide for Ts'iang for at least ten days. Holmes accepted the estimate with philosophical restraint. "I can wait ten days," he said.

"We stayed there two years," Elizabeth told me, with a smile. "It just worked out that way. We couldn't leave Ts'iang on her own, and when we reached her village, her family still hadn't returned from the high plains. That wasn't so unusual, but it meant we were committed for the next three months, at least. Then Ch'ang T'i travelled across to the northern trade route to his home village, to learn about his family. They were dead or missing, as he had suspected, so he came back and married Ts'iang. I think he preferred it that way. Actually Ch'ang T'i was somewhat of a celebrity after his international journeys, and considered a good catch. He found himself a second wife within months of marrying Ts'iang."

Elizabeth smiled at the memory. "And, of course, when winter arrived, we couldn't go travelling about because no one else would, so we stayed, too." Her smile broadened. "Besides, Ch'ang T'i was too old, and Ts'iang had her hands full with her baby, and they needed our help."

I stared at her. "You joined the nomads?"

"Yes. We became shepherds. Well, goatherds, actually. Holmes became quite good at it. But I am afraid I will never be able to judge a good-quality goat."

While they continued to wait for an opportunity to go on their way, they fell into the rituals of nomadic life with an ease that astonished them. And after a time they became tuned to the cadences and rhythms of the seasons that dictated the nomads' way of life. They began to understand the profound simplicity of a life lived in balance with nature.

In the autumn of their second year, they arrived back in Ts'iang's village in preparation for winter and found her family had returned early, too. Holmes had been waiting for such a chance. It had remained his ambition to travel to Lhasa and speak with the Dalai Llama. Holmes also thought he might be able to arrange to sell his account of Tibetan life to one of the international journals while he was there, and thus swell their dwindling supply of funds.

With Ts'iang and the household settled in for winter, and the trade routes still open during the mild autumn, Holmes felt he could impose on Ch'ang T'i to leave Ts'iang and travel to Lhasa with him. Ch'ang T'i was agreeable, and only three days after arriving, they shouldered their packs to leave again.

Elizabeth stayed behind.

The journey to Lhasa was a lengthy one, and Ch'ang T'i was not overly familiar with the route. They hoped to be able to travel fast enough to complete the return journey before winter settled in. But in Tibet pessimism is more practical, so with considerable patience, Elizabeth prepared to wait out most of the winter, if necessary.

"On your own?" I asked.

"The whole village was there," Elizabeth pointed out.

"Yes, but. . . ."

"But, yes, I was the only European," she agreed. "I had nearly forgotten I was English by then. I knew the language well enough, and Ts'iang's people were pure kindness. It was much warmer and friendlier by the fire than traipsing about the Tsangpo Valley in the snow. I had a place there."

One morning, several weeks after they had left, Elizabeth awoke with a start, and froze. She listened with straining ears for the noise that had alerted her. Cautiously she inched her hand towards the knife under her pillow.

Suddenly a strong hand clamped her inching wrist, holding it still.

"It is me, Elizabeth. You have no need for the knife."

She opened her eyes and sat up, dropping the hilt. Holmes was on one knee beside the pallet, leaning heavily on his shepherd's crook. His face was tired and haggard, and half-obscured by the bulky coat and skins necessary to protect him from the cold in the high passes. It was evident he'd only just arrived and come straight to her.

"We weren't expecting you. . . ." Elizabeth stopped as Holmes swayed a little. "You're hurt!" she said, and her eyebrows rose as he pulled his coat aside and revealed a large, bloodstained tear in his clothing.

"We ran into trouble around sunset last night and decided to continue walking until we got home."

"Oh, my god," Elizabeth murmured, appalled at the sight of the wound itself.

"It is not as bad as it looks," Holmes assured her. "A little blood goes a long way. But it might need a stitch or two, and I'd rather not let Ts'iang administer me. Her embroidery is worse than yours."

Elizabeth reached for her clothes. "I will see to it," she told him.

As she strode towards the river, she could see the first glimmer of dawn in the east. If he had been walking since sunset, then Holmes' enforced march had taken twelve hours. What had driven him to push himself in that way?

The pre-dawn air was still and warm, trapped by the cloud layer that had lingered overnight. The cloud was clearing now, and the sun would continue the warming process. Winter had been delayed for a while.

Elizabeth made her way to the river. As she was drawing the bucket to the bank, Holmes appeared by her side, the unfastened coat flapping as he scrambled down the bank. He still carried his pack. "I will save you having to carry the water back."

"I am used to it," she said simply. She studied his dark silhouette, waiting.

"I wanted to talk," he said at last. "It is actually a relief to use English after that bastardized Persian Ch'ang T'i insists on using. I am feeling garrulous—which is a change." He brushed the snow from a large, flat rock, propped a lantern on a corner, and lit it with one of the last of their judiciously preserved supply of matches brought out from the pack. The light flared, and he reduced it to a feeble glow, enough for Elizabeth to see what she was doing. It left his features in deep shadow. He dug deep into the pack, sat on the rock, and held out their medical kit—one of their most precious possessions.

"You're also feeling extravagant," Elizabeth replied. She took the kit. "Lie back."

Holmes obeyed, and watched the sky lighten above Elizabeth's head as she worked. "Our standards have changed since Switzerland, haven't they? We think nothing of the best cuts of meat, yet begrudge a sulphur match."

"The law of supply and demand," Elizabeth said, her voice a little detached as she concentrated on what her fingers were doing. "How did this happen?"

"A trio of outlaws ambushed us in the ravine leading to the last pass. We fought them off, but decided it was wiser to keep on the move rather than make camp and risk them catching up with us again. And you? Any trouble?"

"Only with wolves in the last week or two. They're heading south. I think winter is on its way, at last. We've been lucky." She snipped the thread, and Holmes jumped. "Sorry."

"I deserve it. I was a little too complacent, and this is the result. I have lost my edge."

Elizabeth lifted her head. "Why do you say that?"

"The lack of competition. Lack of danger. My mind has grown lax."

Elizabeth raised his hand to his side, and put his fingers on the edge of the bandage. "Hold that, and sit up," she instructed him, then began to wind the bandage about his ribs. "I do not believe you've grown soft, Holmes. It is just this country—you've no echoing foot-paths or hidden doors out here. All your normally sensitive instincts have merely relaxed." She tore the end of the bandage and tied it firmly. "You do not have to lie awake and listening to know if some-one is approaching across a valley of shale."

"I have grown used to danger from beast and birds rather than man."

"Some people would consider that an improvement," Elizabeth pointed out. She sat back on her heels, studying him in the growing light.

There was nothing of the European about either of them any more. They were dressed alike in long trousers, sheepskin boots, shirts, overshirts, and jackets. As a further measure against the cold, they wore layers of woollen material in the form of overcoats and cloaks, all topped off with oversized coats of goat's wool. They wore the Kurdish adaptation of the turban on their heads, and carried their knives and pistols openly, tucked into the bright cummerbunds. Holmes habitually carried the shepherd's crook and Elizabeth a long staff—invaluable aids when scrambling about the knees of mountains, searching for recalcitrant goats. Both were tanned and extremely healthy, although thinner. They had developed far-seeing eyes, and had learned a philosophical patience for all nature's quirks and delays—though Holmes was still quick to flare over human stupidity.

Holmes remained silent, enjoying the spectacular hues of dawn on the last of the clouds.

"Did you find what you wanted in Lhasa?" Elizabeth finally asked him.

"I did sell my articles." Holmes rearranged his clothing. "And I visited the Potala and spoke to the Llama."

"And?"

He stared out across the river, remembering. "He was indeed a wise man. He had no answers but one—to find what I seek, I must look inside, not for symbols or signs from elsewhere."

Elizabeth remained silent, and Holmes glanced at her. "You knew that all the time, didn't you?"

"You are not one of the weak, Holmes. You already have all the wisdom and strength you need. You simply have to find it."

Holmes nodded. "I have made a crucial mistake," he said.

"I am sure it is not your first."

"And it probably won't be the last, but I swear I will never make the same mistake again."

"I am listening."

He hesitated a little. "If Moriarty and our adventures in Switzerland hadn't happened, I would still have made this trip. Except I would have been alone. And, as we've learned, probably dead. But it didn't happen that way. Even before we left Persia I had begun to realize I didn't need to visit Lhasa. It wasn't a conscious thought, but an unsettling feeling of . . . completeness. I have travelled more than halfway around the globe, most of it on foot and through some of the most god-forsaken country in the world, only to discover I'd brought my happiness along with me." He glanced at her quickly. "I have wasted so much of your time, Elizabeth."

"It hasn't been wasted," she replied softly. "We take back the gift of solitude with us."

"I have put you in danger. That will remain a constant for the rest of your life. Being closely associated with my name is hazardous."

"You have tried to compensate for that," she pointed out, her hand dropping to the hilt of her knife tucked into her belt.

"I have tried to develop your abilities. It is hardly a fair bargain, Elizabeth. You've had very little choice in the matter so far. Perhaps I should give you a chance to decide."

She touched his arm. "It is time to go back, isn't it?"

"Yes, it is time we returned," he replied. "It would be selfish to remain here any longer."

Typically, once he had made up his mind, Holmes could tolerate no delays in implementing his decisions. With seething agitation, he pressed the arrangements to leave.

Elizabeth was equally anxious to depart, for she had been keeping a vigilant eye on the weather. Holmes had returned from Lhasa in late October, and Elizabeth knew the mild autumn would not stay much longer.

With both keen to hasten their departure, they managed to find a guide who was willing to show them the western route along Tibet's low summer valleys and across the mountains straight into Persia. It was the very route, in fact, that Sullah had been adamant they not tackle two years before, and the same route that Ch'ang T'i had been using when Sullah's people had found him, eleven years before.

It seemed to Elizabeth they were destined forever to travel into bad weather. However, she was confident of their guide's knowledge, and she and Holmes were both so much more experienced now at surviving the harsh conditions.

On November 1, 1893, as near as they could tally it, they left for Mashhad with the guide, two yaks as beasts of burden, six goats on the hoof, a dressed sheep, barley meal, a small bag of dried tea leaves, and the shy, warm wishes of an entire village for godspeed and good luck.

"And we needed every bit of luck they offered us," Elizabeth told me. "For we lost our guide in a rockslide just out of sight of the Persian plains, and we had to navigate by stars and moon—when we had a clear night, that is. Usually it was overcast, and we simply followed our noses."

They arrived on Sullah's doorstep on Christmas day, pushing their way the last mile through a storm that settled into a blizzard that lasted three days.

Winter had arrived, and had they followed their intentions, they would have stayed throughout winter once again. But a message from Mycroft was waiting for Holmes—a message that had been sent nearly six months earlier to his last known location via paid carriers, and held by Sullah's household staff until his return to the homestead, which preceded Holmes' by a mere three weeks.

Sullah had been at a loss regarding the message's further progress. That problem was solved by Holmes' arrival, but the contents of the letter were sufficient to prevent Holmes from settling for too long.

Mycroft had gathered a large quantity of facts and information relevant to Holmes' situation throughout his younger brother's absence from London. The distillation of this intelligence was contained in his letter for Holmes to absorb, and upon which to base sound decisions concerning their future.

Amongst many of the significant facts was the news of Straker's imprisonment for murder, and the death of two of Holmes' bitterest enemies—one from natural means and the other in a boating accident in a Scottish loch.

Elizabeth was as quick to grasp the significance of this news as Holmes. She tapped the particular sheet of Mycroft's letter where it lay on the table between them. "Holmes, this means only Moran is loose to cause mischief. If we could somehow contain him. . . ." Hope flared in her. London beckoned enticingly.

Holmes nodded. "Yes, but we must proceed cautiously. Moran's mischief is a potent brew indeed."

There were other, politically important, instructions in Mycroft's letter, and for these, Holmes approached Sullah for help.

"Khartoum?" Sullah repeated aloud, putting the letter down on the low table before him. Holmes had found him in his private salon, from where Sullah carried out most of his daily business of overseeing the extensive organization of his household and grazing lands. "But the Sudan is peaceful now. The Khalifa has smoothed out all the wrinkles. Besides, he is at Omdurman, not Khartoum. That is where you will get most of your information."

"I will start with Khartoum," Holmes answered. "Or finish there. That is where most of the Europeans are, and we can travel to Omdurman as we need to."

"And we can buy what European supplies we need at Khartoum," Elizabeth pointed out, patting her trouser-encased knees.

"Khartoum," Sullah intoned, leaning back into his cushions, his brow wrinkled.

"At fastest speed," Holmes added.

Sullah remained silent, his eyes shut. Holmes and Elizabeth kept the silence, waiting patiently for Sullah to finish his contemplation.

After several long moments, he opened his eyes, clapped his hands twice sharply and called out in Persian for his maps. The requested maps were speedily brought and spread out across the table.

"There is fastest speed and there is safest speed when crossing the deserts," Sullah warned them. "But in winter the two are closer than in summer. And cross the desert you must, if you wish to travel to

Khartoum as directly as possible." He pointed out the route on the maps. "From Teheran to Isfahan, and to Shiraz on the Gulf. You must cross the Arabian Empty Quarter, through to Mecca, down to Jeddah ,and across the Red Sea to Port Sudan. There are ships crossing nearly every day, so that will not hamper your speed." Sullah paused, frowning, staring at the map. "Only an imbecile would cross these deserts without a guide—without someone who knows how." He caught Holmes' impatient motion out of the corner of his eye and held up a finger in warning. "No, not even clever imbeciles who cross the Swiss Alps alone. There is only one person I know who has travelled across the Arabian peninsula often enough to be useful."

"Who?" Holmes asked, restraining his impatience.

"Me," Sullah said simply. He laughed, one of his great bellows. "If you must risk your lives on such a reckless dash across three of the world's worst deserts, it is only fair that I, as your friend, should share the risk. Besides, it is the perfect opportunity to pay my debt to Elizabeth." He put his hand on his heart and nodded his head towards her. "I will lead you both to Khartoum."

Their trip across the deserts was arduous, but rapid. As promised, Sullah led them across the burning plains as swiftly as safe travel would permit. But their pace was not too fast for them to learn and understand just how dangerous it would have been had they attempted the trip alone.

They reached Khartoum in February. Dressed as Arabs, they blended into the indigenous population with experienced ease. This had been Holmes' intention. They had learnt from their time in Constantinople that tongues were looser when Europeans were absent, and Holmes intended to draw out every scrap of information available for Mycroft's associates.

Rumours were endemic, and Holmes soon had a wealth of speculation and gossip. Within twenty-four hours of their arrival, he moved onto Omdurman, leaving Elizabeth and Sullah in Khartoum. There, he completed his extraordinary interview with the Khalifa, who found this strange Englishman in Arab dress much easier to talk to than any other representative of that odd race. He found him such a congenial listener, in fact, that Holmes was able to confirm much that had been worrying the British government for some time concerning Britain's affairs in that corner of the world.

It was Elizabeth who discovered my bereavement, as reported in an old copy of the *Times* she found beneath a dusty pile of periodicals in the hotel foyer on their last evening in Khartoum. She took the paper to their rooms and showed it to Holmes.

"I am sorry he suffered through it alone," he told her.

"Even if we rushed home, the fastest route we can take is the one we're taking," Elizabeth said. "And the paper is three months old. . . ."

"Nevertheless, I am relieved we are continuing on tomorrow." He put the paper aside. "Apart from the report to London, I am anxious to reach Aden. I do not trust any of the wire services in this country and I can arrange for money with the bank in Aden."

Holmes and Elizabeth, accompanied by Sullah, planned to travel by sea through the Suez Canal, and across the Mediterranean to Marseilles, on the French coast. They would wait in France until Holmes received clear information on Moran's activities.

This route to France was well frequented by the British, for apart from journeying by sea, one was forced by the sentinels of desert to travel along the narrow Nile valley. It was with unexpected reluctance that in the Sudan Holmes and Elizabeth purchased and donned European-style clothing. Elizabeth, perhaps, had a little more enthusiasm, though she confessed the constrictive fashions were initially uncomfortable after the freedom of trousers. Sullah, too, converted to European clothing for the duration of their voyage up the Red Sea.

At Suez, Sullah and his people parted company with them, for they were to travel up the eastern Mediterranean coast, taking advantage of the unique opportunity to buy and sell in these foreign markets. Sullah would meet his sons in Constantinople, and continue with his annual carpet sale.

Sullah was almost inconsolable at their parting, and only Holmes' and Elizabeth's reassurance that they would keep in contact as much as they could seemed to calm him.

Two weeks later they were in Marseilles. The cable services between the two brothers fairly steamed as they exchanged cryptic information regarding Moran and Holmes' safety should he return, and based on this new collection of data, Holmes decided to wait before returning to London.

They moved on to Montpelier, which was strategic for two reasons: Holmes was familiar with the city, and knew several people there. One of his acquaintances would be able to host them, and they could thereby avoid using easily investigated hostels, inns, or hotels.

The second reason was purely self-indulgent. Holmes knew the owner of a research laboratory and was able to arrange for work there, gratifying his curiosity regarding coal-tar derivatives, and at the same time distracting his mind from his simmering impatience, which was agitated by the nearness of London and the waiting game he was forced to endure.

The French of that district have an enjoyable custom of not segregating their women after dinner. All the diners sojourn to a lounging room where they consume coffee and after-dinner liqueurs, while the host and hostess lead the conversation.

It was at this point one evening, nearly two months after their arrival in Montpelier, when Elizabeth looked up from a conversation with the wife of Holmes' friend and host, and observed Holmes standing by a small table next to the heavily curtained windows. With apparent disinterest, he had pushed a newspaper around with his forefinger and was scanning an article on the back page. To an observer it appeared he was just pausing and would move off in a moment to rejoin conversation. Only Elizabeth sensed a sudden tension in him, a taut thrumming of nerves and pulse.

He glanced towards her to see if she was watching, and his finger tapped the paper. Then, casually, he moved back to the group he had left.

Elizabeth excused herself and moved over to the paper. With a frown of concentration she began mentally translating headlines. The only one that might have caused the sudden alertness in Holmes was a report on the strange murder of Ronald Adair, in London. She scanned the article. Almost instantly her sight was caught and held by a name within the print. "*Colonel Sebastian Moran.*" It was enough to tell her what had caught Holmes' attention.

She looked around for him, but he had disappeared. She guessed he was making their excuses.

She lifted her skirts and left the room, heading for their suite.

Holmes found her there, packing a small bag. She had already changed into travelling clothes. She paused only long enough to say, "I guessed speed would be the priority. Shall I ask Elise to pack our luggage and send it after us?"

"I have already seen to it." He disappeared into the bedroom and emerged a few minutes later in a dark suit and heavy overcoat. Elizabeth closed the catches on the bag and he picked it up.

"Let us go home," he said.

Chapter Nine

"*AND THAT'S WHEN THE ODYSSEY CEASED,*" Elizabeth finished. "When Holmes saw the newspaper report on Adair's murder, his heart and attention were pulled back to London, and for a while it was as if he had never left."

I nodded, for I had been a part of the end of this particular adventure, and I agreed with her. Moran's murder of Ronald Adair had been the opportunity for which Holmes had been waiting. He'd raced back to London the moment he had seen the report, to solve the case and put Moran behind bars. Moran's imprisonment would remove the final impediment to Holmes' return to public life, and he had spared no energy in achieving that long-awaited goal. It was, indeed, as if he had never left.

The tale of their adventure had taken many months in the telling, for I had soon quit my sickbed, and time for stories was limited after that. Generally we snatched a couple of hours here and there a week, and Elizabeth would take up her narrative where she left off. Of course, the tale I have set down here is extended and detailed beyond Elizabeth's telling, for I have included all the adventures she had told me before, and the stories and viewpoints I have managed to draw from a reluctant Holmes over the years.

And much of my information I received from another, un-expected source, although at first I did not appreciate the worth of that source at all. In fact, my foolishness very nearly lost me an invaluable friendship.

Nearly three years after Holmes' return to London, the three of us went walking through Hyde Park one late afternoon in autumn. A cool breeze was ruffling the last of the withered leaves on overhead branches and the freshness of the day was very pleasant after the lagging heat of summer. We had lingered.

"I believe you're not telling me something," Elizabeth said, addressing Holmes. She paused to negotiate a rut in the path, lifting her skirts a little, the pale green parasol she carried bouncing its ruffles. "You've checked your watch surreptitiously nearly a dozen times during our walk. Have you noticed, John?"

I smiled. "Details of that type escape me, generally. It is only when you or Holmes point them out that I see them."

"Why don't you tell me what it is?" Holmes replied, and there was the faintest strain of a challenge in his conversational tone.

Elizabeth narrowed her eyes. "I am not sure that I should attempt to. You only ever bet when the probability of winning is decidedly in your favour. And as you've pointed out before, only a fool accepts a wager with a certain outcome."

Holmes shrugged. "You're probably wise not to try," he agreed.

"Hello!" came a shout from behind us. "I say, Sigerson!"

The use of Holmes' travelling name startled me and I heard Elizabeth gasp, too. I turned around.

Walking rapidly up the path, trying to catch up with us, was a tall, tanned man dressed in a well-tailored walking suit and brightly polished shoes, wearing one of the latest fashions in hats upon his black hair. He carried a walking cane with a gold handle and ferrule, but it appeared to be an affectation more than a necessary accessory, for he strode along the path with long steps. He held up his cane in greeting as we paused.

Elizabeth gripped my arm tightly. "Sullah!" she breathed.

I felt my own jaw descend a little. This well-do-to Englishman walking towards us was the Persian of Elizabeth's tales? No, it could not be.

The man strode right up to Holmes, holding out his hand, which Holmes took without hesitation, pressing it warmly. Holmes rarely accepted a handshake, and when forced to it, would accept with obvious reluctance, yet he stood now with a small smile on his face, and a pleased glow in his eyes, his hands held in the enormous tanned ones of this man.

This, then, must be Holmes' surprise.

Then Sullah turned to Elizabeth. "Miss Sigerson," he said, with a dramatic flourish of his hat. He took her gloved hand and bowed low over it, and straightened with a twinkle in his eye. He put his other hand over his heart. "The sight of you restores my lost youth," he declared.

Elizabeth's smile brightened, and uneasiness touched me when I saw tears sparkling in her eyes. "Would you mind?" she asked, handing her parasol to Holmes, who took it without protest.

Then Elizabeth astonished me even further by virtually throwing herself at Sullah with a joyful exclamation, her arms around his neck.

I looked away, as a proper gentleman should, and noticed how the strollers passing by were glancing at us, and giving us wide berth. Their expressions ranged from polite non-interest to outraged disgust at Elizabeth's improper public display.

Holmes, of course, ignored them.

I cleared my throat, and studied the gravel at my feet.

Elizabeth tugged at my arm a little, drawing me closer to Sullah, introducing us. Sullah was a fraction taller than I, and his dark eyes seemed to laugh at me while we shook hands. I murmured something, a greeting of some type, then inspected my watch. "Holmes, I should be getting back."

"Soon, Watson, soon," Holmes murmured, but he did not look away from Sullah and Elizabeth, who were chattering away to each other, tripping over their words, interrupting each other. Laughing. Even Holmes had the beginnings of a smile on his face.

Sullah nodded at me. "I do not want to delay you, Doctor Watson. My apologies." He held his arm out to Elizabeth. "Come, you must show me your famous Baker Street." She slipped her hand into the crook of his arm, and they walked up the path together, still talking.

Holmes handed Elizabeth her parasol, stepped ahead of them, and strode down the path, the distance between us lengthening with every step.

"Holmes!" I called, from behind Elizabeth and Sullah.

I saw him lift his hand, and his voice floated back to me. "I'll see you at Baker Street, Watson!"

So I followed Sullah and Elizabeth back towards Holmes' rooms, and tried not to notice the absence of a small, warm hand on my own arm.

The traffic was light—there were many more pedestrians out enjoying the crisp weather—and we turned back into Baker Street quickly. Holmes was nowhere to be seen. He had raced far ahead of us.

We were passing the lane that led to the stables behind Baker Street, when we were halted by Holmes' voice.

"Watson. Elizabeth."

Sullah point down the lane with his cane. "This way, my dear." And he led Elizabeth into the shadowed path.

I peered into the lane suspiciously. Holmes was at the far end of the alley, waiting for us.

By the time we had reached the end of the alley, Holmes had moved away again. We turned into the yard, and Elizabeth gasped and came to a halt.

A large horse float stood in the yard, open and empty. A stable hand was folding blankets at the foot of the ramp.

Held by halter and reins by the other stableboy were two of the most beautiful horses I have ever seen. I am not the disciplined expert some people are, but the quality of these animals shone from their glossy coats and sleek, muscled frames, and from the high-fettled, unsettled motions they made. They were saddled.

Holmes was leaning against the float, with almost a smile on his thin features as he observed Elizabeth's reaction.

"Merlin!" Elizabeth breathed.

The name gave me comprehension. These, then, must be the horses Sullah had given them in Constantinople, brought back to England with what must have been considerable expense and trouble by Holmes, as a surprise—a gift—to Elizabeth.

I thought I understood why Sullah had accompanied them all the way to London. From Elizabeth's tales I judged he would sooner allow a member of his family to undertake alone the difficult and dangerous trip to England, than one of his horses. And Elizabeth had told me these pair were his favourites.

Elizabeth dropped her parasol, lifted up her dress, and ran toward the horses. She threw her arms around the neck of one, and stood for a moment with her cheek resting against its flesh. Then she took the reins and, gathering up her skirts, swung into the saddle. The fabric climbed high, for it was not a sidesaddle, and women's fashions just then were very restrictive. With an impatient click of her tongue, she rearranged them more modestly, then she turned the horse and urged him across the cobbled yard. With a neat jump she cleared a half-barrel, and guided the horse down the alley. The horse's shoes clattered noisily, and I could hear her picking up speed, breaking into a trot. Then she was gone.

Sullah stood silently by, a large grin on his face. It was obvious he was enjoying his part of the surprise.

I walked over to Holmes, who was now examining the other horse. He rapidly discarded his coat, his jacket, and even his collar and tie, which he handed to me. Then he swung up into the saddle, took the reins with a nod to Sullah, and turned the horse and rode away.

I watched him take the barrel with the same ease as Elizabeth, and it occurred to me that I had never seen him astride a horse before. His professed poor horsemanship seemed an exaggeration.

It was the first time I had seen for myself a hint of the changes wrought on Holmes and Elizabeth as a result of their long journey. I had just caught a glimpse of what lay beneath the civilized veneer they had worn since their return, and it intrigued me.

"They will miss dinner," I remarked inconsequentially, almost to myself.

"I do not think they will be very concerned about that," Sullah replied.

We stood staring down the alleyway, where there was nothing to be seen now.

I cleared my throat. "Well. Dinner awaits me." I patted my fob pocket.

Sullah smiled. "A moment, Doctor Watson, please?"

I raised my brow enquiringly.

"Would you care to join me at the dinner table, Doctor? I feel we have a great deal to talk about."

"We have?"

"We have much in common."

"I rather doubt that." I'm afraid I made no effort to eliminate the coldness from my tone.

But Sullah did not take offence. "I meant Holmes and Elizabeth, Doctor." He grinned. "Do you not know how I have envied you all these years?"

I frankly stared at him. "I beg your pardon?"

"Yes! Envied you!" He laughed. "They are difficult people to know and understand. In my small time with them, I never fully satisfied my curiosity. And here you are, a lifelong friend, one who can spend as much time as he wishes to watch and listen and learn about them." His smile faded. "I would very much like to hear what you have learned, Doctor."

I could not find words to express my amazement. Suddenly, my churlishness since I had met him seemed completely foolish. With considerably more warmth, I said, "And all these years I have envied you for being there and seeing some of their adventure."

Sullah nodded slowly, thoughtfully.

"Let us dine alone, then. It is a perfect opportunity to compare notes about those two. I with my observations, and you with your journalistic eye; between us we might be able to dissect the innermost secrets of them both."

As indeed, we tried. Not just that night—even though we sat in Holmes' rooms until the two dishevelled and tired riders returned some hours later. Sullah stayed in England for another three months, and we met frequently. I swiftly grew to count Sullah a good friend.

He had been following Holmes' activities via my articles in *The Strand* magazine, and fulsomely praised my reporting techniques.

"Except you have not acknowledged Miss Elizabeth's part in any of these affairs of which you write," he pointed out sorrowfully.

I tried to explain the reasons for that omission, and Sullah listened gravely, his big, tanned hand curled loosely around the fragile teacup he was using—we were having afternoon tea at the time. He nodded when I had finished my somewhat stilted explanations, and leaned forward to tap the table between us to emphasize his point.

"It is unwise to hide her existence, Watson. Even though both you and Holmes act from the best intentions, it puts Elizabeth at even more risk."

"How is that possible when the public does not know of her?" I demanded.

"Exactly, Watson. No one knows of her. How can your laws punish a person for hurting or maiming or even killing a person who does not exist?"

"Nonsense!" I spluttered, feeling distinctly uneasy. "The public at large may not know of her, but lots of people close to her, to Holmes, to all of us, know who she is. No one would dare try anything."

Sullah held up his hand. "I have upset you. It was not my intention. Peace!" He sat back. "You are probably right, Watson. No one would dare try anything with such a stalwart and loyal friend as you by Elizabeth's side."

"Holmes will always be there, too," I was at pains to point out. "And everyone knows of his reputation."

Sullah nodded. "Perhaps you are right," and he would say no more on the subject. I was happy to leave it be, too.

Sullah filled in the gaps in Elizabeth's narration of their sojourn in the east, much to my content, for I had a very nearly complete picture of Holmes' and Elizabeth's journey now. When he returned to Mashhad we naturally continued our conversations by correspondence. I kept Sullah more fully informed of Holmes' latest adventures, complete with Elizabeth's contributions to his work.

Sullah's discomforting questions made me consider for the first time if our decision to keep Elizabeth hidden from the public might be wrong. I pondered that question a great deal over the next few months but by degrees finally reassured myself with the same answers I had given Sullah: one of us, at least, would always be there to protect her if anything should go wrong.

I once reported in *The Strand* that the years after Holmes' return to Baker Street were the most productive in his entire career. In sheer quantity and quality, the period was unique. As his physician I can attest that he had never been healthier, and his energy was boundless.

And by comparing notes from one date to the next I am able to pinpoint a mellowing in his attitudes toward the softer emotions. Although he would never be a demonstrative man, nor particularly open to the reception of affection or its relatives, except from a select few, he became more tolerant of their manifestation in others: more inclined to amusement rather than irascibility, and most importantly, with more understanding. I believe that of all the pleasures and joys Elizabeth bought Holmes, this was her greatest gift: the rounding and smoothing of a man to a point where he could settle down and enjoy life in retirement, and accept its foibles and follies.

One of Elizabeth's charms was her undemonstrativeness. She would expend as much effort over those labours that would go unnoticed as those that would make themselves felt. Therefore, I wondered to myself—does Holmes appreciate? Does he even know? This question became particularly important to me as time went on, for I well knew Holmes' blindness over his personal affairs.

But during the summer of 1903 I had my answer. For in August of that year, Holmes' deepest fear was realized.

We had accepted a case that at the outset looked simple enough. Its only complication was its location: Perth. Holmes had accepted commissions from Scotland before, as he had from most of England's neighbours. Usually he hated to leave London and the comfort of his rooms, but provided the case was of sufficient interest or promise, he would exert himself and travel. Elizabeth always accompanied him on these jaunts—they were, after all, seasoned travellers, no matter how disinclined. But on this occasion, the circumstances were slightly different, and for the first time since I'd known her, Elizabeth proved intractable.

The client was a woman, old but sprightly. She appeared on our doorstep on the afternoon of Friday, July 31, and was shown up by Mrs. Hudson. Elizabeth met her at the door and brought her into the room, acting out her public role as Holmes' secretary. Elizabeth offered her the sofa, but the woman was too agitated to remain seated, and stood, restlessly moving from one foot to another and wringing a dirty handkerchief that smelt of cheap cologne.

She was peculiarly dressed—the cloth of her dress was of the best quality, but the style was ill chosen, and badly made, and the many trimmings on both dress and hat were the cheap, gaudy type.

Holmes raked his eyes over her frame, and leaned back. "'And who is running your drapery store whilst you are here, Mrs. Thacker?" he asked. "Your husband's business is not successful enough for you to afford hired help."

I smiled to myself at this anticipated display of deduction. Mrs. Thacker stopped her agitated swaying and stared, dumbfounded, as so many of his clients did at this initial exhibition.

He smiled, gratified by her reaction. "Your dress, Mrs. Thacker, gives your occupation away. The quality of the cloth is excellent, but the style—" He paused for the merest fraction of a moment, as Elizabeth, sitting behind Mrs. Thacker with an open notebook and a poised pen, caught his eye and shook her head warningly.

Holmes changed his words smoothly. "But the style is one that no manufacturers use. Nor are the trimmings what a professional dress-maker would choose. Therefore, you made the dress and added the trimmings. The material is an expensive one, and beyond the means of a woman who can afford only a second-class ticket—yes, I can see the stub slipped into your left-hand sleeve. You are a working woman, as your boots display, but you are not a factory worker. Your outfit suggests a shop worker, and the expensive cloth, a draper's. You would not be able to afford the cloth were you a hired hand. Therefore, your husband must own the business. You chose the style as a means of displaying both the cloth and the trimmings, which are from the stock of your store. The fact that you work also tells me that the business is not prosperous enough to hire help."

He leaned forward then. "Your husband is in trouble, is he not, Mrs. Thacker? Only a circumstance as dire as this would force you to close the store and lose potential income, and spend the money to travel from Perth to London to consult me."

At Holmes' assertion, Mrs. Thacker drew in a deep, gasping breath, turned a pasty white about the mouth, and burst into ragged, exhausted tears. She sank back onto the sofa, and buried her face in the malodorous kerchief.

Holmes stood and moved away, barely suppressing an annoyed hiss of breath. Elizabeth moved forward to comfort the woman, coaxing her back into a condition where she could relate her situation and the circumstances of her husband's trouble.

After several minutes, during which time Holmes smoked moodily by the hearth, Mrs. Thacker gave one last tremendous sniff, dropped her handkerchief to her lap, and looked up at us.

"Forgive me, Mr. Holmes. But I am an old woman, and this has plum tired me out. I . . . it is true, what you say. I had to risk closing the store to see you. Horace has been gone nearly a month now, and nobody can tell me anything—not the police, nobody."

Holmes returned to his chair and sat, leaning his forearms on his knees and touching his fingertips together.

"He left no note, nothing to indicate his whereabouts?"

She shook her head. "No. And it's not like him, Mr. Holmes. We're an elderly couple, and we've spent the last twenty years running our store. As you said, it keeps us more or less comfortable throughout most of the year, but we don't have money to spare for extras, and certainly not for a clerk or salesman. So we're kept busy. We wouldn't have it any other way, now."

"And the day he disappeared?" Holmes asked.

"Just another day. Tuesday the 7th."

"Of course. Tell me about that day. Did you have any unusual customers?"

"No. We have built up a trade of regular customers, and all who called we knew. It was an ordinary day in all matters. We closed at six in the evening, and Horace remained behind to count the sales and balance the books, and I went on ahead home to start the supper. I made the supper, and sat to wait for Horace. After half an hour, he was late, and when an hour had gone by, I thought I should return to the store to see what was keeping him. But when I got there, he was gone."

"The store was closed?"

"No. The front door was shut, but not latched. Anyone could have walked in."

"Were there any signs of violence?" Holmes asked.

"No. Nothing. It was as if he had been simply plucked up into the air while doing the books. The books were spread about the counter, and the money was still there. The lights were burning."

By Holmes' still poise, I judged his interest was piqued. He asked further rapid questions.

"And what did the police say?"

She shook her head. "That it weren't no robbery that Horace interrupted or got involved in." She gave a snort. "I could've told them that, what with all that money lying on the counter."

"Quite. Did they suggest any explanation at all?"

"Only that he'd run off on his own. Thrown it in, so to speak."

"Which you do not believe," Holmes added.

"No! We had a happy marriage, happy as usual, that is. There wasn't anything bad enough that would make Horace want to just disappear like that. Especially not after nearly forty years, anyway. He wouldn't know what to do by himself."

Holmes nodded. "Now, I want you to think back to the period of time that he—your husband—disappeared. Think and try to recall if there were any unusual events or happenings around that time. Were there any people your husband spoke with who seemed suspicious or peculiar, or simply strangers to you?"

"No. Nothing like that."

"Did your husband appear to be worrying about a matter which he did not confide in you?"

"No. He was always worrying about the trade, but I knew about that."

"Had the trade fallen off to any marked degree? Or increased?"

"No, it was much as usual."

"Did you or your husband have any regular social activities?"

"No. We didn't have a lot of time, you see. Mostly we visited our children. They're grown up now, and settled down with families of their own. Since Horace gave up on the Freemasons, we've stayed at home."

Holmes narrowed his eyes. "Freemasons? Your husband was a Freemason?"

"No. Not him. He tried to join—thought it would help the business in some way I couldn't understand, though I never did get the right of how he was eligible in the first place. I thought Freemasons were for masons. Still, he tried, and was . . . black-balled. Told no," she added.

"I see." Holmes paused, thinking. Then he sat back in his chair. "Do you and your husband have a rival trade nearby, Mrs. Thacker?"

"Aye. Cartwright's Emporium. On the corner of the street."

"Emporium? How long has it been in business?"

"Only a few years."

"And it is doing well?"

"Oh yes, he does seem to do well."

"One last question. It would not offend you if I guess aloud that you are not Presbyterian?"

Mrs. Thacker looked puzzled. "No. We are not."

"And you are not of the Jewish faith," Holmes maintained.

"No, indeed not. We are Roman Catholic."

Holmes stood. "I will look into this matter for you, Mrs. Thacker. Are you returning to Perth today?"

"I intended to, yes." She studied Holmes. "Do you think I am in danger, Mr. Holmes?"

"No. I don't believe you are. But I would prefer you to stay here than return. I intend to stir up a hornets' nest and I would not like you to be in the path of angry *hymenoptera*."

"Thank you for your interest, Mr. Holmes. It will be a relief to know what has happened to my Horace—no matter how terrible his fate was." It was clear by her words that she suspected the worst. "But I can't stay in London. I have no luggage."

Holmes waved toward Elizabeth. "My secretary, Mrs. Sigerson, will see to the necessary supplies for you."

"Yes, but even so, I would feel better if I returned home. I am a stranger here, and I don't know my way around." She added in a confiding manner, "I would be afraid, on my own. After all, I am a woman, and unescorted."

Holmes replied somewhat impatiently, "Mrs. Sigerson is very capable, and you will be quite safe in her company."

I looked toward Elizabeth. Her face was schooled into a serene expression, but I could see by the light in her eyes that she was surprised and a little indignant.

But Mrs. Thacker looked at Holmes with deep gratitude glowing on her face. "That is so thoughtful of you, sir. I would feel quite lost, otherwise." She looked at Elizabeth. "And so very kind of you, Mrs. Sigerson."

"Not at all," Elizabeth replied, without a hint of irony in her voice.

"I have some business to attend to first." Mrs. Thacker looked askance at Holmes. "I can't afford to miss this opportunity to tour the warehouses and look for new stock."

But Holmes had already dismissed her and begun pulling out train timetables from his files. Instead, Elizabeth moved to Mrs. Thacker's side and tactfully walked the woman to the door, hurrying her along without appearing to do so. She made arrangements for Mrs. Thacker to return to Baker Street later in the day, and closed the door behind her with a sigh.

"You don't mean to leave me in London, do you?" she accused Holmes, moving back to the sofa and dropping the empty notebook onto the cushions.

Holmes looked up briefly from the timetable he was studying. "Yes."

"But you assured her she was in no danger. Why do you need me to stand guard?"

"It is merely a precaution."

"I would serve you better in Scotland," Elizabeth countered.

Holmes put down the timetable and rubbed his temple. I could see he had been expecting this protest. "No, you wouldn't," he replied flatly. "I suspect Horace Thacker has been captured and possibly murdered by the Freemasons. I intend to infiltrate the Perth branch and learn first-hand what became of him. I cannot do that in your company because the society is fraternal. It is also, if I am right, insidiously powerful and dangerous in this area."

"But the Freemasons are a peaceful society," Elizabeth replied.

"Yes, usually they are," Holmes agreed. "But greedy, aggressive men can turn a sect to their own advantages and previously have. This is not the first time I have dealt with corrupt members."

I coughed to gain their attention. "I am afraid I don't understand, either, Holmes. I can't see why you so strongly suspect the Freemasons to have murdered Thacker."

"The Freemasons are a secret society that began somewhere in the seventeenth century. They have roots in the ancient Templars, who were quite openly a bloodthirsty organization. Some of those tendencies have filtered down into the Freemasons—albeit secretly. Most affiliated branches are as innocent as their reputed aims claim.

But some groups go to extraordinary lengths to benefit their members. I am positive that Cartwright of Cartwright's Emporium is a grand master of the Perth Freemasons. To confirm this I must in some way get myself invited to a meeting." Holmes leaned against the mantelshelf.

"But surely they can't simply murder people as you suggest?"

"They can. They have. In one of my unsuccessful cases, Watson—which is possibly why I have not spoken of it to either of you until this moment—I discovered that a certain member had risen from labourer to city councillor in a very short period of time, solely due to the propaganda and political conspiring of his fellow Freemasons. There was even a murder—a single, tactically brilliant murder that cleared the way for this schemer. Unfortunately I was unable to supply even a shred of proof and the police could do nothing."

"But this is outrageous!" I said. "To think a group of men could simply order society as they pleased."

"Groups of men have been doing exactly that throughout history," Holmes replied clinically. "The Freemasons are outrageous only because it is a secret organization, and you have no power over it. They do have their own set of moral codes, but they also have a set of traditional enemies, developed through the intrigues of the past, and who include Jews and Roman Catholics."

"Horace Thacker!" I exclaimed, as all the pieces fell into place.

"Exactly," Holmes replied.

Elizabeth straightened from her perch on the arm of the chair. "That case isn't in your notes, or I would remember it. And it doesn't explain why I must stay in London."

Holmes lit a cigarette. "After the unsuccessful conclusion of the case, I was forced to leave the city at very short notice. My life was threatened, and if I ever returned I have no doubt that the threat would still be in force. I have no wish to bring a similar nemesis upon you."

"I make my own choice," Elizabeth replied.

"I have already explained that the society is fraternal," Holmes added, with something like irritation in his voice.

For the next few minutes Elizabeth stood opposite Holmes, and resisted stubbornly. Unfortunately, intractability was one of the few traits in which Holmes remained her superior. I watched the exchanges with frank curiosity, wondering what it was that was causing Elizabeth to resist so persistently against such outright denial. It was pushing Holmes into a position he had never found himself in before, and I did not envy him his place.

Finally he dragged his fingers through his hair in an old, nervous mannerism I had not seen him use for quite a while. "Elizabeth, please!" He caught at her hand where it rested on the shelf—a rare demonstration. "I would willingly take you anywhere and know that you are as capable as me of escaping danger. But not this time. You would be in greater danger than I." He moved away.

"Because I am a woman," Elizabeth said bitterly.

"Yes."

Elizabeth finally acknowledged there could be no other outcome, and she conceded with far more grace than I would have managed under similar circumstances.

"I will get a cab for you. The overnight train from St. Pancras leaves in thirty minutes." She walked toward the door.

Holmes shut his eyes for a minute, and took a deep breath. "Elizabeth?"

She looked over her shoulder.

"I will miss my companion. Bitterly. But I will not change my mind."

"And I will worry about you." She gave him a small smile. "You pack. John will need to go home and collect his own requirements, so you cannot afford to wait."

At the front door he paused before climbing into the hansom. "I will be as quick as I can, Elizabeth. One conclusive piece of proof is all I need."

"Yes, I know. I will be waiting." She turned to me. "Watch out for him, John. I feel . . ." she broke off, frowning, then shivered, her eyes on some distant point. She refocussed on me and attempted a smile. "Just be careful."

We climbed in while Elizabeth told the driver the destination. Once the cab had turned the corner, Holmes sat forward and smacked the frame of the carriage. His face was grim, and his eyes, sightless, bored through me.

On the train, Holmes was restless. Elizabeth's opposition had rocked his equanimity. Certainly the case had been quite driven from his mind. This was so unusual and out of character for Holmes that I remained warily silent. Elizabeth's quick words to me as I had climbed into the cab continued to echo in my mind.

Her manner and Holmes' moody introspection were unsettling, and I was beginning to fancy I felt the same foreboding at which Elizabeth had hinted. Despite the soothing rock of the train I got very little sleep that night, and I know Holmes had none, for he did not bother disturbing the covers of his berth. I was restless and woke several times through the night, when I would watch with sleep-filled eyes as he strode up and down the passage outside, smoking, completely unperturbed by the swaying of the train.

We arrived in Perth around dawn and Holmes was all for proceeding immediately to Horace Thacker's drapery shop, such was his impatience to solve the case and return. His whole bearing thrummed with tension. I put on my best stern doctor's voice and suggested that as the shop would not be opening for business at all that day, we could investigate at our leisure, and we would be much better employed in settling into our rooms at the hotel and breaking our fast in comfort.

Holmes gave way grudgingly, and I studied him covertly as we made our way to Holmes' preferred inn. I'd seen this type of tension and irascibility before, of course, but only when Holmes had been forced to wait for answers or the development of one of his cases, or when there was nothing on hand to distract him. Yet he had this mystery before him, one with every promise of being a vintage for its strangeness.

He enquired curtly at the desk for rooms.

"Ah yes, Mr. Holmes. We've been expecting you."

Holmes looked up from the register. "You have?"

"Yes, sir. Ever since this cable arrived last night."

Holmes all but snatched the telegram from the clerk's hands and tore it open. I moved to behind his shoulder and read it, too.

"Return at once. Mycroft."

The hand holding the paper began to tremble, and he dropped the cable to the desk and put his hand in his pocket.

"Elizabeth," he said softly. "Something has happened to Elizabeth."

I felt a cold hand clench at my own heart with Holmes' whispered inference.

Holmes looked at the clerk. "When is the next train to London?"

The clerk looked at the desk clock. "You've just missed it, sir."

"I said the *next* train!" Holmes rapped out.

The clerk seemed to shrink back away from the desk. I looked at him pityingly, for I knew the effect Holmes' countenance had on those who attempted to oppose his will. "Six o'clock tomorrow morning, sir," the clerk stammered.

Holmes slammed the flat of his hand down on the desk in reaction to this bad news. He whirled to face me. "Back to the station," he said.

The return to the station was silent. Holmes' eyes were focussed on a point in middle distance, narrowed and glinting with an unveiled danger. His hand tapped a quick rhythm on the top of his cane. Otherwise he was perfectly motionless, and I was afraid to disturb him.

Our first action upon reaching the station was to investigate the swiftest alternatives available to get us back to London. The clerk behind the counter proved helpful, fortunately, but he could not get us back to the city earlier than midnight. I could see the information chaffed Holmes to the quick. It was then I offered my one contribution to the sad, sorry adventure.

"Holmes, look. This timetable. There is a train leaving Carlisle at midday. If we could get to Carlisle. . . ."

A back-light flared deep in his eyes, and he turned back to the clerk. "I want to hire a special. To whom do I speak?"

The journey back was a nightmare of darkest imagination. For the entire trip Holmes stood at a window, motionless, neither smoking nor walking. Nor did he communicate with me just what sort of danger he thought Elizabeth might be in. His only comment was a scathing answer to what, on reflection, seems a foolish question. "It is Elizabeth who is in trouble, or she would have signed the cable herself."

Chapter Ten

MYCROFT WAS SITTING IN HIS USUAL SEAT in the private salon of the Diogenes Club, a drink and ashtray on the table beside him, and several newspapers folded on the table to his right. He watched us approach across the shining tiles, his face unreadable.

"My cabby found you, then," he said, as we reached him. He waved to the chairs beside him, and I sank into one.

Holmes merely pushed his hands into his pockets. "Come, Mycroft, I have expended nearly the last of my admittedly limited patience on the officials of the British railway system."

Mycroft closed the book he held in his lap and rested his hand on the cover.

"The case you were investigating was a ruse designed to have you depart from London and leave Elizabeth behind. They've taken Elizabeth."

I watched Holmes' face for his reaction to this confirmation of his fears.

"I should have seen that," he said after a moment's silence. His voice was flat. "Freemasons!" It was a curse. His eyes cut away from us both and he looked toward the window behind us. "The old woman set the bait perfectly."

"It may comfort you to know the capture of their prize was not an easy one. They had quite a struggle taking her away. Your rooms are in ruins."

"You have been there?"

Mycroft shrugged. "Mrs. Hudson sent for me. The woman was hysterical. She had been held at gunpoint while they attempted to extract Elizabeth from the rooms."

I felt the small wave of horror in me swell as the scene played itself out in my mind.

Holmes ran his fingers through his hair, ruffling it. "I have been a fool!" he said to himself. "They invent a tale that sends me racing for one of the farthest points from London, leaving Elizabeth behind—for her safety."

Mycroft said gently, "I suggest you go home and look for any messages Elizabeth may have left. I have looked and found none, but you know her better than I. I will finish here and follow you."

Holmes turned and walked away. Mycroft looked to me as I stood to follow. "Watch him, Watson. He is straining the limits of his control."

"Yes. I am aware of that."

"My decision to bring you here first was the correct one," Mycroft said, standing up. "The disarray that will greet you at Baker Street would unnerve even the most placid of characters."

The warning was not lost on me. I nodded a farewell to Mycroft and walked swiftly to catch up with Holmes as he hailed a hansom.

At Baker Street, Mrs. Hudson met us at the street door. Her eyes were red-rimmed, and her face had aged.

"You've seen Mr. Mycroft?" she asked Holmes fearfully, half-barring his way to the stairs.

"Yes, Mrs. Hudson, I have," Holmes replied. He pushed her gently aside and climbed the stairs.

I gave her arm a reassuring pat and followed him.

The door to his rooms was a splintered skeleton. The lock was still sitting in the frame, the wood impaled by the nails of the key plate. He pushed the door open. It jammed, half-open, on an over-turned sofa. Holmes stepped over the sofa with one long-legged stride and stood in the middle of the rug, staring at the destruction. He was not observing in his scientific manner, but merely acquainting himself with the unyielding fact of this very personal attack.

His files and papers—the result of years of careful classification—were spread over most of the room, scattered in minutes. The old deal table his chemical equipment sat on had been upturned, and the glass, china, and metal allowed to slide down the slope to shatter and puddle on the carpet. Some noxious chemical had began to eat into the priceless Persian rug. As he turned a slow full circle, taking in the overturned furniture, the fragments of his collection of memorabilia from his travels, and his carelessly scattered possessions, a draught from the smashed pane in the window by the fireplace lifted some of the papers, and floated them over to land at his feet.

I was appalled. A personal attack on Holmes himself would never have achieved the same deep impression that this carefully calculated destruction would. I could see each item of upheaval Holmes observed strike home with the effectiveness of a well-aimed bullet.

Mrs. Hudson appeared by the door.

Holmes looked at her. "No one else has been up here?"

"No, sir. Mr. Mycroft insisted I let no one in."

"Not even the police?"

"Not even them," she replied stoutly. "Mr. Mycroft saw to that."

"That at least is one small mercy in my favour," he said softly. He dropped his bag, shed his coat and jacket, and rolled up his sleeves. Then he crouched down to examine the floor at his feet.

Mycroft arrived two hours later. By that time, Holmes had finished in the main sitting room and was examining the bedroom whilst Mrs. Hudson and I began to clear up the remains of the sitting room.

I showed Mycroft into the bedroom and hovered curiously by the door.

Mycroft pointed to the dressing chair. "You have studied the seat?"

"Yes, yes," Holmes replied, his voice muffled by the bed base. He extracted himself and lifted the pillows, then looked at Mycroft. "All this damage—there must have been a remarkable amount of noise. Did no one come to investigate?"

"Elizabeth apparently shattered the window in the sitting room herself in an attempt to call up some help. But there were men with guns at either end of the street, holding back witnesses."

Holmes pulled the counterpane aside. "And the constabulary—what were they doing?"

"They were rushing to the scene of an accident two blocks away—an accident that, it has now been discovered, was a hoax."

Holmes threw the counterpane to the floor and tipped the mattress over. "So, they were well organized, had large numbers of people to use, and were not afraid to make a lot of noise or create a lot of fear to achieve their ends." He shot a glance at his brother. "The newspapers?"

"I managed to suppress her name and any association with you. That's all I could manage. The police were easier to contain, after I had a word with Tobias Gregson."

Holmes strode into the sitting room and began to sort through his scattered files. "And they've not made any contact since taking her?"

"I rather imagine they were waiting for you to get back from Scotland," Mycroft said.

"When did they take her?"

"About seven o'clock last night."

"The train was barely out of London." Holmes sank suddenly onto the sofa, which now sat on its feet once more. "She could be half a world away."

Mycroft glanced at me, and I read the expression on his face clearly. He was surprised—not at the fact that Elizabeth's abduction had hit his younger brother badly, but that it appeared to be affecting those abilities to think clearly and precisely for which Holmes was famous.

"It is hardly likely, is it?" Mycroft said gently. "They'll want her somewhere nearby so they can use her for the bargaining lever they need her for." His voice was dry, and there was an implied criticism.

"Do not let your dislike of Elizabeth distort your perception, Mycroft," Holmes said softly.

Mycroft pushed at a file with the ferrule of his umbrella. "You persist in that silly misconception."

I confess I stared at the two brothers with dumb amazement. It was the first time I had ever suspected there was any dissension over Elizabeth. It occurred to me as I watched the pair that perhaps family dissension was inevitable. My friends' lives had been bohemian and unfettered, and Mycroft was very set in his ways.

"I refuse to even consider that Elizabeth may be implicated in this. I would trust her with my life—*have* trusted her." Holmes rubbed his temple. His hand trembled only slightly, now he had absorbed the worst of the facts. "As you can see for yourself, they've gone to a lot of trouble to take her." He stood up and strode to the mantel and stuffed a pipe full of tobacco. "At a conservative estimate it would have taken them ten minutes to chop down the door—and Elizabeth had barricaded the door, too. Once they had broken through, she barricaded herself in the bedroom. Unfortunately that door did not prove so solid. A single heave, I would estimate, and the lock snapped." He started his pipe. "Elizabeth is not entirely helpless, and the contest did not end there. I found this—"and he pulled Elizabeth's gold-handled knife from his pocket and threw it to the floor between our feet. "It has blood on it. And we know there were at least three guns involved, so it is safe to assume she probably had to contend with a gun, too."

I picked up the knife and shuddered. The picture Holmes drew was bleaker than the one my own imagination had painted, yet I knew his educated guess was more likely to be the correct one. That this might be Elizabeth's blood on the blade appeared a distinct possibility.

Mycroft sat in a chair. "For goodness' sake, Sherlock, do you not believe I haven't made it my business to know all about Elizabeth long ago? Her loyalty is not in question here."

Holmes took his pipe from his mouth. "You had Elizabeth investigated?"

Mycroft had the grace to look uncomfortable. "You're a public figure. Precautions like these must be taken."

Holmes merely stared at Mycroft, his face immobile. "Do you still have the report?" he asked finally.

"I burnt it," Mycroft replied. "I thought it prudent."

Holmes tapped his pipe out into the grate. "The question still remains—who are they?"

Mycroft looked out the window. "I rather imagine we're about to find out. Here comes Inspector Lestrade, and at a fast clip."

Lestrade made his way up the stairs at a breathless pace. I could hear his boots rattling out a staccato on the wood of the stairs. He stopped abruptly in the doorway, the expression on his face beginning with shock and giving way rapidly to puzzlement and then to unhappy resignation.

"Then I am too late. He has already been here," Lestrade said to Holmes.

Holmes took two paces toward Lestrade. "*Who* has already been here?" he asked, and by his tone, it was obvious that whatever shadows concealed the full shape of the puzzle in his mind, Lestrade's answer would remove them.

"Colonel Moran. He has escaped from Dartmoor. I just heard and came straight around to warn you." Lestrade looked around, and took a breath. "I am too late, I see."

Holmes' face became expressionless as his mind raced to add this new information to the little he already knew. Finally he glanced at Mycroft.

"Moran. The enemy reveals himself."

"The escape was obviously meticulously planned, along with all these arrangements," Mycroft said, indicating the state of the room.

"Yes, and all were executed within a twelve-hour period—or perhaps less. To ensure I would not be warned." Holmes looked at Lestrade. "He escaped yesterday afternoon, Inspector?"

Lestrade nodded. "No one was hurt, then?" he asked, looking about. His gaze fell on Mrs. Hudson's face, and her red-rimmed eyes. "My dear god," he whispered. His face lost all the colour it had acquired from his exhausting race through the hot summer streets to warn Holmes. "The kidnapped woman in the *Standard*. It was Miss Elizabeth."

I was wakened by dim footsteps—slow, measured steps—and for a moment I was returned to a decade earlier, when Holmes tirelessly paced the hearth rug, solving conundrums.

I looked at the clock beside the bed. It was just past midnight. I had been asleep only an hour. The evening had consisted of an exhausting interview with Lestrade and Gregson. The latter had arrived in response to Lestrade's summons. Mycroft had also remained, sitting in the corner by the shattered window, silently absorbing the story as Holmes and I told of the woman who had paraded as the distraught Mrs. Thacker and the detailed, convincing story she had spun.

Holmes was in the novel position of being the victim of a crime, and suffered Gregson's and Lestrade's thorough examination with bad grace. Both those gentleman, however, were astute enough to realize that Holmes was merely venting his anger over his own gullibility, and they maintained their equanimity. Unfortunately, Holmes could also see that they were making allowances for this fact, and the knowledge chafed.

The pair of detectives eventually rose and bid us a good evening. After their departure Mycroft had begun his own series of questions. Holmes submitted to this second inquiry with better humour. Mycroft was not merely gathering information, but questioning Holmes in a manner that was prompting them both to consider every obscure corner of the affair, searching for any facts that their collaborative reasoning might infer.

After a humble and very late supper hastily scratched together by Mrs. Hudson, I had gratefully fallen onto the bed Holmes offered me for the night, and immediately slept.

Sensing the unsettled mind behind the measured steps I was listening to now, I rose and drew on my borrowed dressing gown, and made my way to the sitting room.

Most of the disarray had been reorganized and was stacked, packed, or otherwise pushed into related heaps for Holmes to sort out at his leisure, leaving most of the floor space clear, including his thinking circuit.

Holmes was on the farthest point of his lap about the sofa, and looked up at me.

"Watson, I woke you. My apologies."

"No, do not apologize," I told him. "I came out to see if there is something I can do for you."

"As a doctor or a friend?"

"Both."

"I assume your Hippocratic oath would not allow you to perform a quasi-lobotomy on various parts of my brain?" Holmes asked, with a touch of acid.

"I was thinking of a sedative," I replied, suppressing a smile.

"No." Holmes pushed his hands into his pockets. "I need my wits fully functional, not asleep. So instead, as a friend, talk to me, Watson." He paced the hearth rug. "Take my mind away from the pictures that are plaguing me."

I slid into Holmes' vacant and cold chair. "Yes, I thought something like that was goading you."

Holmes' pace increased slightly. "It is the curse of a good imagination, Watson. The images are persistent." He halted and glanced at me from under his lowered brow.

"You're a logical thinker, Holmes. Surely it has occurred to you that your concern is exciting your imagination and exaggerating the images."

"Yes, yes, I am aware of that," Holmes said impatiently. "But truth and fear are too mixed now to separate, and I cannot halt them. So I must persevere with them."

I studied him professionally. "At least you can reassure yourself she is alive, Holmes. She has to be or Moran would have lost any bargaining leverage."

"Elizabeth *must* be alive," he began bleakly, but the thought was left unfinished. He glanced up at me. "I owe it to Elizabeth to find her. I owe it as an apology. She was right, not I."

"How was she right?" I asked.

"If I had not been so anxious to leave for Scotland, I would have questioned, as Elizabeth did, the similarity of the case with that other to which I compared it. Elizabeth *told* me the notes were missing." He pointed to the sorry pile of documents by the hearth. "They must have been missing since Moriarty's men ransacked these rooms twelve years ago. They were probably taken then. Moran obviously retained them and used the details to dangle an authentic mystery before me. They knew I wouldn't be able to resist the lure of solving this case when I had failed so miserably the first time." His voice was bitter. "If I hadn't been quite so hasty, I would have seen it, too, and known without doubt who it was that was dangling the bait."

"I don't believe she knew consciously that something was wrong. It was just a feeling of uneasiness." I recalled the impression of premonition she had left with me. I had not imagined it, after all.

I looked away and my gaze fell to the table beside Holmes' chair. His watch-chain sat in a small heap beside the whisky glass and, as I pushed at it with my forefinger, a green glitter caught the firelight. The chain spread, and revealed the small Chinese coin that was his fob, and two small, green gems mounted in gold along the length of chain. I had found Elizabeth's two missing gems. Suddenly I recalled Holmes' manner of tucking his hand into his fob pocket when away from Baker Street. And now the chain lay beside his chair—deliberately sought out and carried there.

"Elizabeth is quite capable of looking after herself," I said thoughtfully.

Holmes looked up from the fire, and I saw his eyes go to where my fingers were touching the chain. "You know their history, then," he said. "But there are many ways of overcoming a solitary woman, no matter how skilled or prepared she may be. As this room bears witness, Watson, if you are determined enough and have the numbers, it can be done. And it is that very force which may have been necessary that worries me." He turned and began to pace again, one lap before arriving back at the hearth. "This is the very thing I took all precautions to avoid, Watson. My greatest fear was that my enemies would learn of Elizabeth's importance to me and use that knowledge." He kicked the cold grate. "So, now I am living my nightmare and my passage through it is no easier upon waking."

I pushed the watch-chain back into a neat pile. "Holmes, you're existing on an overdrawn account. You must get some sleep. This pacing is not achieving any results, and will not while your mind is distracted. Let me prepare a sleeping draught for you. I can at least guarantee you eight hours undisturbed by nightmares—either the waking or sleeping variety."

He refused, of course. But I am more deft at handling Holmes since I have had practical examples from Elizabeth. I covertly dropped the powder into his whisky and topped up the glass before going to bed myself.

I woke to find Holmes standing over my bed, wrapped in his dressing gown. His eyes were bloodshot, proof that my sleeping draught had worked.

"We have a visitor, Watson," he said, and walked back out into the sitting room.

Alarmed, I scrambled out of bed, hastily drew on my gown, and followed him out.

It was much later than I had first supposed, for the clock chimed the half-hour after ten as I entered the sitting room. It looked little different from the previous night; Holmes would have had very little time to work before the sleeping draught had taken effect.

Inspector Lestrade was standing by the table, identifying two rugged, useful-looking chaps to Holmes. I guessed they were policemen out of uniform, here to help protect Holmes from Moran's revenge.

"Right, you two," Lestrade finished up. "One by the door, and another across the street. Tell the others they're relieved, and they're to go home and get some sleep. Try not to look like bobbies out of uniform, lads."

They nodded and left the room.

"You had men patrolling last night?" Holmes asked Lestrade.

"Yes."

Holmes picked up a box of broken china and dropped it onto the table with a crash. "There really is no need, Lestrade. I can manage this situation."

"Now, not another word, Mr. Holmes. This is my sort of business, and it is nice to be able to help you out for a change, rather than come to you for help as I usually do."

"If that is the case, there are many other more appropriate ways—" Holmes began, picking up a shard of china that was all that remained of Elizabeth's favourite teapot.

But Lestrade cut him off with a quick wave of his hand, and said firmly. "I insist, Mr. Holmes. Or else I will have to turn this into official police business."

Holmes looked at him, astonished. The threat was quite clear. If Lestrade did turn the affair into official police business, it would be taken out of Holmes' hands entirely, and he would be forced to rely on Lestrade's skills. To Holmes, that was unthinkable.

Lestrade, for once sensitive to atmosphere, added awkwardly, "I like Miss Elizabeth, Holmes. I do not want to see any harm done to her through my own idleness."

Holmes dropped the shard of china back into the box. "I see," he said blandly. "Well, you'd better sit down then, Inspector."

I could almost feel Holmes' bafflement at this sudden appearance of a new element in the equation. It was the first time he had ever come face to face with Elizabeth's true influence on his world, and he had been given much to think about.

Lestrade settled himself on the sofa, and I turned back to the bedroom to get properly dressed.

By the time I emerged into the sitting room again, we had another visitor. Mycroft sat on Holmes' chair, his stick between his knees, both feet placed precisely on either side, and his hands resting on the cane's head. He was studying Lestrade in majestic silence.

Holmes looked up from his sorting, his face thoughtful and his manner subdued. I recognized the sign. He was thinking—hard. He nodded when he saw me.

"Be a good fellow and play host for me while I change?" he asked, and, without waiting for an answer, disappeared into his bedroom.

I sat down on the sofa opposite Lestrade and nodded to Mycroft. "Good morning, Mycroft. You're up and about early." For Mycroft was about much earlier than was his well-established and rarely broken habit.

Mycroft pushed at the carpet with his stick, and I remembered the action from the previous day. He was feeling ill at ease. "I thought I might be of some help," he said. "Moran appears to have all the cards at the moment."

"How do you think you can help?"

"I am not really sure, but something is bound to happen sooner or later. Moran will not leave things as they are, not now. If I am here. . . . "

I studied him. It appeared to me that Mycroft was suffering the same agonies as Lestrade. I wondered if everyone who knew Elizabeth and was privy to the fact of her abduction would eventually arrive upon the doorstep, hoping to be able to help in some undefined way.

Mrs. Hudson chose that moment to enter, bearing her largest tray, spread with an enormous morning tea. She nodded wordlessly to me and to Lestrade and Mycroft, as she transferred the things to the table, placing the box Holmes had been delving into to one side. Just as wordlessly she left again.

"Tea, gentlemen?" I offered.

There was a knock on the street door as we were serving ourselves, and Holmes returned to the room in time to receive the next visitor.

"Gregson. Good morning. Come in, come in. Your colleague, Mr. Lestrade, is here already."

I examined Holmes suspiciously, for I knew the bonhomie was false. His face was inscrutable. He drew Gregson into the room and over to the table.

The two official detectives greeted each other politely. It was apparent they had buried their professional rivalry for the duration, for Lestrade immediately replaced his cup and turned his attention to his colleague.

"We have an interview with the governor of Dartmoor at three o'clock this afternoon," Gregson told him.

Mycroft lifted his chin to study Gregson, his attention caught, as was mine, for if there were any clues to be had on Moran's whereabouts, they would probably be found at Dartmoor prison.

"Are the inmates to be interviewed?" Mycroft asked.

"That is already underway. The prison is conducting its own investigation into the escape."

"That should concern you least," Mycroft retorted. "The man has managed to recruit and establish an entire organization whilst incarcerated, and that should be worrying the authorities far more. He has made the penitentiary system appear utterly useless."

Mycroft's criticism began a three-sided argument on the finer details of penal law and prison reform. The warring parties' voices slowly lifted as the argument grew more heated.

I observed the debate with understanding and a little amusement. These three gentlemen were displaying the symptoms of nervous stress—but their misdirected belligerence was also a natural outlet, and so I let the argument run its course. Time enough to organize the expedition to Dartmoor once their tempers had cooled.

I spared a glance toward Holmes. He had remained apart, standing and gazing out the shattered window with preoccupied detachment.

Around the table, the argument subsided a little and conversation moved on to more productive ground.

"I have a number of men out searching the streets for this Mrs. Thacker whom Holmes described," Lestrade said.

I nodded to myself. That was the first obvious lead to follow, but I rather doubted Mrs. Thacker would be found.

Gregson thought as I did. "She would have gone to ground," he said. "We will not find her now, unless she allows herself to be sighted. Still, the effort must be made. I received my reply from Perth, by the way. No store, no Thacker. There is a Cartwright's Emporium, but it is owned by a business partnership and none of the partners is called Cartwright."

Mycroft added deferentially, "You might see if Mrs. Thacker can be traced in Perth. One confirmed fact in the midst of a wealth of invention cannot be coincidence. According to Sherlock, her accent appeared genuine."

Lestrade nodded, then consulted his watch. "We'd best be leaving. I'd like to get to Dartmoor early and have a sniff around. Gregson?"

"Yes, I'll go with you."

"And I, if I may," Mycroft added.

They fell to discussing travel details and their proposed tasks at Dartmoor, and I moved across to Holmes. "You're coming to Dartmoor, Holmes?"

He shook his head. "I must stay here and wait for Moran's communication."

"Yes, of course," I replied automatically, whilst I examined his face. I could not analyze his mood. It was uncharacteristic of him not to become involved in the discussion—normally he liked to lead the conversation. And he was not irascible or impatient as he would be when waiting idly for developments. And he was not searching for answers—I could at least see that much. Given the little information he had to work upon, Holmes had already drawn his conclusions. In the normal course of a case, he would have immediately put into effect any lines of action available to him. With Elizabeth's life hanging in the balance I expected him to be expending all his energy on the case. But this contemplative figure paused by the window was a stranger to me.

"You must go to Dartmoor, Watson," he told me. "And I will quiz you on the details upon your return."

"Yes, of course," I replied, stupidly repeating myself because of my inattention.

I began to move away, to return to the table, when the glass fragments still precariously hanging in the window frame shattered and dropped musically to the floor. Startled—but not yet alarmed, for I had not heard the sound of a shot—I turned back again.

Holmes had fallen to the floor, a hand clamped to his side. Even as I turned, I saw the blood begin to spread across his shirt front.

Chapter Eleven

I HURRIED BACK TO WHERE HOLMES lay on the floor. He was conscious, and lifted his jacket to look at the wound. I reached to pull the jacket aside so I could examine it, too, but Holmes lifted up his blood-covered hand and, with a grimace, spoke urgently. "No. It is not fatal. Quickly now, Watson; you must show the others the empty house—across the street. He even had the gall to use the same window."

I hesitated. I could hardly call myself a doctor if I left Holmes lying wounded on the carpet. But even as I hesitated, Lestrade and Gregson flung themselves out of the room and rattled down the stairs, shouting for the bobbies to give chase.

Mycroft crossed to my side. "Hurry, Watson. You must show us the way."

Outside the window, I could hear the alarm spreading up and down the street, as the police converged.

"Sherlock will survive for another fifteen minutes, I am sure."

I looked down at my friend, and he nodded reassuringly. "Go."

Mycroft and I hurried down the stairs and across the street to the house to which Holmes had referred. Mycroft appeared to have maintained the agility and sure-footedness that he shared with his brother, despite his corpulence, for he moved as swiftly as I.

I led him to the door of the building, and Lestrade and Gregson followed. Lestrade forced the lock. Behind us stood a pair of police-men in uniform. The two plainclothes officers were not to be seen. The door shuddered aside under Lestrade's impact, and we all pushed our way into the narrow hallway.

Holmes had called it the "empty house" merely as a shorthand means of pinpointing the location of the gunman, for the house had been occupied for several years. This was the house that Moran had utilized as a vantage point when he had attempted to shoot Holmes many years before—in exactly the same manner as on this occasion. Only this second attempt had succeeding in hitting the intended tar-get rather than a substitute wax dummy.

Our forceful entry brought the residents of the house out into the hall to investigate, and both husband's and wife's expressions were startled and indignant.

Gregson looked to me. "Which room, sir?"

I reoriented my bearings, for Holmes and I had previously entered from the rear of the building and at night. I pointed at the appropriate door. "That one."

One of the uniformed policemen remained behind to speak to the tenants, and we rushed into the room.

Only a few short minutes had elapsed since Holmes had been hit, yet the room was quite empty of human occupants. It was prettily fur-nished, neat and tidy, and vacant. I looked around, frustrated. "Gone."

The two policemen in street clothes came into the room and crossed over to Lestrade. "Nobody came out the back way, sir," the spokesman said.

"Right. Begin interviewing everyone out there. See if we have any witnesses."

"Yes, sir." They saluted and left, this time using the front door, and I could hear the householders' indignant tones as they passed through the hallway. Gregson shut the room's door once more, and Lestrade moved over to the window that gave such an excellent view of Holmes' rooms. Mycroft followed.

"Yes, that is the window," I told them, crossing to his side.

"I remember it well," Lestrade replied, bending to examine the sill. "But I think Holmes was wrong for once. The shot didn't come from here. . . . What's the matter, Doctor?"

His question was put sharply. I suppose my face must have sagged in quite a comical way, for I had suddenly recalled that Lestrade had indeed been here on that night in 1894, for he had been the officer who had arrested Moran. In the rush of the chase I had forgotten.

If Lestrade had been here before, why had Holmes insisted that I guide them to the correct window? The answer might have come to me had I the time to consider it, but another, more sinister thought infused itself. Holmes was injured and quite alone in his rooms, and there was a murderer roaming about the streets—free to finish the job he had begun.

"Holmes," I breathed. I pushed past Mycroft and raced out into the street, across the busy thoroughfare and back up the stairs to Holmes' rooms. I burst in through the doorway and came to a breathless halt at the spot where I had left Holmes.

It was empty.

Behind me I could hear the rapid ascent of boots on the stairs, and Lestrade and Mycroft rushed into the room behind me.

I collapsed onto the nearest chair to recover my breath.

Lestrade and Mycroft both inspected the carpet, and Lestrade shook his head, unhappy. "Here's a pretty kettle of fish," he observed colloquially. "Did he leave on his own, or was he taken?"

Mycroft bent to look more closely at the bloodstain, then straightened. "I think you can safely assume my brother has departed for reasons of his own—sending us across the street to investigate the house was a ruse to allow him time to leave unhindered."

Lestrade shook his head. "Then the shot was a fake?"

Mycroft tapped the stain with his cane. "Something injured him," he observed. "But not as badly as we were led to believe. I reserve my opinion on whether it was a bullet or not, but I do recall to your attention that Moran is renowned for his powerful—and silent—airgun."

I concurred with Mycroft, but I kept my opinion to myself, for Lestrade looked baffled and angry enough already. Holmes had made sure I had left him alone, despite his injuries. I didn't believe he could have fabricated either the blood or the unidentified missile that had cracked the glass that remained in the window, but a swift mind could have improvised around the incident, and I knew without doubt that Holmes' mind was keen enough.

Gregson rejoined us then, and he and Lestrade fell to an inconclusive debate over Holmes' motives.

I was troubled by the mystery, too. What on earth had possessed Holmes to throw aside all aid and assistance, and face the certain dangers of confronting Moran and rescuing Elizabeth alone? And how badly wounded was he?

Mycroft was examining the carpet beneath the window again, his face thoughtful.

I watched him curiously. Mycroft was as brilliant a reasoner as Holmes, and I suspected he understood better than any of us why his brother had acted as he did. But Mycroft was contributing nothing to the discussion.

Instead he crouched to study the carpet again, this time lowering himself to his knees to examine it as closely as possible. He reached out a hand to probe delicately with a fingertip. Then, with forefinger and thumb he gently picked up something from the tufts and brought it closer to his face, and studied it.

I rose from my chair and moved closer. "What is it?"

"Some sort of wax," Mycroft murmured, sniffing it gently. He rubbed the red substance between his fingers. "Sealing wax?" he asked himself. "Rough, impure." Then he rose to his feet once more, and looked at me. "I shall return to my club." With that he donned his hat, nodded, and left the room.

His departure broke up Lestrade's and Gregson's discussion. Lestrade fished out his watch once more and frowned. "Time to leave. Can you finish the investigation here?"

Gregson nodded. "Of course."

"But where are you going?" I asked.

"Dartmoor. I have an appointment with the prison governor, remember?"

"No, I had forgotten," I confessed. "Would it be inconvenient if I came with you, Lestrade?"

"No, if you must. Why, Doctor?"

"Holmes wanted me to," I told them. "And that is the only avenue open for investigation, now." Which, from my point of view, it was, for the trail to Mrs. Thacker and Moran was quite cold. It could be traced only by someone as skilled as Holmes, and he had, for reasons of his own, disappeared.

The only other skilled enough to unravel the clues was Mycroft, and he, too, had bowed out of the mystery. I suspected he had done so for the same reasons as Holmes—reasons he had deduced from whatever clues his brother had left behind.

Dartmoor, and the inmates Moran had spent some years associating with, might possibly give us another direction to follow. So I overcame my first impulse to stay at Baker Street and wait for a possible communication from either Holmes or Moran. Instead I primed Mrs. Hudson to act as message-taker, and boarded the train with Lestrade.

Gregson saw us off with a last-minute report on the investigation into Holmes' wounding.

"Traffic was very thick, and nobody heard anything unusual—especially not a gun."

Lestrade was puzzled. "Then there probably wasn't a gun involved," he said. "I cannot see how Moran would be able to obtain a second airgun, and we know the original is still safely locked up. The residents of Baker Street are nervous enough after Friday night's adventure, and would have instantly recognized a gunshot if there had been one."

Gregson looked equally as perplexed. "So what was it that flew hard enough to crack glass and wound a man?"

Lestrade looked at me. "It is a pity you didn't get a look at the wound, Doctor Watson. That would have given us a very good idea of what the weapon was."

"There was no time," I reminded him.

"No. Nor is there now. There's the guard's whistle. Keep on it, Gregson. Goodbye!"

Our trip to Dartmoor was uneventful in the extreme. I imagine Lestrade would make a dour companion at the best of times, and on this journey he was positively gloomy. This suited me, for I was comparably lost in my own cogitation. The silence between us was almost complete, and it wasn't until we were on the very threshold of the governor's office that Lestrade spoke to me.

"I would appreciate it if you would allow me to do all the talking, Doctor. If you just keep your eyes peeled, we should be able to pick up any clues to be had."

I agreed readily, and we went inside.

That was the beginning of a depressing afternoon's work. Lestrade spoke at length with the governor and afterwards interviewed nearly a dozen prisoners who were reckoned Moran's closest associates.

Moran's escape was similar in character to all the operations he had orchestrated to date—the planning was meticulous, the timing perfect, and it was audacious. It was a remarkable escape in the history of the prison, for no other escape, successful or otherwise, had been managed without some type of inside help.

The prison was having new drainage systems and plumbing installed, and workmen had been scattered throughout the buildings for weeks. Sometime during the Friday afternoon, Moran had subdued a workman who resembled him in stature, taken him back to his cell, swapped clothing, and left with the other workmen at the end of the day, all without detection. He had even signed out and collected the man's pay at the gate, passing through the security arrangements apparently without problems, for not one of the guards on duty that evening recalled a single moment of suspicion or any untoward incidents.

Once outside the gate, Moran had melted into the countryside. He hadn't travelled back to town with the men. His planning, it was decided, had included arrangements for transport, clothing, and probably money, but as he had already collected the workman's monthly wages, he had funds enough to travel quite a distance.

He'd had a start of four hours, since it wasn't until the evening cell-check that the substitution was discovered. The workman left behind had been questioned thoroughly and his background scrutinized, and it was concluded he was as innocent as he claimed.

We also spent some time looking at Moran's record and those of all those we spoke to, reading for any conflicting information or other clues. Moran was, according to all we interviewed and his indisputable record, a model prisoner. He behaved as expected and caused no trouble. He associated with none of the prisoners who were considered troublemakers, and even those prisoners deemed his close associates were only vaguely acquainted with him. He wrote no letters and did not appear to communicate with anyone outside the prison, with the sole exception of his sister, who was the only visitor.

The sister, Beatrice O'Connor, lived in London. She had also been questioned. The transcribed notes of her interview were available to us, and made unexciting reading. She was as virtuous in fact as Moran appeared to be by report—a matron at Saint Luke's Hospital, married, and with a blameless reputation which had already withstood countless investigations as a result of her brother's criminal activities.

Lestrade could add to the prison's information about the woman. "I personally interviewed her when Moran was put on trial in 1894. Mrs. O'Connor would have disowned him if she'd known how to go about it. An amazing difference in siblings—virtue on one hand and corruption on the other."

It was not an isolated phenomenon: Moriarty's brother James had been as good and kind as his brother was evil.

"I think we can safely discount Beatrice O'Connor," I suggested.

We emerged from the prison compound into the evening light, and wearily made our way to the station. There we boarded a train for home. Lestrade spent the trip going back over his copious notes, sorting and cross-referencing.

"I suppose this must seem very plodding and pedestrian to you after working with Mr. Holmes," he said, catching my gaze.

I tried to frame a considerate answer. "Holmes is as tied to information as you, Inspector, although I have a feeling he would not have bothered with Dartmoor. He said as much only seconds before the shot was fired, if shot it was."

"Yet he asked you to come. That indicates some importance, doesn't it?"

"Yes, I suppose it does," I said doubtfully. "Yet we've uncovered absolutely nothing. Moran was a saint according to what we've learned."

"Yes. Not like the man we know at all, is it?" Lestrade replied. He returned to his notes again.

I fell back into my brown study. I was at a loss as to what to do.

I had completed the one duty Holmes had charged me with, as useless as that had been. My position now, I thought, was dictated by my being the best person to represent Sherlock Holmes' interests. Accordingly, I should remain at Baker Street. And if I were to emulate Holmes' usual course of action, I supposed my next step was.... And it was on this mental barb that my flow of reasoning became snagged, and stayed snagged well after the train pulled into the station.

Lestrade packed away his papers and stood up, looking about the compartment. "Will you be staying at Baker Street, Doctor?"

"Yes, I thought I might," I replied. "And you, Lestrade? What will you be doing now?"

He scratched his head. "I do not mind admitting that I am not sure what to do. Whatever it is, it will be routine—circulating descriptions of that Mrs. Thacker and of Miss Elizabeth and Moran. Doing the rounds of informers and spies to see what the criminal world can dig up for us. Then there's the investigation in Perth, and Gregson's part of the show to look into."

"Do you believe you will find anything?"

"There's not a lot of hope in any of it, Doctor. I am being frank only because you're familiar with the business, you understand. You see, all the lines of enquiry we could have followed disappeared along with Mr. Holmes." He gave a crooked smile. "This is one of those cases upon which I would normally consult Sherlock Holmes."

During a night of restless tossing about on my pillow I finally came to the conclusion that my best course of action was inaction. I had a feeling, merely an instinct, that Holmes would contact me, and I had best be prepared and available for him to find me easily.

But my heart and mind were in conflict. Despite the logic of my decision, I found inaction barely tolerable. Much as Holmes had, I began to suffer from mental pictures of Elizabeth enduring hardships and indignities in whatever prison they held her, and of Holmes, badly wounded and living on the streets.

I lazed about the sitting room, or else sat at the table with the papers spread before me and gazed out the window.

On the second day, from my vantage point at the window, I sighted several people who appeared to have nothing better to do than loll about on the pavements. I guessed immediately they were watching the rooms, but the purpose behind the vigil escaped me. Holmes was no longer here, and it was hardly likely that I would be in danger.

I gained my answer on the Thursday. Inactivity had finally driven me out into fresh air. In the first cool of the evening I ventured out onto Baker Street, and headed for Oxford Street, intending to walk to the Embankment. I longed for a good, extended stroll.

It had been a hot, still day. The traffic was heavy, and there were a good many pedestrians out, soaking up the small sporadic breezes that had arrived with the evening star. I threaded my way through them, moving fast, trying to blow away the mental cobwebs.

At the Oxford Street corner I looked towards the Arch and saw instead, barely fifteen feet from me, a young man whose features I recognized almost at once, even though it had been quite a few years since I had seen him, and he had been a boy of ten or so, then. It was Wiggins, once the captain of Holmes' street urchins. His clothing was still as tattered as I remembered, and he was walking away from me, dawdling as if he didn't have a care in the world.

I acted instinctively at first. I lifted my cane and called out to him.

Wiggins turned, startled. It would have been rare enough for friends of his to be in this area, so he must have assumed that someone calling his name was of the opposite variety. When he saw that I was, indeed, a stranger, and therefore in the enemy camp, he bolted.

I gave chase.

Wiggins, of course, outclassed me completely. He was younger, and could dodge the crowds more easily, and was faster on his feet. He'd had infinite practice at this type of exercise as a child. Nevertheless I raced after him as quickly as I could, content to keep within sight of him, hoping my adult cunning would best him. If I could catch him, I thought, or at least get within earshot and convince him I was not a threat, I might be able to employ him as Holmes had on occasions. Only this time I would put him to tracing Holmes.

The race led down Oxford Street, away from the park, and I

found, much to my surprise, that I was able to maintain the distance between me and my weaving quarry. Several times I lost sight of him, but then he would reappear, just as I was about to give up.

He ducked sideways and vanished, and when I reached that point, I found a narrow, dank alleyway leading into goodness knows where. Determined to overtake him, I hurried into it. Halfway down its length was a doorway, and as I reached it, a door opened and I was grasped and drawn inside by two powerful hands, and the door shut quickly behind me.

I blinked in the dark. "What on earth is the meaning of this?" I demanded to my unseen captors.

The hands tugged at my coat. "Give us your hat and jacket."

And out of the darkness came a voice that, because of its accent and youth, was recognizably Wiggins'. " 'Urry up, guv. And the cane, too."

"I do not understand," I began, as the hands finally stripped me of my jacket. I felt my hat and stick being removed.

"We've gotta get rid of your watchdogs. Just keep quiet for a moment." Wiggins' voice was reassuringly confident.

I fell silent as requested, blinking as my eyes became used to the dim light. Before me stood a man of approximately my height and weight. He had donned my jacket. As my eyes continued to distinguish more detail, I saw him quickly empty the pockets, the contents of which he handed me. He adjusted my hat, winked at me, and slipped out the door.

The brightness of the daylight dazzled me again, and I listened, blinded, as his footsteps echoed up the narrow alley.

"But what—"

"Shush up, will you?" Wiggins demanded fiercely.

I obediently fell silent and waited, redistributing my possessions about my person once more.

Only a few second later I heard a shout that seemed to come from the entrance to the alley on Oxford Street. "Here! Down here!"

Then the noise of several pairs of running feet echoed along the alley's length, and petered out again.

Only after the alley had been silent for nearly a minute did Wiggins relax, with a gusty sigh of relief. "Thank 'eavens for that."

"That man was impersonating me to draw them off?"

"Correct, guv." Wiggins handed me a faded, disreputable raincoat and a soft, shapeless hat. " 'Ere. Stick these on."

I reluctantly donned the filthy garments. "They wouldn't let me into the Ritz with these," I quipped.

"Don't worry. Where you're going, you'll fit right in."

"And where am I going?" I asked.

"Don't know," Wiggins said blandly. "Ready?"

"Yes." I settled the hat so it came down low over my face. "Who is it that was following me? Is it the people who have been watching Holmes' rooms all week?"

"Don't know," Wiggins replied.

"I see. And you don't know, I suppose, who it is that is impersonating me?"

"That's right," Wiggins replied.

Four days of confinement had chiselled at my temper, and I said sourly, "Then, if you don't know who it was, it will not matter to you what will happen to him if he is caught by these people you don't know."

Wiggins opened the door again then, and I saw his broad, amused smile. "I don't 'ave to worry 'bout 'im. 'E ain't the one wiv the gammy leg. Come on, let's get."

Wiggins' confidence was built on competence, I discovered that evening. He led me for the first part of my strange journey. We continued towards the river, but I never sighted another main street again. Wiggins led me down back alleys and through mews, and finally to the river itself. There, we skirted carefully through Bloomsbury, across Bethnal Green, and south to Whitechapel.

Finally, forty minutes later, he led me into another alley that ended in an enclosed courtyard.

Sitting on an upturned crate was a dockland worker, still grimy with sweat and dirt, whittling at one of the lathes of the crate he was perched upon.

Wiggins led me up to him, then addressed me. "This fellow doesn't know 'oo you are or nothin'. At the other end, 'e'll get a pound for 'is work and go 'ome. So there's no point in askin' questions—same as there's no point in tryin' to drive the price up, understand?" This last he addressed to the docker.

"Aye," the docker acknowledged sullenly. He looked at me and jerked his head, and walked back up the alley.

Wiggins touched his hat brim. " 'Night."

I followed the surly docker and stepped up my pace until I was level with him. He maintained his silence throughout the twenty-minute trip, delivering me at last to a deep doorway on a street indistinguishable from hundreds like it around the riverbanks.

Sitting cross-legged on the doorstep, tailor-fashion, was a dark-skinned Indian, dressed in ragged, white cotton overshirt and trousers, turban, and sandals. He handed the docker one pound, which he fished out from an inner pocket, and uncoiled himself from the step.

"I have been instructed to tell you that your duty has been fulfilled and that you can return to your home now," the Indian told the docker in the unmistakable singsong accent of his native country.

I looked my new guide up and down. "And how much are you being paid?" I asked.

"I have been promised one pound also," the Indian said primly. "This way, please," and he waved me on.

I sighed and moved on.

This leg of the journey was over in fifteen minutes, but had we moved in a direct line we could have reached the destination in three. I was led on a tortuous route up and down streets, in and out of alleys, and I can safely swear that we completed at least one circle, for I recognized the broad doorstep the Indian had been sitting upon when I had first sighted him.

I was handed—literally—exhausted and in considerable pain from my leg, to a very young girl with a sweet face, angelic golden curls, and dirty cheeks, who solemnly took my hand. She gave the Indian his promised one pound.

The Indian bowed to me, his hands together, and disappeared into the thick, warm darkness of the night.

The girl looked up at me. "I am Elizabeth," she told me. Then she tugged with her captured hand. "This way."

She led me quickly into another street, and then into a deserted, dirty courtyard filled with weeds and rubbish, broken wheels, and the carcasses of one or two dories, turned upside down onto trestles and left to rot out in the weather. In the far corner was a ramshackle structure made entirely out of salvaged tin sheet and wood, held together by twine, wire, and the occasional bolt. The roof was corrugated iron and looked to be merely resting there, pinned down only by its own weight.

The door was an old wardrobe door, complete with oval mirror frame. The mirror had long since been broken, and the wood panelling that would have once been hidden behind the mirror showed as much weathering as the rest of the door.

The child Elizabeth led me to the door. "This is our secret hiding-house," she told me. "You mustn't tell anyone about it. Promise?"

"Yes," I agreed, wondering if this was part of the itinerary, or if Elizabeth was adding her own detour into the plan. She opened the door, using both hands, and picked up my hand to lead me inside.

I ducked my head and followed her in.

It was exceedingly hot inside—the playhouse had no windows and had been baking in the summer sun all day. Also, a shuttered lantern sat on the low table in the middle of the room, which added to the heat. Elizabeth closed the door behind me and unshuttered the lantern.

The lantern told me I was here by design, and not through Elizabeth's embellishment. She pointed to a chair in the corner, which looked massive against the child-size proportions of the table.

"Please sit down," she said formally.

I sat down gratefully.

"Would you like some tea?" she asked.

I stared at her. "Real tea?" I asked stupidly.

"Of course," she replied, with adult dignity.

"Yes, thank you."

She moved over to a crate with skewed corners, and removed a cloth that covered a tray with teapot, cups, utensils, and apparatus necessary for tea-making. With an unexpected strength, she lifted the tray and placed it on the table in front of me.

"Is that everything you need?" she asked, as I looked over the tray.

"Yes, that does appear to be everything," I said. My voice sounded distant, for this felt very much like Alice's Mad Hatter's party to me.

"Good. Goodbye." And she smiled brilliantly at me, then opened the door, and swiftly closed it behind her.

I was alone.

I looked around me. The construction materials were as haphazard on the inside as on the out, and it looked very much as if children had built the house themselves. I wondered how stable the structure was, but only for a moment. The tea was hot and the scent made my mouth water, distracting me from my grim thoughts. I poured myself a cup and drank.

I sat alone in that cramped, stuffy little shack for nearly half an hour. In that time I finished the tea, recovered my strength, and had begun to wonder just how long I was to be left waiting there.

Just as I was growing impatient, I heard the latch of the door click, and I turned to see who was entering. I was bitterly disappointed when the Indian of the third stage of my journey entered into the house, stooping low to clear the door frame.

"Just how much further do I have to go?" I asked impatiently.

"Patience, good sir. All will be revealed in time," the Indian advised me. "Would you like some more tea? It is good tea, is it not? From my own country, it is."

"No, I would not like more tea," I answered waspishly. "I would like to continue on with this mad tour of the Thames and get it over with, thank you."

"Then perhaps you'd prefer something stronger?" Holmes asked me, pulling out a hip flask from beneath the cotton overshirt, and proffering it with a smile.

Chapter Twelve

I STRAIGHTENED UP, STARING, AS DELIGHT, anger, and relief all claimed my heart. "Holmes! When am I ever going to learn to look past your disguises?"

"Never, Watson," he told me, settling himself on the dirt floor of the hut, crossing his legs tailor-fashion once more. "It is a human failing to see only what you are shown." He tipped some of the brandy into my teacup.

"Drink."

I drank, glad of the fiery liquid.

Holmes poured himself a cupful and drank, too. His disguise was moderate. He had darkened his skin with some sort of stain, and of course wore the light cotton clothes typical of a poor Indian worker, plus the sandals and turban. One could find dozens of similarly dressed Indians in this area. The rest of the disguise was supplied by Holmes' acting ability—poise, accent, demeanour, gestures, and attitude.

"You had me quite fooled," I remarked. "Though I cannot see why you insisted on pressing the charade to this point—surely you could have revealed yourself in the first instance?"

"You must forgive me for appearing to play with you, Watson," Holmes said soberly. "But there was good reason for the charade. And for the same critical reasons you were left sitting alone in this edifice." He looked around him with a grim smile. "It has the advantage of having only one possible approach—across the yard. And by scaling the wall and perching high up in one corner, I could watch every inch, and wait to see if anyone was interested in you."

I nodded. "I was being watched at Baker Street," I told him.

Holmes laughed—a long, low chuckle. "'Watched' is an understatement, Watson. You had no fewer than three agencies examining your every movement. The watchers had watchers watching them, and those watchers were in turn observed by others." He laughed again. "It has been a merry week in this respect—for you confounded most of your watchers by very elaborately doing nothing."

I stared at him. "You were one of those watchers?" I asked.

"Not in person. I have been busy elsewhere. But mine was one of those agencies to which I refer. I have kept myself informed of your conduct."

"That is a great deal better than I have managed," I replied. "You had me quite worried, Holmes. The last time I saw you I thought you badly wounded. Mycroft convinced me you were not as incapacitated as you let me believe, and for four days now I have been trying to guess what it was you were doing. Have you found Moran, Holmes? Have you any sign of Elizabeth yet?"

He refilled his cup from the flask. "I had better begin at the beginning, and explain myself," he replied. "It seems I have sorely troubled you."

"I thought you had lost your mind," I confessed, "as there seemed to be no sane explanation for disappearing as you did."

"There was one—only one—reason. There were too many people involved and the whole affair was in danger of tripping over one of its many feet." He leaned back against the tin wall and pulled up his knees.

"My midnight pacing had not been entirely without effect, Watson. By reducing the situation down to the bare facts, I could distinguish Moran's motives. If you ignore the complexity of the arrangements, you have the fact that Elizabeth was abducted *at almost the exact moment* of Moran's escape from prison. Moran's motives become somewhat clearer when it is put that way."

"Revenge," I stated.

"No. Not revenge—at least, not entirely. You have overlooked the coincident times, Watson. Moran wanted me to be distracted at the moment of his escape and effectively immobilized for some time afterwards. Elizabeth's abduction ensured that, and allowed him to escape from Dartmoor and travel to London undetected.

"That was as far as I got before your compound stole my senses, Watson. And it wasn't until the next morning, when Lestrade forced me into collaboration with him, that the significance of the dramatic manner of Elizabeth's abduction occurred to me. By involving so many people, and causing such a public uproar, Moran was not only snarling the police force's efficiency, but guaranteeing that they would be involved in the investigation that followed."

"He wants you to find him?"

"No, Watson. He does not. He wants to avoid a confrontation. Moran does not fear the power of the police. It is me he fears. So he involves the police, knowing they would hamper my search for him. He knew I would not be able to keep Elizabeth's disappearance a secret and investigate on my own."

"And that is why you tricked us all?"

"Not completely." His keen eyes glittered with a remembered impatience and anger. "Although I was, indeed, hampered by all the attention.

"I also knew that Moran would follow my every move, either by report or by direct observation. As I stood at the window, I could almost feel his presence out there, watching me. I was like an insect in a specimen jar, Watson. I could not stir and avoid being scrutinized from all directions. It was a most uncomfortable and disabling position."

"So when that shot was fired, you used the situation to climb out of the jar," I stated, borrowing his simile.

Holmes nodded. "Yes. Excellent, Watson."

"I am afraid that was Mycroft's conclusion, not mine."

"Yes, I knew he would comprehend the situation," Holmes replied.

"What was it that struck you, Holmes? We determined that it was not a bullet."

"No. It was a message. Moran communicated his intentions far earlier and more adroitly than even I would have predicted."

"A message?"

"A slip of paper enclosed in a ball of wax and projected by an old-fashioned sling from the rooftop of the building opposite the window. A powerful and almost silent ancient weapon, and a clever piece of thinking on Moran's part. His message is delivered without intermediaries who could be detained and questioned."

"But the blood! You were bleeding!"

"Yes. A moderately shallow cut from a flying shard of glass from the window. Fortunate window-dressing. I could not let you examine the wound because you would know immediately it was not what it seemed."

"It does explain why Mycroft found traces of red wax on the carpet."

"Yes, the ball of wax broke up upon impact—it hit me squarely in the shoulder. My reaction was to clasp the point of impact, and I felt the paper beneath my hand. I knew immediately that this was a message from Moran. I kept it hidden in my hand while I played out the scene and sent you to investigate the empty house. As soon as I was alone, I read the message, which was more or less exactly what I expected it to be."

He withdraw a small, folded piece of paper and handed it to me. It was thick and yellow, and, not unexpectedly, waxy to the touch. Some of the red wax clung to the edges. The writing was in soft, dark pencil. "*Search for me and she dies.*" I turned the sheet over to check the other side, which was blank and featureless.

"Moran's handwriting?" I guessed.

"Undoubtedly."

"Succinct and to the point," I observed.

"It was no more than I had expected," Holmes replied. "So I pushed it into a pocket, snatched up money and other small essentials, raced down the back stairs to Mrs. Hudson's kitchen, and out the back door and across the yard, now conveniently deserted whilst the police searched elsewhere for my would-be murderer. I scaled a few walls, and was alone and well on my way to the east end before, I am sure, you returned to the sitting room and found me gone."

I considered the sequence from Holmes' point of view. "It certainly achieved your aim."

"Yes. And I apologize for worrying you."

"It was necessary," I said, dismissively, "if you are to find Elizabeth."

Holmes' face was grim. "Everything I have done is only for that purpose," he replied.

"So tell me who it was that was watching me. And why."

Holmes composed himself once more. "The watchers," he said, with a smile reminiscent of his earlier mirth. "After I had slipped from the limelight, both the police and Moran were anxious to learn where I was and what I was doing. The police, so they could learn where Moran was through me, and Moran, to decide whether I was obeying his demand to keep well away from him. The only possible means they had of determining my whereabouts was to watch both you and my rooms, utilizing the theory that sooner or later I would contact you. I am quite sure you had a tail like a comet on your journey to Dartmoor, and had you moved from Baker Street again, that same tail would have dogged your every step."

"So Moran's men were also watching the police, and you were watching both."

"Only to determine when you left Baker Street. As long as you stayed in the rooms I could not communicate with you. Every message, delivery, or tradesman would have been suspect, and I am quite sure the police questioned everyone who called at 221B over the past four days, hoping to discover me or Moran, or confederates of either party. It must have frustrated everyone when you stayed indoors."

"I stayed there because I thought you might try to contact me, and I didn't want to be absent and miss any message you might send."

Holmes nodded. "Again, as always, you have done the right thing for entirely the wrong reasons. When you finally did step out for air this evening, the alarm went up amongst both observing parties. They assumed incorrectly that you had received a covert message, and scurried to follow you so that they might locate me."

It was all beginning to make sense to me now. "You were waiting for me to do that very thing," I said.

"Yes. And beginning to wonder if I would have, in fact, to send a covert message to you to get you out and into a position where I could cut off your pursuers."

"So all my guides tonight, and the backtracking and weaving through streets were designed to baffle anyone who had not been fooled by the fellow who took my jacket?"

"It was vital that no one witness our meeting. For that same reason I became one of your guides—I wanted to observe for myself that your trail was clear. And as a last precautionary measure, I forced you to wait alone in this house whilst I watched outside. Had anyone managed to navigate through all my shields and seen you enter the hut, they would have become convinced after some time had elapsed that you had reached your final destination, and burst in upon you— to catch whoever you were meeting with *in situ*."

"You have been exceedingly cautious."

"I cannot afford to become embroiled in official bureaucracy again. I need to be able to move fast and freely if I am to find Elizabeth in time."

"'In time'?"

"Yes, there is a time limit, Watson. I do not know yet what that limit is—that is why I have gone to such lengths to have you delivered here. I said that Moran was not motivated entirely by revenge, but that is without doubt influencing his actions. I know that once Elizabeth's usefulness as a hostage and shield is at an end, Moran will kill her. For revenge."

"Then we must hurry. . . ." I began, feeling an overwhelming sense of urgency descend upon me.

"Hurry to where?" Holmes asked sensibly. "We have a little time, Watson. Let us not squander it by running around aimlessly."

"How much time do we have, do you think?"

"Two days, perhaps. I will know better by tomorrow. For now, let me tell you about Moran. It may be important for a second person to have knowledge of the full facts." He tapped the note I had laid down upon the table. "What does that note tell you?"

I picked it up again. "It is a curious paper—crude. There is no watermark on it, which may mean simply that the mark was on the remaining portion of the page from which the note was torn." I turned it over and back again. "Apart from that and the handwriting, which I will leave to you as the expert, I cannot infer a thing."

Holmes smiled. "This paper did not have a watermark. It is

handmade, and made from very primitive tools and equipment. See the irregular colouration and thickness? There is no point in examining the writing, for we know already who wrote the note. But look at the wax, Watson. See its colour?"

I recalled Mycroft's observations. "Mycroft said it was rough and impure. He thought it might be a type of sealing wax."

"Mycroft did not have a large sample to examine. Lift the sheet and smell the wax, Watson."

I lifted the note and sniffed gently. The scent was strong and exotic, and stirred an obscure memory within me. Holmes nodded at my expression.

"Yes, it is like a calling card, isn't it? I remember this unusual perfume from my time in Tibet. It is used to make candles for burning in the temples as offerings to the gods. And handmade paper is used to send written prayers." He tapped the note. "This told me I should look for a foreign connection. I recalled from my files that Moran had been with the army in India, and I concluded that he had sheltered with Indian comrades whose friendship he had founded whilst in India, and who were now somewhere in London."

"Do you know who they are?"

"Indeed I do. The most notorious of Moran's Indian friends was listed in my files. I learnt that he was in London, and I have, for the past three days, been a guest of Sikmah Rijkmah."

I raised my eyebrows at this announcement. "Disguised as a fellow countryman? Come now, Holmes—you don't even speak Hindi."

Holmes laughed at my expression. "I confess it would have been impossible in a normal household, but Sikmah runs a hostel for migrant workers—and quite naturally the greater proportion of his guests are fellow Hindus. This establishment is quite legitimate, and also serves as an excellent cover for various other nefarious activities in which Sikmah has his busy hand. I sought a room there the same night I abandoned Baker Street, and for three days an unemployed deaf and mute Indian has been loafing about the common rooms of this notorious lodging."

"You're taking quite a chance, Holmes. You're not even sure this Sikmah is involved. You have got only the smell of incense and a peripheral fact in your records, which are possibly quite out of date."

"Yes, it was a gamble," Holmes conceded candidly. "But a gamble with short odds, and it paid off, for on my first day there, none other than Moran's sister Beatrice O'Connor arrived."

"Moran's sister!" I recalled my futile work at Dartmoor. "She was the only one who visited Moran in prison."

"Yes, and that fact should have alerted Lestrade. You would recognize her, Watson, as Mrs. Thacker."

"Of course!" I groaned.

"I had half-expected one or another familiar face to appear in time, because of the peculiar arrangements at the hostel. It is a strangely designed building, Watson. Not at all as one would expect a small, poor hostel to be laid out. The bedrooms are upon the first floor, but not lining a common corridor. Instead they all face a type of minstrel's gallery which in turn overlooks the sitting and dining sections of the ground floor. The arrangement makes for easy observation of the rooms, and the comings and goings of guests—which must be an advantage, considering the calibre of the inmates. But it also lays wide open for scrutiny any antics of the owner. I had been inside the door for only five minutes when I noticed that there was a large, very powerful-looking ruffian sitting on a stool at the end of this gallery, apparently with nothing better to do than scowl at anyone who got too close to him."

"A guard?" I conjectured.

"Yes, a guard. I kept an eye upon the end door, and noted that no one went in or out of the room, except Sikmah on one occasion, and he used a key. The guard took all his meals at his post, and I observed he had a heavy revolver tucked into his waistband. He was relieved by another, equally threatening-looking a warden, and the gun was exchanged.

"You can well imagine my exhilaration, then, when I watched from my cool corner of the sitting room as Moran's sister entered, nodded to the desk clerk, and made her way unaided and without guidance to this very door, where she produced her own key and slipped inside."

"Holmes, do you think Moran is hiding there?"

Holmes looked a little pained at this question. "I do not merely think so, Watson. I made it my task to *know*. And, yes, he was there, for a while."

"Then he is gone again," I said, disappointed.

"Not exactly. Let me explain. Beatrice O'Connor remained in the room for nearly fifty minutes, then left the hostel. Her arrival made it imperative for me to see inside that room somehow. It was impossible to get past the guard, for he was as tenacious as a bulldog in discharging his duties, and he wouldn't be easily tricked or lured from his post. And I was alone. So yesterday I hurried back to Wiggins' quarters, which I am using as a base of operations, changed into my dark clothes, and arrived back at the hostel late last night. I worked my way around to the back of the building, and scaled fences and masonry until I was precariously perched close enough to the end-room window to hear anything. The window was open, of course, for it was a hot night, but heavy drapes prevented me seeing anything other than a one-inch slice of the room, which included the end of a small table and the foot of the bunk which is built into all the rooms.

"Having gained my position, I was very nearly startled off it, for a voice spoke right beside my ear, as if the unseen speaker were addressing me. He must have been standing or sitting against the curtain, and paused for a moment to collect his thoughts, for it had been silent as I had climbed.

"'Very well, then. As you insist upon it, I suppose I must. But I am disappointed, Sikmah. You agreed you would help me, and now you're turning me out.'

"I recognized that voice, although the petulant tone was new. Moran was obviously sheltering in the room. Sikmah answered, and his voice held only a touch of accent.

"'It was not part of our agreement that I risk bringing the wrath of Sherlock Holmes down upon me. I do not wish to bring the interest of the police upon me, either. I especially do not want to face charges for harbouring a dangerous prison escapee. You shouldn't have come here so soon.'

"'How was I to know the ship had been delayed? Ships aren't becalmed any more.'

"'Because most ships have steam. My cousin's ship is a poor one and an old one, and uses only sail. You should be thankful for that. It will draw less attention.'

"'And what am I going to do with the woman for another three days?' Moran demanded. 'Beatrice, I am nearly out of morphine. You must bring me some more.'

"And his sister answered heatedly to this demand. 'No, I will not get more. I was lucky to be able to procure what I did and not be caught. I'll not do any more thieving for you, Sebastian. And you'll risk killing the woman if you continue with the injections. It takes skill and fine judgement to administer it in proper doses, and I'm only a nurse.'

"'I cannot keep her prisoner on my own,' he protested. 'Come now, Beatrice. I will be out of your life forever in three days. Help me just this once.'

"'Now you just listen to me, and listen good, Sebastian Moran. I've got a good man at home, and a good life. It is only because you'll be out of my life that I've even helped you this far—God help me if Jamie ever knew. I'm not happy with this kidnapping business, but I kept my silence because you convinced me it is the only way to keep Sherlock Holmes from stopping you. Fair enough. But it stops here. Now. Show a little backbone, dear brother. She's only a woman. You can contain her for three days, surely, without resorting to morphine again.'

"'Not if I have to find another refuge at the same time. You don't know her, Beatrice. It took four of my men nearly sitting on top of her to merely hold her down. It took a bullet to stop her.'"

"Then Elizabeth is wounded, as you thought, Holmes," I said, trying to banish the image Moran's description painted in my mind.

Holmes nodded. "But then Beatrice said something very interesting. She made a sound of disgust. 'Well, she is not going anywhere in a hurry, now. Look at her. Very well, then, Sebastian, I'll administer one more dose so you can find somewhere else to hide. And I'd better change those dressings again, too—'"

"My god! Elizabeth is in that room, too!" I cried, interrupting Holmes' narrative.

Holmes nodded. "I was just as shocked as you, Watson. It was the last thing I had expected. Only someone very stupid or very desperate would remain with his hostage where both could be found together. It was only when I picked up the threads of the conversation again that I realized Moran was quite as desperate as this act indicated. For he had expected to be on that ship eight hours past, and sailing for the East and safety. Instead the boat had been becalmed and was nearly a week late, and he was perched on the very edge of safety, waiting."

"Is that why you brought me here? To help you rescue Elizabeth?"

Holmes nodded. "Had I been able to devise a plan for removing her from that room unaided and from under the noses of three nervous occupants, I would have carried it out then and there. But I am afraid I wasn't up to the challenge, and against all my inclinations, I remained where I was and tried to learn more. There was one more significant fact. Moran agreed to be out of the room by tomorrow morning. So whatever we do, we must do it tonight. You arrived just in time, Watson."

"And without my medical kit," I sighed. I structured my next question carefully. "Did you hear anything that would indicate where the bullet hit her, Holmes? It would help me to know what sort of wound I might have to deal with."

He shook his head silently. Then he reached up to knock his knuckles, inexplicably, against a sheet-metal fragment of the wall he leaned against. "Very little new information was discussed after that. They continued to argue over the same ground they had already covered, Moran getting more and more peevish as the discussion lengthened. I gave it up then, and went back to rouse Wiggins and lay in some new plans against any possible developments, and to catch up on your movements. That was last night, and you had, according to Wiggins' Arabs, been remarkably sedentary."

"Did you see her, Holmes?"

"No."

The door of the playhouse opened then, and admitted the child Elizabeth. She carried my medical bag in both hands, elbows akimbo to accommodate its depth, which was very nearly equal to her waist height, and shuffled into the room to drop it at my feet.

"Mr. Holmes thought you might want this," she told me, her eyes shining in her grave, perfectly formed face.

"I . . . ummm . . . thank you," I replied, inadequately.

"Elizabeth was once the key member of a band of housebreakers. She did me the favour of retrieving your bag from your rooms today on a strictly commissioned basis, as she no longer breaks into houses."

Elizabeth smiled, and I found myself smiling back. The charm of the little girl was irresistible.

"Elizabeth is also Wiggins' half-sister, and older than she looks," Holmes continued. "Yours is not the first heart and mind to be distracted by those innocent eyes. Elizabeth."

She turned at his address, and Holmes nodded toward me. Elizabeth reached into her pinafore pocket and produced my purse, which she handed over solemnly. "I had to pay Mr. Holmes his promised one pound," she said, "and I do not have any money."

"So she used yours," Holmes said. "Elizabeth is also one of the best pickpockets on the streets. Retired, of course," he added blandly.

I stared at her, astonished.

"Except for emergencies," she replied primly.

Chapter Thirteen

AT TWO O'CLOCK IN THE MORNING I found myself crouched on the bare dirt in front of Sikmah's immigrant hostel, hugging my medical bag to my chest, and closely wrapped in my borrowed coat, which smelt abominably. It was an uncomfortable position, and I had maintained it for not quite an hour already. But the discomfort meant very little to me, for I was more than eager to begin my part in Holmes' plan to rescue Elizabeth.

Holmes had warned me to expect a wait of any length, for he would begin only when the hostel was completely still and settled for the night. He had returned to his hired room, assuming the persona of the deaf and dumb Indian he was using. He planned to slip down to the front door when it was safe to allow me access into the building.

The plan, roughly, was to disable the ferocious sentinel guarding the door to the room Elizabeth was held in, and to remove her. All in stealth, for, as Holmes warned me, "there are at least twenty men on the premises who would object violently to being woken."

At twenty minutes past the hour, the latch of the door creaked, and the shadow about the frame widened and deepened before Holmes' darkened features appeared.

I arose stiffly and moved into the building, squeezing past the half-opened door, and blinking in the musty blackness of the hotel's front room.

I felt Holmes' long fingers on my arm, and his voice murmured into my ear, "Something is amiss, Watson. The guard is no longer there. He was gone when I returned tonight."

I looked about as my eyes adjusted to the lack of light. Before me was a number of worn horsehair chairs and lounges, and beyond them perhaps a dozen long tables and benches. In the corner next to the empty fireplace in the sitting area were several brightly painted figures of deities, their glossy gold tints picking up the feeble glow of the down-turned lights above the stairs, which exaggerated their predatory expressions. On a shelf below each figure was a number of long, red tapers, each standing in its own ball of dried clay. Most were half-burned and had guttered out. None was now alight, but the pervasive, intoxicating perfume lingered in the warm air.

I lifted my gaze upwards to the balcony Holmes had described. Nearly a dozen doors led from it, and at the left-hand end, opposite the stair head, was a corridor that I presumed led to the rear door and any utility and storage areas. A single lamp burning very low sent a pale glimmer of illumination along the balcony, and I looked to the right, where Holmes had located the guard. The spot was empty, but a stool stood against the blank wall, mute testimony to Holmes' description.

We climbed the stairs carefully, making the minimum of noise, and made our way along the balcony. From behind each door we passed we heard either silence, or the natural noises of slumbering men.

At the last door, I took up my post guarding Holmes' back as he bent and examined the lock. It was locked, and Holmes produced his pouch of metal probes and carefully delved into the keyhole. He withdrew the probe, selected another, bigger instrument, and proceeded to unlock the door.

As soon as the click of the lock sounded, we opened the door and slipped inside, and Holmes crossed the room and threw aside the heavy drapes, letting in the starlight. I closed the door behind me, and we both looked toward the bunk.

It was empty.

The room was small enough to be taken in at a glance, and that glance confirmed what Holmes already suspected.

"Moran has already flown," he whispered. "And none of my lookouts raised the alarm, either." He dropped the curtain back into place, picked up a candle from the window ledge, put it on the table before him, and lit it. His features were strained and sombre in the dancing light. "The news of your abrupt disappearance from Baker Street must have terrorized him to the point of flight, Watson. He guessed, rightly, that I was gaining on him." He looked away. "This is a grave development."

I put the revolver Holmes had lent me back in my pocket, and dropped my bag to the floor. "What will you do now, Holmes?"

"I do not know." He looked around the room, and I could see he was assessing it for clues, a habit that was ingrained after years of practice.

Patiently, I perched myself on the single, hard chair in the room, and watched as Holmes quartered the room. The job was swiftly done, for it was very small, and he turned to the bunk. At once he gave a triumphant and almost silent exclamation, and pulled from between the lower mattress and the bunk frame a scrap of lace. I recognized it.

"Elizabeth's," I whispered.

Holmes threw back the thin cover and beckoned me over. "Look, Watson."

I studied the crumpled sheet that covered the mattress. Holmes plucked a long red hair from the pillow, but my eyes were caught by a more sinister clue. Approximately twenty inches below the pillow was a bloodstain, fresh and not small. It would be from the left side of someone laying on the bunk, and more alarmingly, from the lower torso.

"This is not good, Holmes," I said, pointing to it. "Fresh blood, after three days? I hope Mrs. O'Connor is a superior example of her profession."

"It could be an arm wound," Holmes pointed out. "And from what I could learn, Mrs. O'Connor is indeed an excellent nurse." He lowered himself onto a clean section of the mattress and examined the under side of the upper bunk. "Would you pass me the candle, please, Watson."

I gave him the candle, and he lifted it to shine on the upper bunk.

"Ah!" he said. He turned his head to look more closely, then brought the candle out and offered it to me. "We have received guidance from another source," he said. "Look for yourself."

Holmes stood to make room for me. I crouched low and lifted the candle to illuminate the place where he rested his finger, against the base of the upper bunk. The slats of wood were spaced an inch or so apart, and on one was scrawled a word and figure. It took me several seconds to make sense of it, for the writing medium had sunk into the wood and radiated outwards, swelling the lettering almost to the point of illegibility. But by bringing the candle close and puzzling it out, I read aloud "Andhra 7."

I looked at Holmes for explanation, for it was clear it made sense to him.

He was leaning against the post of the bunk. "A light in the darkness, Watson. Against all my expectations, Elizabeth has contrived to rise above her difficulties and leave us a message, and a direction to search in."

"You mean Elizabeth wrote this?"

"Without doubt."

"And what does it mean? Andhra is not English."

"No. It is the name of an area out of Indian antiquity, and also the name or part of the name of a ship. The ship, in fact, that Moran is planning to escape from England upon."

"So '7' is probably a date. Tomorrow. No, today!" I exclaimed.

"Yes. A day earlier than expected. We now know what our time limit is."

I looked at the writing again. "Holmes, this is blood she has used."

"Exactly."

I looked up at him again, a little astonished at the pleased note in his reply. "You're glad of that?"

"Indeed. You mean you don't understand what that means?"

"No," I confessed without shame.

"It means, my dear Watson, that despite injuries and drugs, Elizabeth has more of her faculties about her than Moran realizes, and is hiding it from her captors. They have obviously been speaking quite freely in her presence—as they were last night when I eavesdropped.

And they do not consider her much of a physical threat, for they have not bothered to tether her hands. If they had tied her hands, she would never have been able to reach the slat, nor been able to manipulate her hands to write the message. Nor would she have been able to covertly reopen her wound for the fresh blood necessary to write with."

I must have looked appalled, for Holmes shook his head. "That is not nearly as terrible as it sounds, Watson. It means Elizabeth was more or less rational, for she has grasped the importance of the name of the ship, determined a means of passing that information on, and executed it. So her wounds cannot be totally incapacitating. It also means Elizabeth knows we will be hunting for her despite any threats made by Moran. That gives us hope, Watson. With Elizabeth in the midst of the enemy and still in the game, we stand at least a fighting chance."

I stared at Holmes. This summation displayed military thinking, and it was revealing that he considered Elizabeth—a woman, wounded and handicapped by the soporific effects of drugs—as a key advantage. It was clear that this single, gruesome message conveyed more hope to Holmes than a full battalion of soldiers fighting for his cause.

Fifteen minutes later we were out in the street, our business in that establishment done. We left the place undisturbed. After Elizabeth was safely back in our hands there would be time enough to call in the police.

"And what is our next step?" I asked, as Holmes led me through the streets towards Wiggins' abode.

"Sleep," Holmes replied instantly. "And after that, we must ascertain when the sailing ship *Andhra* is due and at what dock."

Holmes led me back through the narrow streets. It was very late now, and it was possible to discern the faintest wash of light in the sky over our heads, though, as yet, the houses about us remained shrouded in the blackest cloth of night.

Tucked away in an obscure and steep mews, sited at the top of the pitch, was a small house. Holmes entered it, after first gazing about for observers. He drew me in behind him. I stopped with the closed door behind my back, blinking in the darkness, but Holmes took my arm and led me into the house. I sensed there were other occupants under the roof, for Holmes was careful to guide me around furniture and architecture with little noise, and he remained silent.

I was led up a narrow stair and into a room, where Holmes opened a drape far enough for me to see the dim outline of a small, narrow cot.

"Sleep," he told me. "You're quite safe here."

I needed no further assurance. Gratefully I sank onto the meagre mattress and composed myself for sleep.

I awoke some hours later, stiff and cold, for I had failed to cover myself before sleep had descended. I was aware of the sound of traffic somewhere in the distance, but the house itself was still and quiet, and I could hear my own heart beating in the silence.

The room was a dingy box, and the bed I had occupied was similar to those I had used in Afghanistan—and equally as uncomfortable. Apart from the bed and a thick quantity of dust, the room was empty. I did notice, however, that there had been a considerable amount of traffic in and out of the room recently, for the floorboards between the bed, door, and window were swept clean and bare by boots. To prove my theory, in the corner by the window was a now-dry dust mark created by a wet sole.

I rose and pulled my coat about me, and made my way out into the corridor. It was narrow, tall, and quite dim, but there was a runner laid along the centre of the bare floorboards, and the place seemed reasonably clean. From my left, as I stood in the doorway of the room I had slept in, came a quiet chink of china and the unmistakable sound of hot water being poured. My throat contracted dryly at the idea of sustenance. I traversed the corridor and descended the stairs down to the kitchen.

A fire was lit at the far end of the room and, working from its light, the young girl Elizabeth poured tea from the same pot she had served me from the previous evening.

She looked up at me as I entered. "Good morning, Dr Watson. You have risen earlier than we expected you to."

"I was woken by the chill," I replied. "Who is 'we'?"

Elizabeth placed the cup she had poured in front of me. "My brother and I."

Her answer told me whose house this was, and also jogged my memory, for I recalled Holmes saying he had been using Wiggins' house as a base of operations.

"Mr. Holmes has left, then?"

She nodded and sipped her tea. "Hours ago. I think he probably left shortly after bringing you here."

I studied the girl, feeling somewhat confused as to how much I should discuss Holmes' affairs with her. It was evident she was aware of many of the peripheral details, and her oddly adult bearing and speech bespoke highly developed reasoning skills in one so young.

"Did Holmes tell you where he was going?" I asked, circum-navigating the problem.

"To find out about the *Andhra*," Elizabeth replied.

Considering that Holmes had left me here in the early hours of the morning, I thought Elizabeth's explanation was unlikely to be Holmes' only mission. I watched her pour another cup of tea, her movements graceful and controlled.

"Forgive my curiosity, Elizabeth, but how is it that your diction is so flawless, when your brother . . . when his is. . . ."

"Deplorable?" Elizabeth supplied. She smiled. "Henry is lazy. Miss Elizabeth taught him as much as me, but he exerts himself only when it is necessary."

"Elizabeth corrected your accent?"

Elizabeth nodded. "Henry is much better at reading and writing and arithmetic than I. Miss Elizabeth told me that was because he is older, and can grasp more, and I will improve as I grow older, too."

This was a revelation of a part of Elizabeth's life completely unsuspected by me, and I was intrigued by the new glimpses into her character it gave me.

"Did Miss Elizabeth visit you regularly?"

Elizabeth nodded. "As often as she could, whenever she wasn't working with Mr. Holmes. She was virtually a governess to us both—especially after Mother died." She pushed the teacup towards me. "Could you take that to Henry? He is on the roof. You can reach it by going back along the corridor of the room you slept in, and climbing the next flight of steps. The landing at the top leads directly to the roof."

I took the cup of tea and followed Elizabeth's directions, and in short order found myself on the flat pitch roof of the house.

As I stepped carefully across the roof, juggling the hot tea, Wiggins' voice reached me. "Doctor Watson. You're just in time to relieve me."

"Relieve you?" I asked, as I rounded the corner.

Wiggins sat upon the metal case of a roof vent, made comfortable with the addition of a thin cushion, his legs stretched out in front of him.

In his hands was an extended brass telescope—a powerful instrument, by the size of its lenses. At that moment it rested along his legs, but it was obvious he had been using it.

I turned to look at the view myself.

Spread beneath us, reaching over to the river, and expanding up and down its length, was a squalid, crowded urban cesspit. Roofs coated with moss and dirt from the streets presented themselves to my gaze, huddled together in shared misery, concealing the narrow streets that wove between them, and concealing, too, the pitiful humanity that lived, worked, and died down there.

And perched at the river's edge were the equally dismal dockyards of Surrey and the Isle of Dogs.

"I grew up down there," Wiggins said off-handedly. Then he must have recognized some expression on my face, for he laughed heartily. "Yes, Doctor, you are right in thinking that the work I did for Mr. Holmes was possibly the only 'onest money I ever earned." He stood. "Life 'as a 'abit of changing 'orses on you, which is why it is your turn on the lookout. I've got to go to work. Is that my Jenny Lea?"

We swapped items, and as Wiggins sipped his tea, I examined the telescope. It was a beautiful instrument.

"There's no sign of any new ships, but that don't surprise me none," Wiggins continued. "Any ships under wind power would wait for the tide to 'elp 'em upriver."

I lifted the telescope and looked out at the river. It leapt up close to me under the power of the lenses, and I examined the clear details of a handful of docked vessels. None was the *Andhra,* of course.

"You sound as if you know where Holmes is," I commented, lowering the telescope.

"Gone to find out about the ship, of course."

"At four o'clock in the morning?" I asked.

"Mr. 'olmes keeps 'is own counsel. I just do as 'e asks. It's little enough. 'E vouched for me when I applied for this position, you see."

"And Miss Elizabeth gave you elocution lessons and taught you to read and write."

"And my arithmetic," Wiggins replied, unabashed. "Before that I could steal and spend two bob, but I didn't 'ave a clue 'ow to add them together." He took another sip of his tea, and then spoke with perfect diction, his vowels an eerie echo of Elizabeth's mellow tones. "Now I have a chance to do something with my life because I look and act like a successful businessman. Only this way will I ever beat them at their own game."

I looked him up and down. He was dressed in a city business suit, and when using his "proper" voice, he did indeed look like a typical young clerk with good prospects, and his plans had the hallmarks of Elizabeth's original mind and mischievous sense of humour.

"Why did she do it?" I thought, unaware that I had spoken aloud until Wiggins answered, frowning.

"I don't know. I occasionally wonder why she bothers at all. Sometimes when we were being lazy or stubborn, Miss Elizabeth would get hopping mad at us, and lecture us about missed opportunities and the freedom to choose what we wanted to do. . . ."

"Ah . . ." I breathed, for the answer had perhaps just registered its presence to me. Elizabeth had given a similar explanation to me, not all that long ago.

Wiggins shrugged. "Mostly, I think she likes us. And I know she liked my mother immensely. After she died, Miss Elizabeth more or less adopted little Elizabeth. She intervened with the child welfare officers, I know, although she never told me that, and arranged for us two to stay here together."

"Your sister is named for Miss Elizabeth, yes?"

"Yes."

"You have known Elizabeth that long?"

"Mr. Holmes brought Elizabeth here after they had returned from the continent, and she stayed with us while he sorted out Moran." Wiggins drained his cup. "I must dash. I'm supposed to start early today. See y', guv." He grinned cheerfully and strode off across the roof, carrying his teacup, moving back to the roof-access door.

I appropriated the cushion Wiggins had left behind and settled down with the expectation of a long, uneventful vigil. I was pleased to have some solitude with which to puzzle over all I had learnt since arising.

I basked under the pleasant, early-morning sunshine, and occasionally scanned the distant docks and incoming ships with the telescope, while I carried out my long-ingrained habit of noting down the facts and events that had occurred since my leaving Baker Street.

Young Elizabeth appeared an hour or so later, with some sandwiches for my breakfast.

Wiggins had surmised that the *Andhra* would wait for the tide, so I relaxed and enjoyed the peacefulness, aware that Holmes' reappearance would signal the end of inactivity.

So I was much startled and perturbed when my sweeping examination of the docks revealed a small, old-fashioned sail ship making slow progress upriver, aided by a tug and favourable winds against the almost-slack tide. It was nearly noon, and the summer sun was dazzling against the water, making it difficult for me to make out the name. It wasn't until she was tying up at the docks and lowering sail, which conveniently shaded the bows long enough for me to pick out the lettering, that I could confirm that she was, indeed, the *Andhra* we had been expecting.

Andhra's Pride was battered but fast, despite her wind-powered limitations. She was also a ship very much in a hurry, for almost immediately the ropes were secured, men scurried all over her, beginning the unloading process.

That haste put me in a quandary. Holmes had not returned, and Wiggins was away. What was I to do?

Troubled, I climbed back down to the lower level of the house, searching for Elizabeth. The kitchen and all the public rooms I peered into were empty. I stood in the hall and listened for noise of another occupant. The house was silent about me.

I tried calling, but it produced nothing.

Aware that no time must be lost in alerting Holmes, yet sensible to the need for stealth and observation, I frankly dithered, torn by my conflicting duties. Holmes had impressed upon me often enough my affinity for choosing the wrong course of action. Conscious of my procrastination, however, I forced myself to consider the priorities and make a decision.

Hastily I tore out a page from my notebook and scribbled a somewhat cryptic note that I hoped would be decipherable only to Holmes or young Elizabeth, informing them that *Andhra's Pride* had docked, and that I was going to the docks to observe from a closer post. In that way I would be close enough to take appropriate action should the circumstances dictate it.

It was the best I thought I could do. No doubt Holmes would disagree, but for the moment I had to work alone. I dropped the note on the kitchen table, and left the house, closing and latching the door behind me.

Closer inspection proved that the *Andhra's* captain was indeed a man in a hurry. Activity in the vicinity of the wharf was frantic.

I had found a station from which to observe—behind the inevitable pile of discarded, broken packing crates and debris that seems to litter all docks more or less permanently. During my journey to the riverside, it appeared that nothing more remarkable than cargo unloading had occurred.

The captain was overseeing the work himself. He stood upon the observation deck and encouraged the workers to better speed with curses, jeers, and sarcasm. He had the dark skin of a coastal Indian, although his clothing was quite westernized and he wore no turban. He was speaking, I guessed, an Indian dialect, for most of the dock workers were ethnic Indians themselves, to judge by the number of turbans and sweat-soaked cotton trousers and shirts. Occasionally the captain interspersed his curses with English variants for the benefit of the handful of non-Indian navvies.

The cargo being unloaded appeared to be mostly tea. The unmistakable tea chests were being manhandled without benefit of crane or tackle, which was already in use barely twenty yards away, where the new cargo sat. It was an untidy mountain of rough pine boxes of an odd assortment of sizes and dimensions. There were no commercial markings that I could discern through my two-inch-wide view of the activities. The block and tackle was being used to unload what was possibly the last wagonload of the cargo: two or three large and seemingly heavy crates.

The captain was using his own crew exclusively to handle the new cargo. None of the local workers was allowed near it. I saw two fellows with initiative turned back when they approached with offers of help. It seemed an inefficient use of resources to me, especially if the captain was as pressed for time as he appeared to be. With the help of the dock workers they could have the new cargo loaded in half the time.

Nearly two hours later, an officer—probably the captain's second, if the number of stripes on his sleeve was a truthful guide—arrived. He was a tall fellow, but thin as a rake, white and weedy. He was accompanied by another tea chest, this one perched on a trolley being pushed by one of the crew. I judged the chest was the second officer's version of a sea chest, for I saw no other sign of baggage.

He was greeted with a hail from the captain, who hurried onto the deck to greet the officer as he reached the top of the gangplank. They shook hands, speaking quietly, while the tea chest was bumped up on board, when the captain gave directions to the crewman, who disappeared below with it.

Both turned to view the cargo handling. Progress was apparently not to the second officer's satisfaction, either, for a scowl rapidly settled on his features, under the shadow of his peaked cap. He had words with the captain.

Shortly the captain gave a shouted command, and several of the senior crew members working on the new cargo rounded up a number of the dock workers—who had just begun to slow their pace as the last of the tea chests were unloaded—and took them over to the new cargo.

In a short time, the pile of crates began to disappear up the plank and into the ship.

I had very vague and general ideas about cargo handling, gleaned from my short time travelling whilst in the army, but I had a feeling that the speed at which this ship had been unloaded and shortly would be fully loaded again was nothing short of miraculous. The dock workers must have been recruited with the promise of very generous bonuses to extract such efficient work from them.

The speed was deepening my predicament. If Holmes did not appear, I would be forced to act on my own to stop the ship from leaving. Just how I would go about managing that, I had no idea. I had some vague notion, I recall, of marching up the gangplank, and pulling out the revolver I still had in my pocket and holding the captain at bay until help arrived.

Another problem was gnawing at my mind. Where was Moran? This was the ship upon which he was going to make his escape from England, and it had every appearance of casting off and leaving as soon as the cargo was below decks. Would Moran, like Holmes, miss its departure? Or was he already below decks, having stolen aboard whilst I was making my way to the waterside?

And where was Holmes?

My vigil was disturbed by footsteps crunching in the dry grass that lay between me and the warehouses behind me. Startled, I turned, expecting to find either Holmes or Wiggins, or perhaps Gregson or Lestrade had arrived. Instead, the captain and two hefty-looking crew members surrounded me where I perched on an upturned crate.

"Would you be so kind as to accompany me aboard, good sir?" the captain asked in adequate English.

Dismay flooded me. In my preoccupation over Holmes' absence, I had lost concentration and missed seeing the captain's departure. Now I was truly in a bind.

I raised my hand to my forehead to shield my eyes against the lengthening sun. "What on earth for?" I asked, pretending bewilderment and a little belligerence. The thought occurred to me that perhaps my discovery would delay the ship's departure a little, whilst the captain attempted to deal with me. It would lengthen matters if I were as uncooperative as possible.

"You have been spying on my ship, sir, for most of the afternoon. I wish to invite you aboard to discuss your reasons for this conduct."

"Spying? Me? Now look, sir, that is preposterous. Why on earth would I wish to spy on a little boat?"

"That is what my second officer and I would like to know," the captain replied quietly, not at all moved by my bluster.

"That's damned silly. I have just been sitting here, minding my own business and enjoying the sunshine. This isn't a private dock. I am free to come and go as I please."

"Yes, I am aware that this is a public dock," the captain said, and his tone suggested that the fact was most inconvenient to him. "However, it is quite obvious that you have been watching my ship very carefully. You were sighted not long after we arrived, and have been monitored all this afternoon. For a member of the general public you have a singularly deep interest in my 'little boat.' Please, come aboard and let us talk about it."

"No. I can't, I am afraid. I have, in fact, an appointment elsewhere." I pulled out my watch. "In fact, I am already late—fell asleep in the sun—stupid of me, I know."

The captain remained entirely unmoved by my reply. Stoically he repeated, "Please accompany me on board, sir."

"No."

He sighed, and waved a hand at the crewman who stood closest to me. "Then, I am afraid my man here will have to shoot you."

Chapter Fourteen

FORCED BY THE THREAT OF BODILY HARM, I left my perch on the packing crate, and allowed myself to be led across the dock and up the gangplank of the ship, the captain and his armed crewman close behind me.

The second officer was on the main deck, watching the loading. He turned as we approached, and his face sagged when he saw me. He let out a curse.

"A stranger, you said, Sarawan!" he snarled at the captain.

The voice told me what my eyes had not seen. Ten years in prison had not smoothed Moran's tones. They had only deprived him of the flesh of easy living, and sucked the mark of an outdoors-man from his skin. The excess skin lay in folds and creases about his frame, prematurely aging him. But the eyes were unchanged: they held the same hatred and venom I'd last seen in the empty house over a decade earlier.

The captain was puzzled. "So he is."

"He is only Sherlock Holmes' right-hand man, by Christ!" Moran snarled. He looked at me. "The years have treated you kindly, Doctor Watson. As you can see, they have done very little for me."

"One of the side benefits of being a criminal, I see," I remarked.

"Where is Sherlock Holmes?" he asked abruptly.

"I don't know," I replied truthfully, and without hesitation.

Moran chuckled. "Yes, I expected that answer, or one similar. You're not going to force me to apply the tedious process of torture and question, are you, Doctor?"

"That's not necessary. I am telling the truth. I don't know."

Sarawan, the captain, spoke up. "He may not, Colonel. He's been here all afternoon, alone."

"It will be easy enough to find out," Moran murmured, studying me. "It is not very complex information I am looking for, so I do not have to be careful how I go about extracting it. I can apply whatever messy and expendable process I believe will give me the answer soonest."

"My answer would remain the same."

"I beg to disagree, Doctor. With your medical knowledge, you should know the physiological effects sudden and overwhelming pain can have on a body. Now, if we were to apply mental pressure at the same time. . . ." He looked me up and down thoughtfully. "As a doctor, you depend upon the use of your hands as an aid to diagnosis, and also as a writer of your damnable chronicles, too. What if we were, say, to cut off your right index finger and thumb? Or are you left-handed? We could cut off both, perhaps. Have you ever tried to cope without that opposable digit, Doctor? It is simply impossible to lift anything. Imagine going through life trying to cope without being able to pick things up—your clothes, your food, your pen. . . ."

This grisly discussion was quite disturbing in that scurrying, mercantile atmosphere. I controlled the shiver it gave me and tried to maintain my steady gaze. I remained silent. Moran would never believe I truly did not know where Holmes was, and it possibly would delay the ship's departure even longer if I could let him think he might get a different answer with a little more effort.

But Sarawan was more concerned about his ship.

"Colonel, the cargo . . ." he interrupted quietly. "We cannot afford to delay."

"This is more important, Sarawan. Take the doctor to my cabin."

"But the arms!"

"Damn it, Sarawan, if Sherlock Holmes has plans to stop me leaving on this ship, then your revolution is going to go without its guns, too. Think on that. And take Watson below."

I was roughly pushed below decks and into a cabin that was quite large, and on a ship of that size an exorbitant waste of space. Moran's tea chest sat in the corner by the porthole. The cabin had been Sarawan's until a short time ago—his compass and charts, navigation equipment, lay scattered over the desk, and the thick captain's log rested as a paperweight on the last chart he had been using.

Moran turned to Sarawan. "Leave us. You see to the loading."

Sarawan nodded and hurried away, looking relieved.

The crewman was openly wielding the pistol, now that we were in relative privacy. Moran waved him forward.

"I am going to search his pockets. Keep it trained on him."

Obediently, the crewman cocked the gun and pushed it up against my ear. The cold metal was sufficient to keep me totally immobile whilst Moran searched my clothing. He found, quite naturally, the gun. My other possessions were harmless, and he let them be. The gun he put in the desk drawer. He cleared the desk in one sweep of his arm, sending charts and the log scattering across the floor.

"Put him in the chair," Moran ordered, pulling the seat up close to the table.

I was pushed into the chair, and the gun was brought back to rest against my neck again. Moran crossed the cabin and delved into a locker, and extracted a flat black box, which he brought back to the desk.

"Recognize it?" he asked me.

I did recognize its type. It was a first-aid kit, a comprehensive, all-encompassing kit that one would expect a responsible ocean-going captain to have available. Although the more esoteric items could vary from one to another, scalpels and blades were standard items.

Moran opened the lid and extracted the scalpel, and carefully fitted a new blade to it. His movements were slow and deliberate.

"Please do tell me when to stop, Doctor," he told me.

"Why bother? You do not believe me."

"I don't believe the song you're singing now. Let's change your tune a little, and see if I believe you then. Majah, his arm, please."

The gun lifted from my skin, and Majah grasped my right

forearm and pinned it to the leather desktop. He put most of his body weight into the effort, and I couldn no more shift my hand than I could fly.

Moran delicately separated my thumb and moved it away from my hand, and I was powerless to slide it back. He looked at me with mock kindness. "Last chance, Doctor. Do we operate?"

"Why bother, Moran? Doctor Watson has been telling you the simple truth." It was Holmes' voice.

Moran looked up, startled. "Well, well, so you were here all along, Mr. Holmes." He nodded to Majah, and the inexorable weight lifted from my arm. I gratefully slid my arm off the desk, and swivelled around in the chair.

Majah had turned to point the gun at Holmes, who stood in the doorway, dressed in his Indian costume, his dock worker's gloves in one hand. Holmes pointed at Majah. "There's no need for him. I have too much to lose by attempting anything foolish."

Moran considered this. "All right. Majah, give me your gun, and leave us."

The crewman was obedient to the last. Without a murmur of protest he handed over the weapon and left the room, closing the door behind him.

The two opponents faced each other across the cabin.

"Your tan is dripping," Moran remarked.

Holmes rubbed at the skin dye, which was washing away in the high summer heat. "It has served its purpose." He pulled off the turban, and wiped his face with it.

Moran rose and walked around the desk, and sat down in the captain's chair. "So, Mr. Holmes, despite my warning, you have persisted in searching for me."

"You took extraordinary measures to ensure I would not. That was your mistake. You should have left Elizabeth alone, Moran."

"I think not. Look at you. You are alone, and I have both you and your companion under my control. I see no sign of reinforcements. You thought the police might foul your plans, and now you are here, alone and unmasked. I think it was a rather effective ploy, myself."

"You are not out of England yet."

"Mere details. Shall we negotiate face to face?"

"You have no room for negotiations, Moran. The police are on their way here now. You do not think I would have foreseen this possibility and made arrangements against it? Even Watson had his own safety provisions. This ship has been watched from afar for as long as Watson was on the dock. As soon as you brought him aboard, the alarm went up. I give you mere minutes of freedom."

Moran, with a chuckle, lined the revolver up on the tea chest sitting innocently in the corner. He cocked it, and aimed carefully, then looked toward Holmes as he pulled the trigger, watching for his reaction. The noise of the shot was loud in the enclosed room, and I jumped despite myself. The shot drilled messily through the thin packing case.

Holmes appeared to remain completely unmoved, despite Moran's instantly turning the revolver back upon him, and cocking it with one quick, practised motion of his thumb. If Moran had expected Holmes to show any appreciation for his marksmanship, he was disappointed. But I saw something that Moran would not notice beneath the faded remains of the stain; Holmes had turned quite pale. I saw him clench his hand to hide its tremor.

Moran smiled. "Another, Mr. Holmes? Or shall we make arrangements for my escape? I have one last shot at my disposal, for this is a dual firer. No?"

He turned with casual speed and fired into the tea chest once again. This time, Holmes moved to launch himself at the man, but Moran instantly swung back around, lifting my own revolver from the desk drawer, and levelling it at Holmes. Holmes halted, knowing as surely as I did that Moran needed very little excuse to fire.

"Surprise," Moran said softly. "I have six more shots to use."

"Then I suggest you use them, Moran, for that is the only way you will be able to leave this cabin alive."

There was something in my friend's tone that I could not fathom, and I was quite at a loss to understand the definite note of doom I could sense in his words. An undercurrent was sweeping through the room, and I was being left upon the shore. Moran understood, however. I could see it in his gloating face and triumphant smile.

It was then it happened. There was a loud explosion, and the ship's whole structure rose and fell in an uneven, terrifying heave and shudder beneath our feet. I recoiled violently, and swung towards the porthole, hoping to see some evidence or explanation for the alarming explosion.

Moran, too, drew in a startled oath.

I turned my head rapidly back at the sound of his exclamation and was in time to see Holmes catapult himself at Moran, one hand pushing aside the arm holding the revolver. My friend's face was that of an implacable enemy bent on justified revenge.

Moran recovered swiftly from the distraction, but not quite swiftly enough to beat Holmes' matchless speed and reflexes. The gun fell to the floor, and they came together.

The competition was over very quickly. Moran was in poor condition after his restricted years in prison, and Holmes, in addition to long years of experience and honed skills, was motivated by a powerful incentive.

As Moran's fingers closed about his throat, Holmes brought from beneath his Indian's costume a gold, curved-bladed knife, which he plunged with one powerful stroke into Moran's sternum, burying the blade to the hilt.

As soon as Moran crumpled to the deck, Holmes bent and placed a foot on the man's chest, beside the knife hilt, and extracted it with one sharp tug. Then, with the bloody instrument poised to strike again if needed, he meticulously checked that all signs of life were gone—that Moran was indeed dead. The callousness of the task painted for me the picture Elizabeth had once, in vain, tried to convey: the dangerous and ruthless savage that lay beneath their shell of civility. Now I understood just how deep and fundamental that change had been.

Holmes moved rapidly across to the splintered tea chest.

"Hurry, Watson. Quickly now, all speed. We've got to get this lid off. Hurry, man!"

He was applying the blade of the knife to the nailheads as he spoke, and trying to prise off the lid. Bewildered, I hurried to obey. The lid had been loosely secured beneath four bent nails, and between us we forced the nails aside and prised the lid up, splitting it into two in the process.

Holmes lifted the fragments and threw them across the decking, and looked down into the chest, with a face that seemed feverish. And for a moment I thought he might faint. He grasped the edge of the crate.

"He'd already moved her!" he whispered hoarsely.

I stared down into the empty crate and studied the telltale blood-stain on the coarse grain of the wood. The eddying undercurrents swirled back to pick me up and enlighten me. Holmes had thought Elizabeth was in the crate. The bloodstain told that she had indeed been a prisoner inside for a while. But not now. Moran had moved her elsewhere.

And Holmes had not known that.

I recalled his pallor when Moran had fired upon the chest. And his remorseless words of doom that had followed the second shot. He had indeed suffered pain enough to awaken the savage.

The ship listed slightly. Holmes crossed to the door and turned the key, locking it. There was a further, minor explosion out on the deck, and the boat listed again, with a creak of strained beams. There were many cries and hoarse, panicked shouting in foreign tongues.

"She could be somewhere in here," Holmes said, looking about. He spotted the doors of a wardrobe and crossed to tug at the handles. He dug out his metal probes.

"Or anywhere else on the ship," I pointed out.

"No. I have been watching this door since Moran came aboard. No one has left the cabin except him and the crewman who wheeled the chest in." He began picking the lock.

My attention was distracted by another occurrence. My feet were wet. I looked down at them, alarmed.

"Holmes!"

He spared barely a glance at me.

"Holmes! There is water leaking in."

"It is not leaking, Watson."

"Not? Then what is this water doing here?"

He selected another probe. "Rising, I would assume. I suggest you stand on the other side of the cabin."

I struggled up the tilting deck to the other side of the cabin, as he had suggested. "Holmes, it is getting higher." And it was. It was across at least a quarter of the floor. "Where is it coming from, if the ship isn't taking on water?"

Holmes lifted his head, his expression exasperated. "It is not leaking, Watson, because I did not make a mistake with those charges. The ship is sinking." The ship gave another deep groan, adding its own emphasis to his forecast of doom.

I stared at him.

"You had better get out while you can, Watson," he told me, turning back to the locks. "I will search the rest of the cabin."

I was quite frozen to the spot. Nothing could have induced me to leave Holmes behind, even though I had no way of assisting. Nothing, that was, until Holmes spoke to me quietly.

"Go. There is no point in all of us dying together."

The ship sank beneath the surface as I was making my way from the cabin, and I was sucked down into the water with it. I am a confident swimmer, so I allowed myself to be pulled deeper until I was free to strike for the surface.

I came up and looked around. The now-racing tide had pulled me well out into the river. My coats and boots were weighing me down, so I paddled slowly through the flotsam toward the dock. There appeared to be a large number of men on the dock, some wet, some dry, and there were still a few in the water, being helped up by those already ashore. It appeared that the majority of people on board had made it safely onto land.

The police had arrived. A handful of bobbies were taking down details in their notebooks, and as I hauled myself up the pier, Lestrade crossed the dock to kneel and lend me a hand.

"Was Holmes aboard when she blew?" Lestrade asked me, lifting his voice above the babble behind him.

"Yes. How did you guess?"

"I got a telephone call from him this morning. He gave me the details about Moran, the hostel, and this ship."

I turn and scanned the lapping wavelets. Nothing. My beating heart was rapidly counting seconds ticking away—each second an eternity. The water remained undisturbed by human presence.

"Where is he?" Lestrade hissed, vocalizing my own worry.

Flotsam had been rising to the surface continually, but now no more new rubbish appeared. The water became still.

"Damn it, where is he?" Lestrade muttered again.

It was too long.

I stripped off the repulsive coat and bent to remove my boots.

"Watson?" Lestrade asked.

"I am going back." I stopped, needing my breath to work on the water-swollen boots. They finally came off.

Lestrade had turned away and whistled piercingly. He waved his arms and five men, three of them uniformed bobbies, ran towards him. They were barely within hailing distance when he began to dispense crisp orders in a decisive manner not at all like his usual laconic self. Then he touched my shoulder.

"I have got a man here who's good at underwater stuff, Watson. He'll go."

"Not fast enough," I said, standing and moving to the edge of the jetty.

"Let him go. You're too tired——"

"Out of my way, Lestrade."

"There he is!" The cry went up from further down the shore. A policeman was pointing down the river and we gazed out at the middle of the flow where the man was directing us to look.

The distance blurred my vision and I could see only a small, dark figure.

There was a splash as the underwater man dived in and began swimming strongly out to the drifting figure. He reached it and slowly they began the return trip back. As they came closer I could see two distinct figures: Holmes, swimming alone, and the policeman, trailing.

Many willing hands reached down to help them up onto the dock.

Holmes hauled himself upright, water draining from him in rivulets, and faced us.

"Your timing, Lestrade, as always, is immaculate."

Lestrade found us twenty minutes later, in a sun-warmed corner of the warehouse they had opened temporarily to shelter the cumbersome investigation of the sinking of the *Andhra's Pride*, and the illicit cargo of guns and ammunition.

"I have to ask just a few questions," Lestrade said apologetically. "The details we can sort out later."

"Of course," I agreed. "What do you want to know?"

"Moran. He is dead?"

I recalled my picture of Moran, staggering and clutching the gold knife handle with its green gems, staggering and falling.

"Undoubtedly," I answered.

"How did he die?" Lestrade asked.

I hesitated for a fractional moment, thinking through my answer. Holmes had killed Moran with ample reason, so if I replied truthfully, it would not harm my friend. However, the legal complications that would ensue could tie Holmes up in official bureaucracy for many weeks.

I waved a hand towards the Thames and looked Lestrade in the eye. "The ship sank," I replied levelly, carefully avoiding Holmes' gaze. It was not really an answer at all, but was as close as I could stretch the truth.

Lestrade nodded. "And why did the ship sink?"

"I don't know," I said instantly and quite truthfully. "There was an explosion, and the ship began to take on water. Actually, it simply fell apart."

"An explosion? The ship was sunk deliberately? By whom?"

I looked at Holmes, troubled. "I don't know that it was deliberate," I said slowly. "If it had been deliberately sunk, then it must have been one of us, mustn't it? Yet we were both in the cabin with Moran when the explosion occurred." I didn't voice the rest of my thoughts. I knew it was not I who had set charges to sink the ship and thereby kill several quite innocent men. And Holmes had by far the strongest reasons for such an act. I recalled his statement about not making a mistake with the charges.

"The *Andhra* was carrying a load of illicit munitions, including gunpowder and explosives," Holmes said, burying his hands deep into the pockets of his borrowed overcoat. "And they were using naked candles in the holds. It would take only a very small mistake for a tragedy of this sort to happen."

Lestrade nodded again. I could see he was not entirely happy about the mystery, but he accepted Holmes' hypothesis. He was called away, then.

"Holmes, what of Elizabeth?" I asked him.

It was two days after the sinking of the *Andhra* and we were back at Baker Street. Those two days had been busy, indeed. The police investigation had included a search of Sikmah's hostel, which resulted in several arrests, and Holmes and I both participated in that event.

Moran's sister, Beatrice O'Connor, had been found and detained. I was witness to Holmes' interview of her—an occasion I do not care to repeat. She had been abusive, hysterical, and uncooperative. Despite her circumlocutions, it became plain after weary hours of talk that hers had been the driving mind behind Moran's revenge. Moran had, after ten years of continual persuasion, convinced his sister that she could be rid of him forever—relieved of her monthly duty visits and the disgrace to the family—if only she would help him escape and flee England.

Once her assistance was assured, he had given her the information necessary to revive the last remains of Moriarty's network of criminals and Moran's own circle of comrades.

And in the end, Moran had betrayed her, too. He had carefully hidden from her his plans for revenge. Elizabeth's abduction was explained away as necessary and Moran had promised fervently she would be returned, unharmed, once he had left British waters.

"I looked in every corner or space in that cabin that could possibly hide a body. Elizabeth wasn't there. Therefore I must infer that the tea chest came aboard empty. Moran was bluffing me, and successfully, too."

Lestrade, Gregson, and Mycroft sat in the sitting room, considering Holmes' words for a moment.

"We know she left the hostel," Holmes continued, from his position by the hearth. "The room Moran had occupied was quite empty when Watson and I searched it, and your investigation and search would have uncovered her if they had merely moved her to another room."

Gregson spoke up. "My inspectors interviewed Sikmah thoroughly. He swears he doesn't know where she is. I have to believe him."

Holmes nodded. "He wanted Moran to move her out of his hostel. He was very anxious to disassociate himself from the abduction. I think we can believe him. He says Moran removed her early on Thursday evening, in the tea chest. My sentries confirmed that a tea chest left the hostel on the Thursday in the company of an Indian woman in native dress, who left from the kitchen door."

"Moran in disguise?" Lestrade hazarded.

"Undoubtedly. News of Watson's disappearance panicked him completely. He assumed, correctly, that I was on to him and watching him, and he took steps to escape undetected, almost as soon as the news filtered through."

Mycroft tapped his cane head. "So we know she left the hostel in the chest. And we know she wasn't brought aboard the ship. Moran's sister swears in one breath that she is alive, and in the next, recants and states she is dead. She is of no help. We must find her ourselves."

When writing up Holmes' cases for *The Strand*, I would try to pick those that displayed his extraordinary powers of detection, or those that had strange or novel circumstances. Above all, I chose cases that came to successful, or at least definite, conclusions. There were exceptions to this habit, but they had overriding merits of their own.

In putting down the final act of Elizabeth's story, I am aware that it would serve poorly indeed as material for *The Strand*. For despite all Holmes' skills, he could not discover what had become of Elizabeth, and the circumstances, far from being strange or novel, were depressingly grim. Too, there is no neat finish to this tale, but that is my fault.

There are only a few, painful incidents left for me to record. The first occurred several weeks after Moran's death, as an early sign of autumn was whistling up the streets. I called in at Baker Street, as I had almost daily, for any possible news of Elizabeth.

I found the lower floor deserted. Upon climbing the stairs, I discovered why. The tell-tale bottle sat upon the mantelshelf, and the shelf all around it had been cleared. Peppered upon the wall immediately behind the bottle were the gouges and cracks of plaster that showed where bullets had strayed.

Holmes sat in the far corner, his revolver dangling from a slack grip as he let his arm fall from the arm of the chair.

I peered closely at the bottle. It was difficult to tell if the level had dropped, for plaster dust covered the glass.

"Holmes, you disappoint me," I said, trying for a light tone that would not reveal how deeply disappointed I really was.

"Look again, Watson. It hasn't been touched. Yet," he added dryly.

I refrained from examining the bottle again, and instead attempted to change the direction of the conversation. "Your aim is appalling." I gestured towards the halo of chipped plaster about the bottle. "Elizabeth would have cracked the seal with one shot." And I winced mentally at my ineptitude.

Holmes looked at me with an expression that was at once exasperated and hurt. Then, without warning, he lifted the revolver and fired; barely without aim. The bottle shattered, sending liquid and glass fragments to the four winds. A fair proportion splattered my sleeve and jacket. Philosophically, I brushed it away.

Holmes threw himself to his feet with an impatient flex of his knees. He dropped the gun onto the cushion he had vacated, and whirled and stalked to the window. There he stood, silent for several long minutes as he observed the progress of traffic upon the street.

"I am sorry, Holmes."

He shrugged, an elegant, barely seen movement.

A little encouraged, I decided to pursue the issue.

"Holmes, I crossed paths with Lestrade today—"

"You waste your time, my friend," Holmes replied.

"I do not understand."

"I mean you waste your time on a fruitless mission—searching Lestrade out from the midst of those endless corridors at Scotland Yard."

"I didn't say that—"

"No, not in so many words." Holmes turned to face me again. "I find your sudden lack of faith in my skills as a detective fascinating. After seventeen years of documenting my cases, and publicly applauding my professionalism, you have suddenly taken it into your head that I am wrong. Not only am I wrong, but two of the people whose careers I have consistently had to prop up are eminently correct."

I could feel my indignation swelling. "It isn't that at all, Holmes, and you know it. I cannot understand your conclusions. Even I am convinced there is a strong possibility Elizabeth is still alive."

"Because there is no body," Holmes replied, his tone acrid.

"Yes! And the longer you delay your search—"

"Elizabeth is dead," Holmes stated emphatically. "And in all probability we will never find a body."

"You do not know that."

"I know!" His face was grim. "I have explained my reasoning to you *ad nauseam*. I refuse to pander to your imagination any longer, Watson. Do not raise the subject again. Not ever."

But I could not leave it alone. I found Mycroft at his club the next evening, and mentally blessed him for his dependability, when it seemed that the rest of my world had decayed and was crumbling away.

He was quite willing to hear me out. He listened with the same absorbed concentration that his brother used with clients and remained silent for long moments after I had finished my hesitant, confused monologue.

"For a man who has spent nearly twenty years working with my brother, you remain surprisingly undisciplined in your thinking, Watson. Let me play devil's advocate, and summarize: Elizabeth has disappeared, and the evidence shows that she is either unable or unwilling to return. If she is unable to return, it is because she is either dead or physically unable to manage it. Sherlock has determined that she is dead, but you do not believe him. You believe she is still alive and in need of our help."

"Yes," I agreed.

Mycroft smoked in silence for a second. "Let us discard all the evidence that points towards her death. I am sure Sherlock has demonstrated that proof with exhausting attention to detail."

I winced at his description.

"Yes, I can see he has. Let us deal, instead, with your hypothesis that she is alive and in need of our help. What proof can you offer?"

"Very little. That's why I am here. Holmes refuses to consider the possibility, and I haven't his abilities for searching out clues. The major clue is, of course, the lack of a body."

"Murderers have been convicted without a body before now," Mycroft pointed out. "But you have a point. Has there been any sign of her existence since her disappearance?"

"Beatrice O'Connor swore she was alive."

"I believe you must exclude the ravings of vengeful old ladies, Watson. Besides, she was not in a position to know the truth. She was arrested in Scotland, and it must have taken her at least twelve hours to get there. Those twelve hours include the vital hours covering Elizabeth's disappearance."

"Well, then, what of the proof that Elizabeth had been in the tea chest? Why, if Moran had killed her, would he drag proof of her captivity with him onto the ship?"

"Circular reasoning, Watson. Sherlock argued that it was to fulfil his need for revenge. Moran already knew he'd been seen leaving the hostel, and that he had possibly been detected. Either she escaped, or he got rid of the body and took the empty chest along with him to terrorize Sherlock. It doesn't prove anything else." Mycroft leaned forward. "And you overlook a fundamental clue, Watson. Elizabeth is clever and resourceful. She has proved on more than one occasion that she can overcome physical pain and discomfort that would immobilize anyone else, and fight her way back to safety. If, as you fear, she is hurt or injured or otherwise immobilized, why has it taken her so long to solve her problems and reach one of us?"

I sat, defeated. "Then she is dead."

"That is not what I said," Mycroft replied. "What of the other possibility?"

"Which other possibility?" I asked dully.

"That she is unwilling to return."

"You do not seriously consider. . . ." I trailed off, confounded.

"There is considerably more evidence in support of that than your theory, Watson. Take, for example, my argument a moment ago that she is resourceful and clever. She is as capable as Sherlock of seizing an opportunity and shaping it to her purposes. And Elizabeth knows from practical experience and from Sherlock himself how to feign her death and assume another identity."

"Why did she leave the clue of the ship's name for us to find, then?"

"Because escape was not a possibility then. Death at Moran's hand was more likely. Also she probably wanted to show Sherlock where to find Moran."

"And there is no body," I added, a little bitterly.

Mycroft nodded. "And there is one more overwhelming piece of evidence in support of this theory: Sherlock is adamant she is dead. Unyielding to the point of obsession."

"How is that proof?"

"My brother is not altogether witless, Watson. He would have considered this hypothesis himself. Given its validity, one is next forced to consider why Elizabeth might not wish to return. Given the range of possible answers, is it any wonder Sherlock has insisted so stubbornly that she is dead?"

There is no fool like an old fool. My reaction to Mycroft's theories was, I suspect, similar to Holmes'. After that initial period of blank rejection, however, I realized that he had not actually disagreed with me that Elizabeth was alive, but had merely offered another, more feasible explanation for her absence.

Yet I, the fool, could not leave it there. I found myself avoiding Baker Street. Like a dog with a bone and a sore tooth, I was snappy and irritable, barely human.

I was jolted out of my mood by an entirely unexpected letter from Persia. Sullah's daughter, Tayisha, now twenty-one and graduated from college, was to be married in London the next spring. Sullah would not be making the journey. Would I, as his representative, give the bride away?

I grasped at the ideas Sullah's letter had given me, as a drowning man would grasp at straws, and drew myself out of the morass with the aid of newborn hope.

I couldn't leave London without at least notifying Holmes, no matter how strained the friendship had become . . . or that is what I told myself. Accordingly, I found myself at Baker Street one evening.

Holmes appeared completely unmoved by the news of my plans.

"Go," he said irritably. "Go if you must."

"I must," I said firmly. "I know it will upset a number of plans, but I must go. Will you be good enough to notify *The Strand* for me, Holmes?"

He sat up a little straighter. "Why?"

"There are two stories due. . . ." I began to explain, but Holmes waved a languid hand of dismissal.

"Don't trouble yourself," he said. "I will write them."

"You?" My voice must have been thick with disbelief, for the look Holmes sent me was hard, yet I thought I saw a glimmer of humour in it, too.

"Yes, me. What is so extraordinary about that? I've always disliked the way you flood the tales with drama, so I will relieve you of the burden and write them as they should be written—as a proper treatise on scientific deduction."

"In that case, I bid you good night," I said coolly, picking up my hat and overcoat.

"Good night," Holmes answered absently, already turning back to the fire and his pipe.

That was the last time I saw Holmes in the old Baker Street rooms, and I was never again to write up any of his adventures for *The Strand*.

Recklessly, I withdrew all my liquid funds and undertook the long, expensive journey to Mashhad, with the minimum of preparation or delay. I was buoyed up by my hopes, and delay would have been unbearable. I even forgot to warn Sullah I was coming, and was forced to dash off a telegram from Teheran with the time of my arrival in Mashhad. Here I was delayed, somewhat, by the lag of modern technology. I was forced to hire a guide and horses to travel with me to Mashhad, for neither train nor carriage was to be had. I was acquainted with a small portion of my foolishness within five minutes of sitting in the saddle—I hadn't sat upon a horse since my army days.

Nevertheless, I persevered, consoled by the thought of comfort upon my arrival.

On the last day out from Mashhad, we were approached by a number of horsemen, and my guide muttered uneasily in his native tongue.

"Be cautious," he added to me.

I nodded. As was the custom in those parts, we halted and waited for the larger party to pass by. But it slowed as it approached, sending alarm through me. The lead horses were only ten yards away when a shout went up.

"Watson! Hello!"

It was Sullah.

They had been on the road two days, hoping to intercept me and save me the difficulties of negotiating transit from Mashhad to Sullah's home. Having found us, the small party of men stopped where they were and set up a fire to boil water for tea. I had developed a liking for the strong, minty beverage, and I was more than happy to alight and sit for a while.

All my delight at meeting Sullah faded, however, as I watched him dismount, helped by two strong men. He negotiated his way to the camp stool they had set up for him by my side, his walking sticks taking most of his weight.

I had failed to hide my dismay.

"It happens to all of us, eventually, Doctor. You should understand that better than I," Sullah chided me, seating himself slowly and carefully.

"Yes, but it still affects me when I see it in old friends, especially those I expected to outlast me."

Sullah laughed, and it was still the same belly-shaking roar. "So why have you come so far and at such haste?" he asked.

"I am replying to your letter in person," I replied. An appalling consideration had struck me. Did Sullah know about Elizabeth's disappearance? It was not the sort of news one gave within seconds of greeting the other.

But Sullah was examining me with his perceptive, wise eyes. So I fell to a half-truth. "I needed a holiday, too."

We were at Sullah's home before I found the privacy and the moment to break the news, if news it was, to Sullah. He had not mentioned either Holmes or Elizabeth throughout our short journey, and I wondered if that was because the majority of his household still believed Holmes was a Norwegian called Sigerson.

So I held my tongue. On the first day after our arrival, however, I got my chance.

Sullah found me at sunset, sitting on a flat rock, facing east. "Holmes used to sit there, contemplating Tibet from afar."

I nodded. "I guessed it was this one."

Sullah gathered his sticks in one hand, and lowered himself to the rock. "You're troubled."

"I came to talk to you of Elizabeth, Sullah. And I do not know how to break the news."

He sighed. "There is no need. I know. Tayisha wrote to me."

"Is that why you have avoided mentioning their names for two days?"

"Partly. And I sense, old friend, that they are very much on your mind. If you are truly here for rest, then it would be an unkindness for me to stir the memories." But I heard a note of query in his tone.

I had come thousands of miles to explain myself and ask the question that Sullah was giving me the opportunity to ask. Yet it took all my will to state it aloud. I hesitated. Finally I jumped in with both feet and bad grammar, letting it tumble out how it would, from the beginning: Beatrice O'Connor, Moran, the child Elizabeth and Wiggins, Elizabeth's tutelage and admonition of lost opportunities, Holmes' failure. And finally, my new hopes.

"She was happiest here in the East, here where she had perfect freedom. It was important to her—I suspect, in the end, more important than Holmes was to her. I thought . . . if she were still alive, she would return here."

After a long moment, Sullah said softly, "Perhaps. If she were alive."

"Then she hasn't."

Sullah remained silent.

I studied him. "Your first loyalty is to Elizabeth, of course," I said slowly.

"Someone must watch out for her."

"I thought I was."

Sullah gazed at the ground for a long moment. Finally he spoke softly and with pure kindness.

"I believed your loyalty was to Holmes."

"It was—it is."

"Then why are you here, my friend? Holmes believes her dead. Have his skills deteriorated to the point that you no longer trust him as you once did?"

I could find no answer to this.

"What if he needs you? And you are here on a mission that could only bring hurt to both of you, no matter what its outcome. A friend does not do this thing."

I searched out Sullah tonight after evening prayers and gave him a copy of this chronicle. "You can consider it yours, Sullah," I explained. "But if ever—"

Sullah nodded. "I understand."

We said our goodbyes then, for neither of us pretended that Sullah would ever make the trip to England again. I didn't need to call on my medical skills to know that he would barely last the year. Sullah was aware of his body's betrayal, but he had made his peace.

I, too, intend to make mine. Tomorrow I am going home.

—J.H. Watson, MD
Mashhad, Persia
March, 1904

Footnote

IT IS A MATTER OF RECORD that Sherlock Holmes wrote two stories for *The Strand* magazine, and they were among the last handful of cases ever published. The remainder were written by Watson, but they were all reports on earlier cases.

Shortly after that, Holmes retired to the Sussex Downs to study bees. The year was 1903.

The friendship between Watson and Holmes was restored, although it probably never regained its old glory. However, it worked well enough for the two to operate together on the eve of World War I to outwit and defeat Von Bork, a spy from the German emperor's army.

When hostilities between England and Germany became formal, Watson returned to his old regiment, the Fifth Northumberland Fusiliers. No records exist of Sherlock Holmes' war service, but given his talents it is probably a safe assumption that his work was solitary, covert, and exemplary.

However, that is another story. . . .

Chronology of Events

(Events particular to Watson's last chronicle are in italics.)

1878   Watson graduates as Doctor of Medicine—London University
Second Afghan war begins

Watson travels to Bombay

Date uncertain: events of *The Adventure of the "Gloria Scott,"*
Holmes' first case, while still in college

1880   Battle of Maiwand—Watson received his wound in the
shoulder (which later became a wounded leg)

Two unnamed cases while Holmes was living in Montague
Street

Year uncertain: the events of *The Adventure of The Musgrave
Ritual*, third case in Montague Street

1881   Watson returns to London, meets Sherlock Holmes, and
together they move into 221B Baker Street

October: the events of *The Adventure of the Resident Patient*

1882   March 4 (year imprecise): events of *A Study in Scarlet*,
Watson's first introduction to Holmes' work

Events of the Trepoff Murder case in Odessa, a case
mentioned in passing by Watson

Events of the case of the Atkinson Brothers at Trincomalee, a
case mentioned in passing by Watson

Events of the case concerning the Royal family of Holland, a
case mentioned in passing by Watson.

1883   Early April: the events of *The Adventure of the Speckled Band*

Date uncertain: the events of *The Adventure of Silver Blaze*,
Watson living at Baker Street

*Early spring (year uncertain): the events of The Adventure of
the Yellow Face, Watson living at Baker Street*

*August (year uncertain): the events of The Adventure of the
Cardboard Box, Watson living at Baker Street*

Summer (year uncertain): the events of *The Adventure of the Greek Interpreter*

October (year uncertain): the events of *The Hound of the Baskervilles*

1887 February (year uncertain, Watson still living at Baker Street): the events of *The Adventure of the Beryl Coronet*

April 14: Holmes falls ill in Lyon, from overwork. Watson summoned.

April: the events of *The Adventure of the Reigate Squire*

July 7/September (both months are mentioned), year uncertain, might be 1886: the events of *The Sign of Four*

Autumn: the events of *The Adventure of the Noble Bachelor*

(Month uncertain): Watson's marriage to Mary Morston

Late September: the events of *The Five Orange Pips*. In the story Watson says his wife is visiting her mother, yet his wife (Mary Morston, whom he met in the case of *The Sign of Four*) is an orphan.

Events of *The Adventure of the Paradol Chamber*, a case referred to by Watson, but never written up

Events of the British barque *Sophy Anderson*, a case referred to by Watson, but never written up

Events of the Camberwell poisoning, a case referred to by Watson, but never written up

1888 March (year uncertain): Watson buys medical practice in Paddington

July: first of two possible dates for the events of *The Adventure of the Norwood Builder*. Hilton Cubitt refers to the Jubilee of the previous year, and Watson is living at Baker Street (which is anachronistic for both possible dates, see 1889). Logically this is the more likely year, for if Cubitt had been referring to the second Jubilee, it would have been natural for him to qualify that he meant the second Jubilee, not the first.

20th March: events of *A Scandal in Bohemia*

Summer: the events of *The Adventure of the Crooked Man*, shortly after Watson's marriage.

June 3, Monday (year uncertain): the events of *The Boscombe Valley Mystery*

June (year uncertain): the events of *The Adventure of the Stockbroker's Clerk*. Watson dates this case three months after the purchase of his private practice.

July: the events of *The Adventure of the Naval Treaty*, occurs in "the July which immediately succeeded my marriage" (Watson).

July: the events of *The Adventure of the Second Stain*. In this story, Watson states that the case's international ramifications mean the year and date should remain vague. Yet he states the year and the month in passing reference in an earlier story as July 1888. This is contradicted in the actual story, in which Watson states the events occur in autumn. Assumed that Watson is attempting to misdirect.

July: the events of *The Adventure of the Tired Captain*

1889   Early spring (year uncertain): the events of *The Adventure of the Copper Beeches*. In this case, Watson appears to be living at Baker Street, which would place the date as pre-1887, yet Holmes talks about the cases of *A Scandal in Bohemia* and *A Case of Identity*. Assumed Watson is a temporary guest.

Friday, June 19th: the events of *The Man with the Twisted Lip*. Watson's wife calls him "James." It is from this slip it has been established that John Watson's second initial must stand for Hamish, which is Scottish for James.

Summer: the events of *The Adventure of the Engineer's Thumb*

December 27 (year uncertain): the events of *The Adventure of the Blue Carbuncle*

November: the events of *The Adventure of the Dying Detective*, occurred in the second year of Watson's marriage

Year uncertain: events of *The Valley of Fear*. Watson states it is the end of the 'eighties

1890   Month uncertain : events of *A Case of Identity*

June: events of *The Red-headed League*

1891   Holmes in France working for French government

January 4: Holmes "crossed swords" with Moriarty

January 23: Holmes "incommoded" Moriarty

Mid-February: Moriarty "seriously inconvenienced" by Holmes

Friday, April 24: the events of *The Adventure of the Final Problem*: (AM) Moriarty visits Holmes; (PM) Holmes visits Watson

Saturday, April 25: Moriarty visits Homes (AM)

Sunday, April 26: travel to Brussels

Monday, April 27: Brussels, Holmes telegraphs London police; travel to Strasbourg; evening: receive reply; move on toward Geneva

Tuesday, April 28 to Sunday, May 3: Travel up the Rhone Valley to Leuk; across the Gemmi Pass (in snow) along the Daubensee, through Interlaken to Meiringen

Sunday, May 3: stay at Englischer Hof., Meiringen

Monday, May 4: intend to cross the hill and spend the night at Rosenlaui. Stop off at the Reichenbach Falls. There the Swiss boy delivers the message which sends Watson back down the hill to Meiringen. Moriarty confronts Holmes. Next week spent travelling through Alps, across the Italian border, through Turin, to Florence.

Wednesday, May 6: reports of Holmes' death in European papers.

Sunday, May 10: Holmes reaches Florence

Tuesday, May 12: Holmes leaves for Constantinople

May: Holmes in Constantinople. Leaves for Persia.

September: Holmes reaches Persia, then leaves for Tibet

November: Holmes reaches Tibet

1892   Late March: the events of *The Singular Experience of Mr John Scott Eccles* ("A Reminiscence of Mr Sherlock Holmes"). Perhaps because it was a reminiscence, Holmes can be forgiven for getting his dates wrong—he was in Tibet at the time he claims this case took place.

1893   October to early December: Holmes travels back to Persia

December: Colonel James Moriarty writes a report which causes Watson to respond with his story of Holmes' confrontation with Moriarty at Reichenbach; publication of *The Adventure of the Final Problem*.

1894   Holmes travels to Khartoum via Mecca

Late February to late March: Holmes travels to Montpellier

March 30th: the events of *The Adventure of the Empty House*

Date uncertain: the events of the case of the papers of the ex-resident Murillo, a case merely referred to in passing, but not written up

Date uncertain: the events of the case of the steamship *Friesland*, a case merely referred to in passing, but not written up

Summer (?), date uncertain: the events of *The Adventure of the Norwood Builder*. Watson writes that "Holmes had been back for some months" and refers to the above two cases.

Late November: the events of *The Adventure of the Golden Pince-Nez*

1895   February (year uncertain): the events of *The Adventure of the Missing Three-Quarter*

Saturday, April 23: the events of *The Adventure of the Solitary Cyclist*

Month uncertain, but prior to July: events of the case of the death of Cardinal Tosca, referred to by Watson, but not written up

Month uncertain, but prior to July: events of the case of Wilson, the Canary trainer, referred to by Watson, but not written up

July (1st week): the events of *The Adventure of Black Peter*

November, 3rd week: the events of *The Adventure of the Bruce-Partington Plans*

Date uncertain, winter: the events of *The Adventure of Charles Augustus Milverton*

Month uncertain: the events of *The Adventure of the Six Napoleons*

Date uncertain: the events of *The Adventure of the Three Students*

1896   Early in year: the events of *The Adventure of the Veiled Lodger*

1897   March: events of *The Adventure of the Devil's Foot*. Holmes is forced to take a holiday in Cornwall because of ill health.

       Winter (month uncertain): the events of *The Adventure of the Abbey Grange*

1898   Tuesday, May 14 (year uncertain): the events of *The Adventure of the Priory School*. This is the earliest possible date, for Lord Holderness was married in 1888, and his son, the subject of the case, was ten years old.

       July: second of two possible dates for the events of *The Adventure of the Norwood Builder*. (See 1888.)

1899   Summer, month uncertain: events of *The Adventure of the Retired Colourman*

1902   Late June: the events of *The Adventure of the Three Garridebs*

       September 3: the events of *The Adventure of the Illustrious Client*

       Early September: the events of *The Adventure of the Creeping Man*

1903   January: the events of *The Adventure of the Blanched Soldier*. Holmes himself related this tale, although it wasn't published in *The Strand* until over a decade later.

       August: Mrs Thacker visits

       September: Watson travels to Persia

       Month uncertain: Holmes retires to the Sussex Downs to study and indulge in bee-keeping.

1904   March: Watson returns home.

1907   July: events of *The Adventure of the Lion's Mane* (after retirement, in Sussex). This is the second case Holmes narrates himself.

1915   August 2, the eve of World War I: the events of *His Last Bow*. The reunion of two old friends.

       Watson joins old service (Fifth Northumberland Fusiliers), shortly after this case.

Undated cases:

The Adventure of Shoscombe Old Place (Watson at Baker Street)
The Adventure of the Red Circle
The Disappearance of Lady Frances Carfax (after Crimean War)
The Adventure of the Three Gables
Summer: *The Mazarin Stone* (Watson not at Baker Street)
November: *The Adventure of the Sussex Vampire*
October: *The Problem of Thor Bridge* (Watson at Baker Street)